A year ago I would have thoi
gentleman to take my hand to
a year of encounters with the seamier side of humanity had honed my Spidey senses, which now tingled from my scalp down to my toes. I clutched my mug with both hands and took a step away from him. "Excuse me. I just remembered I'm late for an appointment." I spun around and hurried off before he could respond.

Acclaim for the Anastasia Pollack Crafting Mysteries

Assault with a Deadly Glue Gun

"Crafty cozies don't get any better than this hilarious confection...Anastasia is as deadpan droll as Tina Fey's Liz Lemon, and readers can't help cheering as she copes with caring for a host of colorful characters." – *Publishers Weekly* (starred review)

"Winston has hit a homerun with this hilarious, laugh-until-your-sides-hurt tale. Oddball characters, uproariously funny situations, and a heroine with a strong sense of irony will delight fans of Janet Evanovich, Jess Lourey, and Kathleen Bacus. May this be the first of many in Winston's Anastasia Pollack Crafting Mystery series." – *Booklist* (starred review)

"A comic tour de force...Lovers of funny mysteries, outrageous puns, self-deprecating humor, and light romance will all find something here." – *ForeWord Magazine* (Book-of-the-Year nominee)

"North Jersey's more mature answer to Stephanie Plum. Funny, gutsy, and determined, Anastasia has a bright future in the planned series." – *Kirkus Reviews*

"...a delightful romp through the halls of who-done-it." – *The Star-Ledger*

"Make way for Lois Winston's promising new series...I'll be eagerly awaiting the next installment in this thoroughly delightful series." – *Mystery Scene Magazine*

"...once you read the first few pages of Lois Winston's first-in-series whodunit, you're hooked for the duration..." – *Bookpage*

"In Winston's droll second cozy featuring crafts magazine editor Anastasia Pollack...readers who relish the offbeat will be rewarded." – *Publishers Weekly*

"...a *30 Rock* vibe...Winston turns out another lighthearted amateur sleuth investigation. Laden with one-liners, Anastasia's second outing (after *Assault With a Deadly Glue Gun*) points to another successful series in the works." – *Library Journal*

"Winston...plays for plenty of laughs...while letting Anastasia shine as a risk-taking investigator who doesn't always know when to quit." – *Alfred Hitchcock Mystery Magazine*

Revenge of the Crafty Corpse
"Winston peppers the twisty and slightly edgy plot with humor and plenty of craft patterns. Fans of craft mysteries will like this, of course, but so will those who enjoy the smart and snarky humor of Janet Evanovich, Laura Levine, and Laura DeSilverio." – *Booklist*

"Winston's entertaining third cozy plunges Anastasia into a surprisingly fraught stew of jealousy, greed, and sex..." and a "Sopranos-worthy lineup of eccentric character..." – *Publishers Weekly*

"Winston provides a long-suffering heroine, amusing characters, a...good mystery and a series of crafting projects featuring cloth yo-yos." – *Kirkus Reviews*

"A fun addition to a series that keeps getting stronger." – *Romantic Times Magazine*

"Chuckles begin on page one and the steady humor sustains a comedic crafts cozy, the third (after *Death by Killer Mop Doll*)... Recommend for Chris Grabenstein ("John Ceepak" series) and Jess Lourey readers." – *Library Journal*

"You'll be both surprised and entertained by this terrific mystery. I can't wait to see what happens in the Pollack household next." – *Suspense Magazine*

"The book has what a mystery should...It moves along at a good pace...Like all good sleuths, Anastasia pieces together what others don't...The book has a fun twist...and it's clear that Anastasia, the everyday woman who loves crafts and desserts, and has a complete hottie in pursuit, will return to solve another murder and offer more crafts tips..." – *Star-Ledger*

Decoupage Can Be Deadly

"*Decoupage Can Be Deadly* is the fourth in the Anastasia Pollock Crafting Mysteries by Lois Winston. And it's the best one yet. More, please!" – *Suspense Magazine*

"What a great cozy mystery series. One of the reasons this series stands out for me as a great one is the absolutely great cast of characters. Every single character in these books is awesomely quirky and downright hilarious. This series is a true laugh out loud read!" – Books Are Life–Vita Libri

"This is one of these series that no matter what, I'm going to be laughing my way through a comedy of errors as our reluctant heroine sets a course of action to find a killer while contending with her eccentrically dysfunctional family. This adventure grabs you immediately delivering a fast-paced and action-filled drama that doesn't let up from the first page to the surprising conclusion." – Dru's Book Musings

"Lois Winston's reluctant amateur sleuth Anastasia Pollack is back in another wild romp." – The Book Breeze

A Stitch to Die For

"*A Stitch to Die For* is the fifth in the *Anastasia Pollack Crafting Mysteries* by Lois Winston. If you're a reader who enjoys a well-plotted mystery and loves to laugh, don't miss this one!" – *Suspense Magazine*

Scrapbook of Murder

"This is one of the best books in this delightfully entertaining whodunit and I hope there are more stories in the future." – Dru's Book Musings

"*Scrapbook of Murder* is a perfect example of what mysteries are all about—deft plotting, believable characters, well-written dialogue, and a satisfying, logical ending. I loved it!" – *Suspense Magazine*

"I read an amazing book recently, y'all — *Scrapbook of Murder* by Lois Winston, #6 in the Anastasia Pollack Crafting Mysteries. All six novels and three novellas in the series are Five Star reads." – Jane Reads

"Well written, with interesting characters." – Laura's Interests

"...a quick read, with humour, a good mystery and very interesting characters!" – Verietats

Drop Dead Ornaments

"I always forget how much I love this series until I read the next one and I fall in love all over again..." – Dru's Book Musings

"*Drop Dead Ornaments* is a delightful addition to the Anastasia Pollack Crafting Mystery series. More, please!" – *Suspense Magazine*

"I love protagonist Anastasia Pollack. She's witty and funny, and she can be sarcastic at times...A great whodunit, with riotous twists and turns, *Drop Dead Ornaments* was a fast, exciting read that really kept me on my toes." – Lisa Ks Book reviews

"*Drop Dead Ornaments* is such a fantastic book...I adore

Anastasia! She's clever, likable, fun to read about, and easy to root for." – Jane Reads

"...readers will be laughing continually at the antics of Anastasia and clan in *Drop Dead Ornaments*." – The Avid Reader

"I love this series! Not only is Anastasia a 'crime magnet,' she is hilarious and snarky, a delight to read about and a dedicated friend." – Mallory Heart's Cozies

"It is always a nice surprise when something I am reading has a tie in to actual news or events that are happening in the present moment. I don't want to spoil a major plot secret, but the timing could not have been better...Be prepared for a dysfunctional cast of quirky characters." – Laura's Interests

"This is a Tour de Force of a Murder/Mystery." – A Wytch's Book Review

"A series worth checking out." – The Ninja Librarian

"I flew through this book. Winston knows how to make a reader turn the page. It's more than a puzzle to solve—I was rooting for people I cared about. Anastasia Pollack is easy to like, a good mother, a good friend, and in a healthy romantic relationship, the kind of person you'd want on your side in a difficult situation." – Indies Who Publish Everywhere

"Lois Winston's cozy craft mystery *Drop Dead Ornaments* is an enjoyable...roller-coaster ride, with secrets and clues tugging the reader this way and that, and gentle climbs and drops of suspense and revelation to keep them reading." – Here's How It Happened

"Anastasia is a take-charge woman with a heart for her family– even her ex-family members who don't (in my opinion) deserve her kindness... What I like best about Anastasia is how she balances her quest for justice with the needs and fears of her family... I can't wait to read more of her adventures and the progress of her relationship with her family and her boyfriend." – The Self-Rescue Princess

"...a light-hearted cozy mystery with lots of energy and definitely lots of action and interaction between characters." – Curling Up By the Fire

"I thought the plot was well thought out and the story flowed well. There were many twists and turns...and I enjoyed all the quirky characters. I was totally baffled as to who the killer was and was left guessing to the very end." – Melina's Book Blog

"(Anastasia's) wit and sarcasm lend a bit of humor to this cozy, and the story kept me intrigued right up to the end." – The Books the Thing

Handmade Ho-Ho Homicide
"Handmade Ho-Ho Homicide" is a laugh-out-loud, well plotted mystery, from a real pro! A ho-ho hoot!" – *Suspense Magazine*

"Merry *Crises*! Lois Winston has brought back Anastasia's delightful first-person narrative of family, friends, dysfunction, and murder, and made it again very entertaining! Anastasia's clever quips, fun stories, and well-deserved digs kept me smiling, and reading the many funny parts to my husband...does that count as two thumbs up in one? What a great journey!" – *Kings River Life Magazine*

"Once again, the author knows how to tell a story that immediately grabbed my attention and I couldn't put this book down until the last page was read.... This was one of the best books in this delightfully lovable series and I can't wait to see what exciting adventures await Anastasia and her friends." – Dru's Book Musings

"This was such a fun quick read. I can't wait to read more of this series." – A Chick Who Reads

"The story had me on the edge of my seat the entire time." – 5 Stars, Baroness Book Trove

"Christmas, cozy mystery, craft, how can I not love this book? Humor, twists and turns, adorable characters make this story truly engaging from the first to the last page." – LibriAmoriMiei

"Take a murder mystery, add some light-hearted humor and weird characters, sprinkle some snow and what you get is *Handmade Ho-Ho Homicide*—a perfect Christmas Cozy read." –5 stars, The Book Decoder

Books by Lois Winston

Anastasia Pollack Crafting Mystery series
Assault with a Deadly Glue Gun
Death by Killer Mop Doll
Revenge of the Crafty Corpse
Decoupage Can Be Deadly
A Stitch to Die For
Scrapbook of Murder
Drop Dead Ornaments
Handmade Ho-Ho Homicide
A Sew Deadly Cruise

Anastasia Pollack Crafting Mini-Mysteries
Crewel Intentions
Mosaic Mayhem
Patchwork Peril
Crafty Crimes (all 3 novellas in one volume)

Empty Nest Mystery Series
Definitely Dead
Literally Dead

Romantic Suspense
Love, Lies and a Double Shot of Deception
Lost in Manhattan (writing as Emma Carlyle)
Someone to Watch Over Me (writing as Emma Carlyle)

Romance and Chick Lit
Talk Gertie to Me
Four Uncles and a Wedding (writing as Emma Carlyle)
Hooking Mr. Right (writing as Emma Carlyle)
Finding Hope (Writing as Emma Carlyle)

Novellas and Novelettes
Elementary, My Dear Gertie

Once Upon a Romance
Finding Mr. Right

Children's Chapter Book
The Magic Paintbrush

Nonfiction
Top Ten Reasons Your Novel is Rejected
House Unauthorized
Bake, Love, Write
We'd Rather Be Writing

A
Sew Deadly
Cruise

LOIS WINSTON

Cover design by L. Winston

ISBN:978-1-940795-48-5

DEDICATION

In loving memory of my Aunt Selma who was so much more
than an aunt to me.

ACKNOWLEDGMENTS

Authors often have ideas that may or may not work. I owe a huge debt of gratitude to Judy Melinek, Cynthia Rice, D.P. Lyle, Ruth Glick, Wesley Harris, Stacey Pearson, and Kia Dennis of CrimeScene Writers and Jen Prosser of Sisters in Crime Guppies for answering my legal and medical questions, thus preventing me from making some huge mistakes.

And finally, as always, special thanks to Donnell Bell and Irene Peterson for their superb editorial skills.

ONE

I stood in the bedroom and stared at the snow-covered street and twinkling Christmas lights.

"Something wrong?" asked Zack, coming up alongside me and offering me a glass of wine.

"Of course not."

He raised an eyebrow. "Then why are you standing there worrying that ring back and forth on your finger?"

I glanced down at the ring on the third finger of my left hand. "Was I?"

"You were. What's on your mind?"

"I was thinking about everything that's changed over the past year."

Twelve months ago *normal* best defined my life. That changed the day my husband dropped dead at a casino in Las Vegas and turned my world upside-down, inside out, and seven ways to sideway. Clueless me thought he was at a sales meeting in Harrisburg, Pennsylvania.

My cluelessness soared to galactic heights in the days that followed as I learned the true extent of Karl Marx Pollack's deception. He had gambled away our lives, leaving me to deal with astronomical debt, his murderous bookie, *and* his communist mother.

I'll probably be paying off the debt for decades to come, but thanks to surging adrenaline, pure survival instincts, and my trusty X-acto knife, I survived the bookie. Unfortunately, as my unwelcome permanent houseguest, Lucille, the communist mother-in-law from Hades, is the gift that keeps on giving.

My name is Anastasia Pollack. I'm the mother of two teenage boys, the crafts editor at a third-rate women's magazine, and as of a few minutes ago, newly engaged. The engagement ring represents the only good thing to happen in my life since Karl's death.

"Not to mention the last twenty-four hours," said Zack, pulling my attention from the past back to the present.

"Worst Christmas Eve ever," I said.

"I thought I'd lost you."

Tears began to pool in my eyes and spill onto my cheeks.

Zack clasped my left hand and held it up between us, the diamond's sparkle vying with the Christmas lights. "I hope my timing wasn't off. Maybe I should have waited."

"As if Alex and Nick would have let you." My fifteen and seventeen-year-old sons had been in on the surprise proposal. For all I knew, they'd bullied Zack into it.

Zack chuckled. "True but even if they had, Ralph never would have forgiven me. You don't mess with a master of the Bard of Avon."

"I'm not sure he'll ever forgive either of us when we board him with the vet for a week while we're on our cruise."

Ralph was the African Grey I'd inherited from my great-aunt Penelope Periwinkle. After spending decades in her college lecture hall, the parrot was nearly as much a Shakespearian scholar as his now-deceased mistress. Having an uncanny knack for spouting situation-appropriate Shakespearian quotes, Ralph hadn't disappointed when earlier this evening Zack went down on one knee, whipped out a small velvet box from behind his back, and flipped it open to reveal the antique engagement ring now encircling my finger.

"Come to think of it," I said, "I'm not sure who actually proposed to me, you or Ralph."

"Very funny. I don't think it's legal to marry a parrot in New Jersey."

I raised myself up on my toes, lifted my chin, and planted a kiss on Zack's lips. At the same time—and not for the first time—I wondered what a guy who looks like he emerged from the same genetic stew as Pierce Brosnan, Antonio Banderas, and George Clooney sees in a cellulite-riddled, pear-shaped, slightly overweight, debt-ridden, middle-aged suburban mom like me. After all, the guy had dated supermodels and Hollywood celebrities.

"Your proposal couldn't have come at a better time," I said after our lips parted.

"So you only agreed to marry me because a psycho kidnapped and nearly killed you last night?"

"A psycho and his psycho wife."

"The psycho wife made the difference?"

"Let's just say I've come to realize life is too short to postpone happily-ever-after any longer."

Zack knit his brows together as he scrutinized me, his tone growing more serious. "Ever-after will last a lot longer if we can keep you away from any future psycho killers."

"I'll admit, it is getting a bit redundant."

"Is that what you call it? Redundant?"

I took a sip of wine and shrugged. "For lack of a better word. You do realize I don't go searching for dead bodies, right?"

He heaved an enormous sigh as he shook his head. "And yet you keep finding them."

"Blame Karl. I never stumbled across a murder before he died."

Along with the debt and the communist mother-in-law, ever since Karl dropped dead, I've found myself in the unenviable position of reluctant amateur sleuth. I've lost count of how many murder investigations I've gotten sucked into the last year, beginning with the ones committed by the murderous bookie. At least he's now spending the remainder of his days in a federal facility—the kind with bars and barbed wire.

So are the other killers I've come in contact with, but at some point I feared my luck might run out. Better to quit while ahead. I'd promised my sons. I'd promised Zack. Yet somehow those dead bodies continue to find me and pull me in.

Zack tapped a finger against my temple. "I get the sense something else is churning around upstairs. Out with it."

"How do you do that?"

"Do what?"

"Read my mind."

He cupped my chin, caressing my cheek with his thumb. "Not your mind, your eyes and mouth. The expressions on your face make you an open book."

Good grief! "I know I can't lie with a straight face, but—"

Zack laughed. "Relax. Not to everyone. Just me. My career training makes me extremely observant."

I wondered which career he meant—the one he admitted to or the covert one I suspected. I hesitated, chewing on my lower lip, before saying, "There is something."

"Aha! Does it have to do with alphabet agencies?"

From the day I first met Zachary Barnes, I suspected he led a double-life. Why would a world-renowned photojournalist want to move from a Manhattan high-rise to an apartment above a garage in a New Jersey suburb? He'd claimed he needed more privacy when he wasn't globetrotting and continues to deny any affiliation with covert government organizations. Still, he does own a gun, makes frequent trips to our nation's capital, and has a habit of taking off to places like South America and Madagascar at a moment's notice.

But there was something besides his possible James Bond secret identity gnawing at me. "You've never mentioned anything about your family. Why haven't I met any of them?"

"You've met Patricia."

"She's *ex*-family." Zack had been married briefly in his twenties. Realizing their youthful mistake, he and Patricia Tierney parted friends and continue to remain friendly. Her kids even call him Uncle Zacky.

Zack grew thoughtful for a moment before indicating the bed with a tilt of his head. "Have a seat."

Once I perched myself on the edge, he joined me, taking my hand in his. "Like you, I'm an only child, and like you, both my parents were only children. I have no aunts, uncles, or cousins. My mother died when I was eleven. Her parents raised me. They both died years ago."

"And your father?"

"Out of the picture since my mother died."

I gasped. "He deserted you?"

Zack's jaw tightened as he shrugged. "No great loss. He wasn't much of a father when he was around."

"I'm sorry."

"Don't be. My grandparents gave me a good life. I never missed him." He placed our wine glasses on the nightstand and changed the subject. "So how should we celebrate our engagement?"

"I'm assuming you have something in mind?"

"You better believe it."

~*~

The next morning my sons ambled into the kitchen and greeted us with the subject I'd been dreading ever since Ira surprised us with cruise tickets for Christmas. Ira is the half-brother Karl never knew existed. He and his three extremely spoiled kids entered our lives last summer. They were far easier to tolerate when they lived on the other side of the state. However, wanting to be closer to us (his choice, not mine), Ira had recently purchased a McMansion on the other side of town.

"How do we survive a week stuck on a ship with Uncle Ira and his brats?" asked Alex.

"Not to mention Grandmother Lucille," added Nick. Unfortunately, he didn't notice the commie in question had arrived in the dining room and taken her seat at the table where, in her usual fashion, she waited to be waited on.

"I can hear you," she roared. "Why are you talking about me?"

"This is going to be fun," I muttered under my breath as I headed into the dining room. I pasted a smile on my face and said, "Ira is treating us all to a cruise, Lucille."

"How does that concern me?"

"He also bought you a ticket."

She knit her bushy steel-gray eyebrows together and snorted one of her trademark harrumphs. "Why would I accept a gift from that man?"

Lucille refuses to believe Ira is her beloved Karl's half-brother. Even a DNA test wouldn't change her mind, not that one is needed since Ira is the spitting image of my deceased husband, although several years younger, more than a few pounds thinner, and still in possession of a full head of hair.

Instead, Lucille has decided Ira is scamming me. To what end I have no idea, given that Ira is extremely wealthy and generous to a fault, while I'm up to my eyeballs in Karl-generated debt—something else Lucille refuses to believe.

"So you're not going?" asked Nick, joining us in the dining room and doing little to contain his delight.

"Absolutely not!"

My son turned to me and grinned ear-to-ear. "Well, that solves one problem, Mom."

I answered with a Mom Look that needed no translation.

"I'll grab the orange juice," he said, quickly ducking back into the kitchen.

Lucille's refusal to go on the cruise might have made Nick's life easier, but it added one more layer of complication to mine. I didn't trust my mother-in-law alone in my house for more than a few hours, let alone seven days. The woman couldn't toast a bagel without risk of setting the kitchen on fire.

Three alternatives sprang to mind. "If you're not going to come with us, Lucille, you and your dog can move to Sunnyside for a week."

The Sunnyside of Westfield Assisted Living and Rehabilitation Center owed me big time. If Medicare didn't cover the cost of housing Lucille for a week, I'd remind the director that I'd saved their reputation by catching a killer for them last summer.

"Absolutely not!" said Lucille, smacking her palm on the table.

"Then you can cover the cost of someone moving in to care for you and Mephisto while we're gone."

This time Lucille curled both her hands into fists and pounded the table with such force she not only rattled the silverware and plates, she knocked over her glass. Luckily, Nick hadn't yet returned with the carton of orange juice. "His name is Manifesto!" she bellowed at the top of her lungs.

If looks could kill, Zack and the boys would now be planning my funeral. But really, who names a dog for a communist treatise? My mother-in-law, that's who.

I ignored her outburst and continued. "Your third option is to move in with Harriet." Harriet Kleinhample was Lucille's second-in-command in the Daughters of the October Revolution. The organization consisted of thirteen octogenarian communist rabble-rousers who blindly followed my mother-in-law. Reason escapes me as to why.

She answered me with a growl that I optimistically took as agreement to the third option.

"What makes you think Harriet won't bring her back to the house?" asked Alex after I returned to the kitchen.

"She probably will, but I plan to steal your grandmother's house key so she can't get in."

Nick offered me a high-five. "Way to go, Mom!"

"I'm marrying one extremely devious lady," said Zack, shaking his head as he plated the scrambled eggs onto a serving dish.

"What if she breaks a window to get in?" asked Alex.

I hadn't considered that. The alarm would go off, alerting the police, but Westfield's finest all knew Lucille lived here. They'd picked her up on various transgressions from jaywalking to vandalism to protesting without a permit on an almost weekly basis, locking her up on more than one occasion.

However, they'd believe her when she said she couldn't find her key. As a favor to me, they'd probably even repair the broken window.

Now I had to worry if my house would be standing when we returned from a cruise I didn't want to take. Or worse yet? I might come home to find twelve squatters residing within Casa Pollack.

TWO

Six weeks later Mama, Zack, the boys, and I slowly snaked our way along the security line within the cavernous Gemstones of the Seven Seas cruise terminal in Bayonne, New Jersey. "Are there several ships leaving today?" asked Nick.

"Just ours," I said. "Why?"

He twisted around to scope out the vast, crowded interior, his eyes growing wide. "All these people are going on the same ship as us?"

"All these and then some," said Mama. "The Gemstone Empress holds four-thousand passengers plus fifteen-hundred crew members."

When I raised an eyebrow in her direction, she offered up an overly dramatic sigh. Then she said, "I met Poor Lou on this ship."

Poor Lou Beaumont would have become Mama's sixth husband if not for his untimely death by knitting needle to the heart. I draped my arm around her shoulders and muttered, "Of all the cruise ships Ira could have chosen..."

"Lou died before you met Ira," Zack reminded me.

"True, but had he consulted us before booking this surprise Christmas present, Mama could have told him to choose a different ship. She doesn't need a week of being confronted with bittersweet memories every time she rounds a corner."

My mother waved a gloved hand in dismissal. "I don't mind, dear. I plan to spend the cruise reliving all those wonderful times we had on the ship, not crying over them. It's just that..." Her eyes took on a faraway look.

"What, Mama?"

"I keep thinking about how, if Lou hadn't died, I never would have married Lawrence."

Now it was my turn to sigh. Mama's marriage to Lawrence Tuttnauer was one more strike against my husband's long-lost half-brother. If not for Ira, Mama would never have met Lawrence, let alone married him. Shortly after walking into our lives, Ira introduced Mama to his widower father-in-law. By the end of the summer Flora Sudberry Periwinkle Ramirez Scoffield Goldberg O'Keefe had become Flora Sudberry Periwinkle Ramirez Scoffield Goldberg O'Keefe Tuttnauer.

Mama never has any trouble finding husbands. She looks twenty years younger than her actual age of sixty-six and wears several sizes smaller than yours truly. On top of that, she looks like a young Ellen Burstyn from back when the actress starred in *Same Time Next Year*. As a result, Mama attracts men like boy bands attract teenybopper groupies.

However, Mama had a lousy track record when it came to keeping those husbands. With the exception of my father, most died within a year of their vows.

Lawrence had broken the dead husband cycle. Mama's

marriage to him ended in divorce after his arrest for a laundry list of felonies. However, more importantly, if Mama hadn't met and married Lawrence, several of his victims would be planting daisies come spring, not pushing up daisies from six feet under.

Alex paused from his nonstop texting and pulled his eyes from the screen. Worry clouded his features. "Sophie and her dad are stuck in traffic on the Turnpike. What if they don't arrive in time?"

Alex's girlfriend had cajoled her father into canceling their planned ski trip to join us on the cruise. I liked Sophie, but sometimes I worried about the speed of their relationship. She and Alex had only met at the beginning of the school year after Shane Lambert and his daughter relocated from North Dakota to Westfield. Alex fell head-over-heels for the newcomer who reminded me of a petite version of Nicole Kidman.

"The ship doesn't sail for another four hours," said Zack. "If they're on the Turnpike, they're only a few miles away."

"They can always walk," said Nick.

Alex rolled his eyes at his brother. "And what do you suggest they do with their car, Doofus?"

Nick waved his hand in a dismissive gesture. "Ditch it on the side of the road. It's not like Shane can't afford to buy another car after the cruise. The guy has a bazillion dollars."

I directed a Mom Look his way.

"What?" he said. "It's true."

I shook my head. A bazillion dollars—if there was such a thing—was probably a gross exaggeration. However, having won one of the largest lotteries in history, Shane Lambert wasn't hurting for funds. Rather than lecturing my son, I said, "I think there may be a law against deliberately abandoning a vehicle on the

Turnpike."

Nick offered up a shrug. "So he pays a fine."

"Shane would give his car away before he'd abandon it," said Alex, defending the ethical principles of his girlfriend's father.

"Whatever," said Nick. "I'm just saying there are ways to avoid missing the cruise."

"No one is going to miss the cruise," I said.

We finally inched our way up to the front of the security checkpoint. I placed my carry-on, purse, and coat on the conveyor belt and stepped through the body scan. While I waited for my items to make their way through the X-ray machine, I heard the opening bars of "Defying Gravity" coming from inside the scanner. The TSA agent monitoring the video screen chuckled.

"Must be a fellow *Wicked* fan," said Zack, matching her chuckle with one of his own.

"Then she has excellent taste in musical theater." I caught the agent's eye and gave her a thumbs-up.

Once I'd retrieved my belongings, I checked the Missed Call display. "Tino."

"They're probably stuck in the same traffic jam as Shane and Sophie," said Zack.

My phone dinged a text message: Call ASAP.

Tino answered on the first ring. "Hey, Mrs. P. Change of plans."

"What's going on?"

He answered with a loud yawn. "Sorry. Haven't slept."

"Where are you?"

"Back at Ira's house. Finally."

"Back from where? And why haven't you slept?"

"We've been at the hospital since four this morning."

Zack's brows knit together. I mouthed "hospital" to him before continuing to speak with Tino, "Let me guess. Isaac climbed out his bedroom window again, and this time he fell and broke a leg."

"Worse. Ira was rushed into surgery with acute appendicitis."

"Oh dear! Is he okay?"

"He is now. He's out of recovery and resting in his room. I've notified the cruise line for him. You're to go to Guest Services as soon as you board the ship."

"Why?"

"Ira arranged to move you to his suite instead of the three cabins he booked for you, the boys, and Flora. They'll have your new cruise cards waiting."

I gritted my teeth. "How nice of him." Personally, I'd rather have a shoebox-sized cabin next to the boiler room as long as it came with complete privacy.

"He said to tell you to enjoy the cruise. He'll book another family vacation for everyone once he recovers."

"How long?"

"The next cruise?"

"No, the recovery period."

"Six weeks minimum."

"At least he has you to take care of him and the kids."

"Yeah, thanks a heap for that, Mrs. P."

"Regretting the manny job already, Tino? I thought you were bored with cyber-security and enjoying this new challenge."

"In retrospect, bleary-eyed boredom from sitting in front of a bank of computer monitors eight hours a day doesn't seem so bad compared to six or more additional weeks playing drill sergeant to Ira's three juvenile delinquents."

"I thought you were making a difference." Once Tino had stepped in after Ira's last nanny quit, his kids' behavior had definitely improved—not greatly, but Tino hadn't been on the job all that long.

"Only if I sit on them twenty-four/seven. I thought I could do some good. You know I'm not a quitter, Mrs. P."

"Of course not." The guy had served with distinction as part of Special Forces in the Middle East. He had the medals to prove it.

"I've never quit at anything in my life, but I'm raising the white flag on this one. Those kids are even too much for me. I'd rather be back in Iraq than have to spend one more day than necessary in this house."

"Does Ira know?"

"I had decided to give him a month's notice after the cruise. Now I'll have to wait until he's fully recovered before I even bring up the subject."

I heard a loud crash in the background. Tino cursed under his breath. "Gotta go, Mrs. P. Have fun on your cruise. I'll see you when you get back—assuming I'm still alive."

He hung up before I could wish him the luck I'm sure he'd need.

"What's going on?" asked Zack.

I glanced at both my sons. Each had their noses buried in their phones. "It appears the Karma gods are smiling down on Alex and Nick."

At the mention of their names, they pulled their attention from their screens and eyed me. "Huh?" they said in unison.

"Ira, his kids, and Tino won't be joining us." I then filled everyone in on the details.

"Best news ever," said Nick.

"Really?" I asked. "*Ever?*"

"Well, at least this week."

As we ascended the escalator that led to the gangway, I whispered to Zack, "I have to admit, as bad as I feel for Ira, not to mention Tino, I can't disagree with Nick."

"Neither can I. Now we can look forward to a relaxing vacation free of Ira's family drama."

"I do feel guilty, though. I know Tino took this job at my suggestion."

"Tino's one tough dude. Besides, he loves a challenge. I'll bet he whips those three hellions into line before Ira fully recovers."

"I hope you're right."

"How about we toast to his success with one of those decadent cocktails your mother waxed poetic over last night?"

"Sounds like a plan."

Little did I suspect at that very moment the sadistic deities who get their jollies messing with my life were currently rolling around in the clouds, laughing their derrieres off.

THREE

Shane and Sophie arrived in time to meet us for lunch at the Pearl of the Sea Buffet, a massive spread offering everything from basic American fare to international cuisine, not to mention an obscene selection of desserts. Many of the sugary confections were heart-shaped in celebration of Valentine's Day, which would occur during our cruise. And of course there were all those frothy umbrella drinks, which turned out to be unlimited and on the house, compliments of our upgraded status.

If I didn't exercise massive self-control, I'd easily gain ten pounds over the next week. Unfortunately, when it came to sweets and anything containing wine, rum, vodka, or tequila, my willpower took off for parts unknown. Hence, my pear-shaped figure that squeezed into a size eight only on a good day.

"Is that all you're eating?" asked Mama after I heaped my plate with nothing but leafy greens, cucumber slices, and a few drops of low-fat Italian dressing. She'd opted for the veal Parmesan, pasta with red sauce, and creamed spinach.

Why hadn't I inherited her metabolism? She ate like a sumo wrestler, yet never gained an ounce. Wasn't a woman's metabolism supposed to slow down after menopause? Leave it to my mother to be the lucky exception to the rule. "I'm not very hungry thanks to that enormous cocktail-of-the-day we were offered at guest services."

She eyed me suspiciously but said nothing. I knew Mama knew I had lied to her. She always did.

We were walking back to the table when Mama stopped dead in her tracks. "Is that who I think it is?" she said, her voice filled with excitement.

I followed her gaze. Several thousand people filled the Pearl of the Sea Buffet. None looked familiar to me. "Who?"

Mama pointed with her chin. "Over there. I do believe that's Victor Hogan."

Again, I asked, "Who?"

"You know, dear. The author. The one who writes all those juicy celebrity biographies."

I had no idea what Victor Hogan looked like. I knew him by reputation alone. I'd never waste my time reading the type of unauthorized, gossipy books he wrote. Mama, on the other hand, devoured them. "So?"

"I'd love to meet him."

I recognized that dreamy voice. Mama was definitely back in husband-hunting mode. If Victor Hogan was on this ship, he'd best prepare himself for an all-out campaign from Flora Sudberry Periwinkle Ramirez Scoffield Goldberg O'Keefe Tuttnauer. I followed behind her as she hurried back to our table and dropped her tray. "I'll be right back," she said, rushing off.

Zack raised an eyebrow in question.

"You don't want to know," I said.

A few minutes later Mama returned.

"Well?" I asked. "Mission accomplished?"

She heaved a huge sigh as she dropped into her seat. "I lost sight of him in the crowd."

I sent up a swift silent prayer to whichever deity watches over daughters of multi-married mothers. The last thing I needed was a stepfather who consistently made the pages of the tabloids.

As soon as they'd finished eating, Alex, Nick, and Sophie headed to the Teen Scene for a welcome mixer. "I'm off as well," said Mama, pushing back from the table. "There's a seniors get-acquainted gathering in the Ruby Bar. Perhaps Victor Hogan will be there."

I shook my head as I watched my mother, dressed in a two-piece Lily Pulitzer lemon yellow sweater set, crisp white linen pants, and yellow espadrilles, catwalk her way from the dining room. "There goes a woman on the prowl for Husband Number Seven," I said to Zack and Shane.

Shane chuckled.

Zack's voice sounded his surprise. "And she's set her sights on Victor Hogan?"

"You've heard of him?"

"Of course."

"I haven't," said Shane.

"He's almost as famous for getting sued as he is for the unauthorized books he writes about celebrities, athletes, and British royals," said Zack.

"She thinks she saw him a few minutes ago," I said. "That's why she rushed off earlier."

Zack groaned. "If Hogan is on this ship and Flora meets him, she's going to be in for a rude awakening. The guy certainly isn't worthy of hero worship."

"Nothing I can do about that." I stood and raised my coffee cup. "I'm going for a refill. Can I bring either of you anything?"

"I'm good," said Shane.

"Same here," said Zack.

I wandered around until I found a coffee station with less than a dozen people in line. As soon as I joined the queue, someone stepped behind me and said, "They need more caffeine stations on this ship."

Without turning around, I acknowledged his comment with a nod of my head and added, "Definitely."

He moved alongside me. At first I didn't think anything of it, until he said, "That's a rather unique ring you're wearing."

I turned to face him. The voice belonged to an older man. "Thank you."

"Have you had it long?"

Zack had given me his great-grandmother's engagement ring, which had been passed down first to his grandmother, then to his mother. The platinum setting featured a one-carat emerald cut diamond surrounded by a border inset with a vine motif accented with smaller diamonds. The vine and diamond pattern repeated around the circumference of the band.

However, I had no intention of imparting any information about the family heirloom to the stranger standing beside me. Instead, I said, "That's a rather personal question."

He placed a hand over his chest. "You're absolutely right. Forgive me, my dear. It's just that I haven't come across an Art Nouveau setting like that in several decades."

"Are you a jeweler?"

"I've dealt in antiques and estate jewelry from time to time." He offered me a tight-lipped smile and reached for my hand. "May I take a closer look?"

A year ago I would have thought nothing of allowing an elderly gentleman to take my hand to examine my engagement ring. But a year of encounters with the seamier side of humanity had honed my Spidey senses, which now tingled from my scalp down to my toes. I clutched my mug with both hands and took a step away from him. "Excuse me. I just remembered I'm late for an appointment." I spun around and hurried off before he could respond.

I made my way back to our table, glancing over my shoulder several times, relieved to find no overly inquisitive septuagenarian following close on my heels. Zack and Shane were deep in conversation when I arrived but clammed up as I settled into my seat.

"Forget something?" asked Zack, his brows knit together as he stared at me.

"Huh?"

He pointed to my mug. "Didn't you go for a refill?"

I glanced down at the empty coffee mug, still wrapped in a death grip. "Long lines," I said. "I'll get some later."

He reached across the table and pried my fingers loose. "What's going on?"

"It's probably nothing."

He studied me for a moment, then said, "Or it's definitely something."

"What happened?" asked Shane. The grooves that years of outdoor construction work had etched into his forehead deepened with concern.

I shook my head and laughed. "I think my imagination got the better of me." I told them about my encounter.

"Cruise ships often attract grifters, pickpockets, and jewel thieves," said Zack.

"They prey mostly on elderly widows," added Shane.

"Well, thanks for that!" I said. "I may be a widow, but I hardly consider myself *elderly* at the ripe old age of forty-three."

Shane's face grew beet red. "Boy, did that ever come out wrong."

Zack laughed as he turned toward him. "You think?"

"What I meant was we should warn Flora, especially if she's brought any expensive jewelry onboard."

"Nice recovery, man," said Zack, patting Shane across the back. He then turned to me. "What did this guy look like?"

"Probably in his seventies. Dapper. Well dressed. About six feet, muscular build. Closely cropped white hair. The kind of guy who probably belongs to an exclusive country club and spends his days working out with a personal trainer when he's not on the golf course."

"Chances are, on a ship this large you won't run into him again," said Zack, "but if you happen to notice him, point him out to me."

"I will, but I'm sure he's nothing more than a harmless old man."

"You don't get rattled by harmless old men."

No, I don't. So was I suffering from a form of PTSD, or were my Spidey senses trying to tell me something?

~*~

Shortly after the Gemstone Empress left port, the boys and Mama returned to our suite. We all bundled up against a whipping winter wind and headed out onto the deck to meet Shane and Sophie. Standing at the railing, the seven of us watched as the ship cruised past the Statue of Liberty on our way out to sea and toward The Bahamas. In little more than twenty-four hours bathing suits would replace parkas, not that I had any intention of parading my cellulite-dimpled thighs around several thousand other passengers and crewmembers.

After a few minutes a series of bells sounded over the ship-wide loudspeaker system. Moments later the captain came on, alerting all passengers of the mandatory muster taking place in half an hour. According to our cruise cards, our muster station was the Emerald Lounge on the Atrium Deck.

"What's a muster?" asked Sophie.

"It's like a fire drill," said Mama, our self-appointed cruise expert. "A crewmember will explain that in case of an emergency, they'll pass out life jackets once we all arrive at our stations, then lead us to the lifeboats."

Sophie's eyes grew wide. With one hand she latched onto Alex's arm. Her other hand grabbed for her father. "You mean like in *Titanic*?"

"It's just a formality required by Maritime Law," said Shane. "Nothing to worry about, Soph. It's no different from the monthly fire drills you have at school."

"But sometimes there are fires in schools," said Sophie. "What if we hit an iceberg?"

"We're heading south," said Alex. "No icebergs."

"Besides," said Nick, "thanks to global warming, all the icebergs are melting. Even if we hit one, it wouldn't do more than put a small dent in the ship."

I heaved a sigh. Time for another Mom Look. "Not helping,

Nick."

"We're not going to hit an iceberg," said Zack. "Or anything else. This ship is equipped with modern technology that wasn't around when the Titanic sailed. We're perfectly safe, Sophie."

She eyed Zack skeptically. "You're sure?"

"Positive. You have my word."

Sophie exhaled a shudder, which could have been from nerves, the freezing temperatures, or both. "Why don't we get out of the cold and head down to the Emerald Lounge now?" I said. "I hear hot cocoa calling."

The seven of us tramped out of the whipping wind into the warmth of the ship and headed for the Atrium Deck. We found the concourse jam-packed with passengers. Making matters worse, crewmembers were busy setting up dozens of tables running down the center of the floor from one end of the concourse to the other.

I wonder what all these tables are for," I said.

"Duty-free shopping," said Mama, once again informing us of her superior cruise knowledge. "Along with the shops that will open once we're out in international waters, these tables will be filled with designer watches, purses, jewelry, and cruise clothes.

"This is worse than the crowds and street vendors in Times Square," I said.

"Everyone probably had the same idea as us," said Mama. "They'll shut down the bars and restaurants prior to the muster. This is the last chance to grab something to eat or drink until after the muster ends."

As we entered the cavernous Emerald Lounge, I spied an empty table toward the back and made a beeline for it before anyone else snagged it. With Mama holding down the fort, Sophie and I grabbed a few unoccupied chairs from other tables and dragged them over to the table while Zack, Shane, and the boys stood in line at a beverage station off to one side for our hot cocoa.

Another series of bells sounded, followed by a repeat of the muster announcement. Then another and another, every five minutes as people poured into the Emerald Lounge.

A crewmember came around and checked our names off a master list. Ten-minutes after the arrival deadline, the loudspeaker began paging dozens of no-shows. "This happens on every cruise," said Mama. Some people think they're too important to follow the rules."

"The joke will be on them when it's a real emergency and they miss the last lifeboat," said Nick.

This time I didn't need to spear my son with a Mom Look. His brother did it for me. "Stop being a jerk, Nick." He punctuated his words with a wallop to Nick's arm.

I glanced at Sophie. Her knuckles had turned white from gripping her cocoa mug. Zack leaned in and whispered in my ear, "I think Nick needs to find a girlfriend."

Sophie had begun to think of Nick as a younger brother, and he was certainly acting like one right now—the pesky kind. I thought my sons had gotten beyond sibling rivalry, but Nick's behavior lately loudly proclaimed three's a crowd. "Maybe he'll meet someone on the ship he can hang with," I whispered back.

Twenty-minutes later another series of bells sounded, alerting us to the official start of the muster. The crewmember who had checked off our names pointed out the location of the lifejackets, which he said would be handed out if needed. He then directed our attention to a series of TV screens mounted on the walls around the room. A safety video gave instructions for donning the lifejackets and explained everything we'd need to know in the event of an actual emergency.

When the video ended, another series of bells sounded, followed by a woman's voice. "Good afternoon, ladies and gentlemen. I'm Lily, your cruise director. I want to welcome you aboard the Gemstone Empress for your weeklong cruise to The Bahamas. We have a huge array of activities available for you while onboard, so be sure to check out *GemEvents*, your daily ship newsletter for times and locations. If you haven't done so already, don't forget to reserve your seats for our evening shows and sign up for the various ports-of-call shore excursions we offer. My staff and I will be happy to assist you with any questions you may have. Happy cruising!"

An hour and a half after we first arrived for our hot cocoa, we were finally dismissed. "I'm going to drop my coat back in our suite," said Mama, "then head over to the Sapphire Lounge to play some Bingo."

"Let's check out the bumper cars," said Nick.

Sophie frowned. "I'd rather check out the shops."

Alex rolled his eyes. "You want to go *shopping?*"

"So do I," I said, not that I planned to buy anything, but I thought it might be a good idea not to force Alex to choose between his brother and his girlfriend. "The rest of you go do guy things. We'll meet up later."

Zack and Shane looked toward each other. "Bumper cars it is, then," said Shane.

"Minus the coats," said Zack.

As we filed out of the Emerald Lounge, I thought I saw the man from lunch. I pulled on Zack's arm and pointed. "That's him."

Zack turned to look in the direction I had indicated. "Where?

I can't see anyone who looks like the guy you described."

Neither did I. "I could have sworn I saw him."

~*~

Twenty minutes later Sophie and I stood at a glass counter perusing the wire racks of earrings in one of the shops. "What about these?" she asked, pulling a pair from one of the displays. She removed the earrings from their plastic container and held them up to her ears, checking her reflection in a nearby mirror. The earrings consisted of a grouping of three silver flowers with small topaz stones mounted in the center of each bloom.

"Lovely. I think you should wait to buy them, though."

"Why?"

I pointed to the sign above the display that indicated Yellow Elder was the national flower of The Bahamas. "You might find a larger selection once we arrive in Nassau."

"And they'll probably be cheaper on the island. Dad will appreciate that."

I had to commend *bazillionaire* Shane Lambert for instilling proper values in his daughter. "If you don't find anything you like better in our various ports of call, you can always buy these later. My mother mentioned cruise lines steeply discount everything toward the end of each cruise."

"So they add huge markups at the beginning of the cruises for suckers like me?"

"For first-time cruisers who don't know any better."

"In other words, suckers." Sophie placed the earrings back in their box and returned the box to the rack.

"Wise move, young lady."

I spun around to find the man from lunch standing behind me. Instinctively I placed my arm around Sophie and drew her closer to me. "Are you following me?"

"Not in the least but I'm glad I bumped into you."

"And why is that?"

"I wanted to apologize. I'm afraid we got off to a rocky start earlier." He pointed to my left hand, clasped around Sophie's forearm. "I may have appeared a bit aggressive in my excitement over seeing your ring. I didn't mean to frighten you."

"You need to work on your people skills."

"So I've been told. Will you accept my apology?"

"Accepted. Now if you'll excuse us, we have to be going."

"Wow," said Sophie as I hurried her out of the shop, "you're really rattled. Hard to believe you're the same person who kept me from getting kidnapped. What happened between you and that guy earlier?"

I told her about my first encounter with the man. "According to your dad and Zack, he might be a thief. They often target women on cruise ships."

"First the lifeboats, now thieves? I'm beginning to regret talking Dad into cancelling our ski trip for this cruise."

That made two of us. "Something about that man bothers me. I think your dad and Zack might be right about him, that he's up to no good."

"And you never met him before today?"

"No, why?"

Sophie tilted her head and wrinkled her nose. "There's something familiar about him."

I stopped walking and turned to stare at her. "In what way?"

She shook her head. "I don't know, but I get the feeling I've seen him somewhere."

I didn't like the sound of that. After winning the lottery, Shane and Sophie had experienced the darker side of coming into such an enormous windfall. He'd legally changed their names and moved them across the country in an attempt to keep his daughter safe. I pulled out my cell phone. "We need to round up everyone."

FOUR

"What's going on?" asked Mama, the last to arrive at our suite. "I was on a roll."

"Bingo will have to wait, Mama. Have a seat."

She settled onto one end of the leather sectional couch in the middle of the suite's expansive living area, which included a full-size dining room table, large enough to seat twelve, and a baby grand piano. Ira had spared no expense, booking the ship's premiere accommodations for himself and his kids. It wasn't going to be easy returning to my too-small, worn-out mid-century rancher.

Once I had everyone's attention, I filled Mama and the boys in on my lunch encounter at the coffee station, finishing with, "A few minutes ago the same man approached Sophie and me."

"What did he say?" asked Shane. He jumped to his feet and strode across the room to hover nearer his daughter.

Sophie sat on one section of the sofa, between Alex and Nick. She turned to me. "You tell them."

I related the encounter and gave everyone a description of the man. "Zack and Shane think he might be a grifter who preys on women. You need to be careful, Mama."

"I know the con, dear. I've had some of those gigolos hit on me during past cruises. They love to go after older widows who look like they have money."

Another older widow reference? I shook off my irritation to concentrate on what was really important. Mama had no money, but that didn't keep her from dressing like she did, thanks to her ongoing affair with Mr. Lord and Mr. Taylor. "What did you do?"

"I make it perfectly clear that I live only on Social Security and the cruise is a gift from my children. That always sends them scurrying."

"*Children?*" My eyebrows shot northward. "How many siblings do I not know about, Mama?"

She offered me a sheepish grin. "It sounds more convincing."

Zack laughed. "Very savvy, Flora."

And yet she'd had at least one shipboard romance that hadn't ended well. After Lou Beaumont's death, Mama discovered some secrets he'd hidden from her. Her current bravado sounded too much like revisionist history to me.

"Of course, the gentleman could be completely innocent and only lacking in social graces," she said. "I've certainly met my share of men like that over the years."

Sophie shook her head. "I'm on Team Anastasia. I got some bad vibes from the guy."

I glanced at her. She hadn't mentioned that earlier. "Sophie also thinks he looked familiar."

Alarm deepened the weathered creases of Shane's face. "What do you mean?"

"I think I've seen him somewhere."

"In Westfield?"

"I don't know, Dad. It could be nothing. Maybe I spotted him in the cruise terminal. Or at a school event. He could be someone's grandfather, right?"

"Maybe we're all getting overly paranoid," I said.

"With good reason," said Zack. He addressed the three teens. "For now, keep your eyes open, don't go anywhere alone, and steer clear of anyone who makes you uncomfortable."

"Even the least bit," said Shane. He directed his next comment to his daughter. "And let us know if you see this guy again."

~*~

Due to Ira's emergency surgery, we found ourselves joined by five strangers at dinner that evening. According to Mama's cruise expertise, passengers outnumbered the total seats in the dining room for the combined early and late seatings. This resulted in a waiting list for both. "So where do people eat if they don't get a spot in the dining room?" asked Sophie.

Mama ticked off the other choices. "At the Pearl of the Sea Buffet, the various casual dining spots around the ship, or the premier celebrity chef restaurants."

With an overabundance of senior citizens as passengers, the five-thirty seating, which Ira had booked because of his kids, looked like the cruise equivalent of the Early Bird Special at any major chain restaurant in Florida.

The dining room had been decorated for Valentine's Day. Pink, red, and white balloons created a sculpted archway at the entrance. A faux crystal bud vase with a single carnation in one of the three colors decorated each table.

A waiter directed us to a round table already occupied by two men and three women, four of them old enough to qualify as grandparents, the fifth bordering on the edge of senior status. As we approached, I overheard Nick whisper to Alex and Sophie, "I vote we ditch the old folks after tonight and eat on our own at one of the other spots."

"I'm in," said Alex.

"Ditto," said Sophie.

"Welcome, folks," said the man at the far end of the table, his voice overly boisterous as he raised a pilsner of beer in our direction. He wore a garish Hawaiian shirt patterned with nasty looking cartoon monkeys lobbing coconuts at each other as they scampered up and down palm trees. "Now that we're all here, how about if I start the introduction ball rolling?"

Without waiting for a reply from any of us, he placed a massive pudgy hand on the shoulder of the woman seated to his left and said, "We're Orson and Birdie Gilbert." With his other hand still holding his glass, he indicated the couple to his wife's left. "And this here is Birdie's twin sister Bunny and her husband Dennis Marwood."

Aside from similar silver-gray pixie cuts, Bunny and Birdie looked nothing alike. Either Bunny towered over her sister, or Birdie had slumped low in her chair. The top of her head came no higher than her sister's chin. Her sunken features and emaciated frame were suggestive of someone who had recently suffered through a serious illness. I doubted she weighed a hundred pounds. Three Birdies might come close to equaling one Bunny— maybe three-and-a-half.

In contrast, each woman's husband was her polar opposite. Dennis definitely needed to put on a few pounds. With his deeply etched wrinkles and unkempt wiry hair sticking out from all directions under a well-worn feed cap, he reminded me of a scarecrow—one still standing in the cornfield from the previous growing season.

Unlike his brother-in-law's flamboyant garb, Dennis wore a traditional red and blue checked short-sleeved button-down shirt. Slightly frayed around the collar and in need of ironing, the shirt added to the scarecrow motif.

The twins had dressed in matching pink T-shirts emblazoned with the cruise logo. Birdie's, at least two sizes too big, hung from her shoulders. Bunny could have used a size or two larger, the fabric straining across her ample bosom.

Orson, a burly man with a steel-gray comb-over, sported broken capillaries on his bulbous nose. Coupled with his ruddy complexion and the slight tremor in the hand that still rested on his wife's shoulder, I suspected the beer wasn't his first of the day.

Neither the sisters nor Dennis did more than glance toward us.

Orson continued speaking, mentioning the two couples lived in a retirement community on the outskirts of Princeton, then added, "We've been cruising together with Gemstones of the Seven Seas ever since we retired twelve years ago. The Gemstone Empress is like a second home to us."

Perhaps the dour expressions on the faces of Birdie and the Marwoods had to do with the dining room captain performing a last-minute reshuffling of seats after Ira cancelled. They certainly didn't look thrilled to be sharing a table with us.

Finally, Orson turned to the fifty-something woman seated on his right and rested a beefy palm over her hand. "Your turn, my dear."

I caught Birdie's lips tighten at the endearment and familiarity with which her husband addressed the woman, his hand remaining in place on hers. Did Orson make a habit of hitting on single, younger women whenever they cruised, or was he merely a clueless guy of a certain bygone era?

Birdie glanced over at her sister before she reached for her wine glass. Bunny shook her head, frowning as Birdie downed the glass's contents in one long swig.

The woman in question had continued to study her menu while Orson spoke. Without so much as a sideways glance in his direction, she slipped her hand out from under his, raised her chin, and offered us a stiff smile. No doubt she'd choose a seat several chairs removed from Orson Gilbert's overly friendly paw for the remainder of the cruise. "Lenore Rosedale," she said, her voice as taut as the severe bun that pulled her chestnut hair so tightly off her face that it gave the impression of a facelift performed by an overzealous plastic surgeon.

We waited, expecting her to add something in addition to her name. When she didn't, Zack broke the awkward silence by introducing our group. Afterward, with the waiter hovering impatiently, pen and notepad at the ready, we turned our attention to the dinner selections.

Mama had taken the empty seat next to Lenore. "I remember you from Bingo this afternoon. Are you traveling alone?"

"I am." Lenore gazed off in the distance for a moment, blinking several times in rapid succession to ward off the tears gathering behind her eyes. "This is my first cruise since I lost my husband."

"Same here," said Mama.

Nick executed a double take. His jaw flapped open as he stared at his grandmother.

I stopped him with a Mom Look and a slight shake of my head before he could spill the Lawrence beans. Technically, Mama *had* lost her husband—to the federal prison system. If she wanted to pretend her ex had died, let her. Our dinner companions didn't need to know the truth about Lawrence Tuttnauer.

After the waiter took our orders, the twins returned to conversing between themselves while their husbands turned their attention to their phones. However, Lenore appeared to relax and open up once Mama engaged her in some friendly Bingo-related conversation. The two seemed on their way toward becoming BFF cruising buddies.

Once dinner ended, Mama announced the two had decided to hit the casino. "You're not going to the show?" I asked.

"We've both seen it on our last cruises." She and Lenore pushed themselves away from the table, and Mama offered us a wave. "Don't wait up, dear."

"Bingo this afternoon, now the casino," I muttered to Zack as I watched the two women snake their way around tables toward the dining room exit. "I hope she doesn't blow her entire Social Security check for the month on a quickie with a one-armed bandit."

"I don't think slot machines have had arms in years," said Zack. "They're all push-button now."

What did I know? Even though I've lived my entire life in New Jersey, I'd never visited Atlantic City. My sole experience with casinos had to do with learning my husband had dropped dead in one after blowing quite a bit more than our life's savings.

"Besides, continued Zack, "I seriously doubt she's gambling with her own money."

"Ira?"

"Is there any doubt?"

Ira Pollack believed money solved all problems. After

Lawrence's arrest and conviction, Ira's guilt over having played matchmaker between Lawrence and Mama led him to assume the bulk of Mama's expenses. Without any qualms, Mama channeled Blanche duBois and gracefully accepted Ira's self-imposed penance. Unlike the character in *Streetcar Named Desire*, Mama relied on the generosity of one particular quasi-relation rather than strangers. However, giving Mama carte blanche might change Ira's philosophy once he opened his credit card statements at the end of the month.

The teens voted to take in a showing of the latest Marvel movie in the Crown Jewels Theater while Zack, Shane, and I opted for the live Vegas-style review in the Scepter and Orb Theater, given that Ira had previously booked our seats prior to the cruise setting sail. We bid good evening to the twins and their husbands and followed Mama and Lenore's path out of the dining room.

Before entering the theater, I decided to duck into the ladies' room. As I headed back to where Zack and Shane waited, I saw the elderly man from earlier in the day approach Zack from the opposite direction. We both arrived at the same moment.

"Hello, Junior."

Junior? I stared first at the man, then at Zack. Suddenly I realized why Sophie found the man so familiar. How had I not noticed the resemblance before now?

"How the hell did you get out early?" asked Zack.

"If you must know—"

"Oh, you better believe I must."

"A benefactor interceded on my behalf." The man turned to me and smiled. "Well, my dear, if this isn't an interesting coincidence."

Zack looped his arm over my shoulder and pulled me closer to him. "Is it? I find that hard to believe, considering you're not up for parole again for another year."

"The system works in mysterious ways."

"As well as corrupt ones, given I was never notified of your release."

"That's between you and the U.S. Postal Service. Take it up with them."

"Or maybe I should take it up with the parole board. Who is this benefactor, and what did you promise him in exchange for his intercession?"

The man's eyes glinted as he smiled, but when he didn't answer, Zack said, "Not to mention how unusual it is for parolees to be allowed to leave the state, let alone the country."

The man spread his arms. "Yet here I am. With the full knowledge of my parole officer."

Zack took a step closer to him. His eyes narrowed, and his tone grew low and menacing. "I'm only going to say this once, Emerson. So listen carefully. Keep your distance. From me, my fiancée, her family, and our friends."

The man twisted his mouth into a sneer. "Is that a threat, son?"

Zack's grip on my shoulders increased. I twisted my neck to stare at the tic beating within his clenched jaw and the angry blood vessel throbbing along his temple. I'd seen him nearly lose control on several occasions, but all involved threats to my life. They paled in comparison to the seething anger I now witnessed.

"*Son?* You lost the right to call me that the day you murdered my mother."

FIVE

The man Zack had called Emerson showed no reaction to the accusation other than silently glaring at Zack for a beat before turning and walking away. I, on the other hand, found myself juggling a myriad of conflicting emotions. Hurt and anger topped the list. I wriggled out from under his arm and stepped in front of him. "Care to explain?"

He turned to Shane. "Looks like we won't be joining you at the show."

"Understood." Shane placed his hand on my upper arm and offered a reassuring squeeze before leaving us to enter the theater.

Zack and I silently walked back to our suite. Once inside he placed his index finger to his lips, pulled out his phone, and tapped the screen several times. I stood with my arms crossed over my chest, waiting for more than a minute as he stared at his phone. Then I watched as he slowly canvassed the entire suite, pointing the phone in every possible nook and cranny.

After about ten minutes Zack pocketed the phone and said, "I need a few minutes before we talk."

"For what? To figure out more half-truths to tell me? You just had a few minutes. What was that all about? Searching for Pokemon?"

"I was making sure the suite isn't bugged."

"By your *father*?"

"Nothing would surprise me."

"And you say you're not a spy. Yet you just happen to have a cell phone that detects listening devices." Fighting back tears, I said, "How can I believe anything you say any more?"

Zack ran a hand through his hair as he expelled a huge sigh. "Okay, I deserved that." He pulled the phone back out of his pocket, tapped the screen again, and showed it to me. "It's an app anyone can download, which is what I did while you were standing watching me. But I still need to make a phone call before we talk."

I waved him away. "By all means. Call your handler. That is what you spies call them, isn't it?"

"Actually, I'm calling my attorney."

"If you say so." I walked into the bedroom and slammed the door behind me. A childish reaction I regretted immediately, no matter how satisfying it felt. I grabbed a folded blanket from the foot of the bed and wrapped myself in it. Then I stepped out onto the darkened balcony and curled up on one of the deck chairs. Hugging my knees to my chest, I closed my eyes and allowed the tears to spill silently down my cheeks.

I'd left the slider open and didn't hear Zack until sometime later when the other deck chair creaked from his weight. He cupped his hands over my clasped fists that held the blanket against my body. "You have every right to be angry with me."

I opened my eyes and turned to face him. "I certainly do. Why would you keep something so critical from me? You led me to believe your father had simply walked out on you after your mother died."

He didn't answer immediately. Finally he said, "The last time I spoke about what happened was the day I testified against him at his trial."

I shifted onto my side to face him better. He sat on the edge of the deck chair, leaning toward me. I had never seen him so raw, so emotionally exposed, and I dreaded what he'd say next. "You testified?"

"If I hadn't, he would have walked." He sucked in a lungful of air, exhaling forcefully before continuing. "I saw him kill my mother."

I gasped. Before I could say anything, he plowed ahead. "Emerson owned the local pharmacy in our town. My mother often filled in when one of the employees took vacation or sick days. Apparently, one day she found some major discrepancies in the accounts. She did some further digging and realized he was trafficking in narcotics."

"She confronted him?"

He nodded. "She didn't realize I'd come home and was in my room. They were down the hall in their bedroom, shouting at each other at the top of their lungs. Even with my door closed, I heard every word. My mother said she was calling the police. He told her to put down the phone. The sound of her heels on the hardwood grew louder as she raced down the hall toward the staircase, I'm guessing to get to the downstairs phone. I opened my door a crack just in time to see him rush her from behind, slamming her to the floor."

In the dim light that filtered onto the balcony from within the suite I saw Zack squeeze his eyes shut. "Emerson lifted weights; my mother was tiny. He hoisted her over his head and hurled her down the stairs. To this day, I hear her scream in my nightmares."

I hated that I had forced him to relive his mother's murder. My heart broke. I strained to speak around the lump that had formed in my throat. "What did you do?"

"I was terrified of what would happen if he knew I'd seen him. I remained in my room, both hands clasped tightly over my mouth, stifling the sobs building inside me.

"I remember shaking violently as he descended the staircase. I thought surely he'd hear me, but he didn't. A moment later he returned with one of her shoes. He snapped the heel and dropped both pieces on the landing. The bastard actually dusted his hands as he made his way back downstairs to call the police."

"He staged evidence of an accident?"

Zack clenched his jaw. "That's when I knew for certain he'd killed her. When the police arrived, I heard him tell them he'd come home to find her at the bottom of the steps."

I shuddered. Zack stood and pulled me to my feet. "You're shivering. Let's go inside."

Once in the suite and settled on the sofa, I asked. "You refuted his account to the police?"

Before answering, he headed for the bar and grabbed the bottle of bourbon. "Join me?"

I nodded, needing something to help calm the emotional upheaval running rampant within me.

"Not then," he said, answering my question. He shook his head as he partially filled two glasses. "I waited in my room until he drove off behind the ambulance. Then I ran the half-mile to my grandparents' house and told them what had happened. They called the police."

He handed me a glass and joined me on the sofa. "Based on what I'd overheard, they were able to secure warrants to search the pharmacy and the house. They arrested him later that evening. He kept demanding to see me. I refused. I didn't see him again until I testified at his trial."

"I'm sorry."

"No, I am. I should have told you, especially knowing how Karl deceived you for years. Can you forgive me?"

At least he understood the crux of my hurt and anger. "Of course. I love you. Whatever happens, we'll get through this together."

He cupped my face in his hand and stared into my eyes. "You really are the best thing that has ever happened to me. I don't know what I'd do if I lost you."

"And I don't know what I'd do without you. I'm not going anywhere. You're stuck with me."

"I was worried for a moment."

I nursed a sip of the bourbon, then asked the one question still nagging at me. "Why didn't you tell me?"

"For one, I didn't think it was fair to burden you with ancient history, not with all you've had to deal with this last year. But it was also selfish of me. I wasn't keeping my past from you as much as burying it for my own sake. And I thought it worked. Until tonight."

Under the circumstances, I don't know how Zack didn't totally lose it when his father approached us. "The call you made?"

"What about it?"

"Was that to find out why he was released early?"

He frowned into his glass. "My lawyer was just as shocked at the news. He's going to make a few calls first thing tomorrow morning."

"Most of what I know about parole comes from the movies and TV. It's probably not at all accurate, but I thought victims and their relatives are notified of parole hearings."

"Both parole hearings and when a felon is released. That's the way it's supposed to work and always has—until now."

"Did you confront your father at the previous parole hearings?"

"No, testimony is confidential, whether given to the board in person or in writing. The parole board doesn't even necessarily meet with the convict."

"So your father hasn't seen you since you were eleven years old?"

"That's right."

Something wasn't adding up. "He called you Junior, but you called him Emerson."

"I was christened Emerson Dawes, Jr., but I couldn't go through life with the name of the man who killed my mother. I took my maternal grandfather's name."

"You legally changed your name?"

"I did."

Something he had in common with Shane and Sophie, if for different reasons. Maybe this was why Zack and Shane had grown so close in a relatively short period of time.

"Did you remain in the same town?"

"No, my grandparents dragged me to a therapist who recommended a fresh start. We moved to California."

"And your father never knew any of this?"

"How could he? Unless..."

His gaze locked with mine. "He knew you immediately, Zack, knew you'd be on this cruise. He recognized my ring."

"Someone's been feeding him information."

"Maybe for a long time. Who would have that sort of power?"

He shook his head. "It's more a matter of money than power. The parole board is a dumping ground for political patronage. It's rife with abuses. Not all of the appointees are the most upstanding of citizens. Grease a few unscrupulous palms, and you can sway votes in your favor."

"Why after all these years, though?"

"I don't know. Maybe it took him all this time to make the right connections."

Like a recent addition to the prison population? Someone who had laundered money for the mob and had far-reaching tentacles? My heart dropped into my stomach. Blood roared in my ears. "Someone like Lawrence."

Zack reached for my hand. "It's not Lawrence."

"How can you be sure?"

"Different systems, for one thing. Lawrence is in a federal penitentiary. Emerson was in a state prison, not to mention in a different state."

"So who greased those palms for your father? And why?"

"That's what I need to find out. He's not on this ship by coincidence. He's up to something."

I worried the *something* had everything to do with revenge that had festered and grown within Emerson Dawes for thirty-five years. After all, if not for Zack, his father would have gotten away with murder—literally. "What are you going to do?"

"For one, tell the captain he's got a killer on his ship. If the crew is alerted to keep an eye on him, there's less chance he'll have an opportunity to carry out whatever he's got planned."

"And then?"

Zack stood and began pacing across the expanse of the living room. "Figure out his plan and thwart it."

~*~

Zack placed a call to see if the captain was on duty. After learning he was on the bridge, Zack suggested I stay in the suite while he went to speak with him.

I offered him a stink eye. "Seriously?"

He threw his hands up in resignation. "What was I thinking?"

"Obviously, you weren't."

He chuckled, then kissed me. "Obviously not."

My emotions somewhat assuaged, I linked my arm through his as we left the suite.

We passed few people as we took the staircase from our deck up to the bridge. Most passengers were either taking in the various evening's entertainments, losing money at the casino, or having dinner in one of the shipboard restaurants.

We were met on Deck Twelve at the entrance to the bridge by one of the ship's officers. "May I help you, sir?"

His name badge read Xavier, which could have been either his first or last name. The ship's stewards and the dining room staff all wore badges indicating their first names and countries of origin. However Xavier's badge was pinned to an official-looking naval-type uniform. Still, he might be no more than a flunky posted at the entrance to the inner sanctum, his only duty to keep passengers from pestering the captain.

Zack explained we had important information the captain needed to know.

"I'm afraid passengers are not allowed on the bridge, sir."

"Unless they shell out more than a hundred dollars for a bridge tour," I said, having read of the pricey tour in our cruise packet.

Xavier scowled at me before continuing to speak to Zack. "As First Officer, I can handle whatever concerns you have, sir. The captain is a very busy man. If the subject requires his attention, I'll relay your message to him."

"You think he might be interested in knowing there's a killer on his ship?" I asked.

Given that Xavier's jaw nearly dropped to his feet, I'm guessing he'd probably expected to hear a complaint about the dearth of coffee stations at the Pearl of the Sea Buffet or the television programming that consisted solely of infomercials and a single sports channel that only played international soccer games. "Wait over there," he said, indicating a seating area off to our left. He then race-walked inside the bridge.

"Looks like he agrees the subject requires the captain's attention," I said, dropping into one of the upholstered chairs.

"Subtle," said Zack, but I did notice he fought to hold back a grin.

I leaned against the seat cushion and stared at a coal-black, star-filled sky, the likes of which never occurs in New Jersey. Thanks to all the light emanating from the cities and suburbs, our skies never grew dark enough at night to see much more than the International Space Station and the planes coming and going from Newark Liberty, JFK, and La Guardia.

Xavier returned a moment later, ushered us inside the bridge, and escorted us to a cordoned off area. I assumed this was the place where passengers who had paid for the bridge tour were penned for the presentation.

Xavier left us and approached a man stationed in front of a

high-tech command center filled with computer screens and console panels that wrapped around three sides of the bridge and overlooked the bow of the ship. The First Officer stood approximately six feet tall. The man he spoke with had nearly a foot on him.

The giant of a man glanced in our direction. With his chiseled jaw, ice-blue eyes, blond hair, and perfect posture that filled a crisply starched white uniform, he looked like a Nordic sea captain right out of Central Casting. He exchanged a few more words with Xavier before joining us.

"I'm Captain Halvorson," he said with a slight Scandinavian accent as he extended his hand toward Zack. "And you are?"

At six-two Zack needed to raise his chin to look the captain in the eye as they shook hands. "Zachary Barnes. This is my fiancée, Anastasia Pollack."

The captain dipped his head toward me, adding a slight chivalrous tap to the brim of his cap, "Ms. Pollack." He then turned back to Zack. "What's this about a murderer on my ship?"

Zack explained in broad strokes without going into either detail or personal history.

"The cruise line routinely performs background checks of all prospective passengers," said the captain. "A recently paroled murderer would have been flagged and not allowed onboard."

"He's likely traveling under an assumed name with a bogus passport." Zack began to explain the unusual circumstances surrounding the release of Emerson Dawes. "There's also the suspicious coincidence of him showing up on this particular cruise."

"Why is that?"

"Because, Captain, I'm on this ship. Emerson Dawes is my

father."

The captain stiffened, his eyes narrowing. "Are you worried for your safety, Mr. Barnes?"

Zack squeezed my hand. "Mine and my traveling companions. My fiancée's sons and her mother are also traveling with us, as well as a friend and his daughter."

While on photography assignments, Zack had faced down drug smugglers in South America and camped out in the jungles of Madagascar in search of lemurs and pochards. Nothing fazed him—with the exception of discussing his past. I could tell he really didn't want to dive into the weeds any more than necessary with the captain. However, as a mother, I knew that it's always best to yank a bandage off as quickly as possible. "When Zack was a child, he witnessed his father kill his mother," I said. "His testimony convicted Dawes."

The captain looked down at Zack. "You might have led with that, Mr. Barnes."

The muscles of Zack's jaw tensed. "The bottom line, Captain, is that given the corruption that had to have occurred for his release, it stands to reason, those same forces were instrumental in getting him on this ship. He's a dangerous man who has been denied parole at every one of his previous hearings."

The captain thought for a moment. "If he's on the ship illegally, we can hold him in the brig until we dock back in the States."

• Who knew a cruise ship had a brig? But this was the best possible news. Emerson Dawes couldn't carry out his nefarious plan—no matter what it was—from a locked cell.

However, the captain would have to find him first. He obviously wasn't listed on the passenger manifest as Emerson

Dawes. "With four thousand passengers on board, it's going to take time to track down a man traveling under an assumed name no one knows."

"It shouldn't take very long," said the captain. "The ship's manifest contains the passport photos of all passengers. I can arrange for you to view it. Once you identify the photo, we'll have his name and cabin number. In addition, all public areas of the ship are monitored with security cameras. We can pull the footage to track his movements."

I wish I had the captain's confidence, but I'd dealt with enough killers lately to know it's never that easy, even with surveillance cameras and a crew of fifteen hundred.

However, before the captain could give the order for us to view the manifest, a flurry of activity erupted across the bridge. Xavier rushed over to us. "Excuse me, Captain. Sorry to interrupt you."

"Yes?"

Xavier scrutinized us, hesitating before continuing. "We appear to have a Rising Star situation, sir." He leaned closer to the captain and continued in a voice too quiet for me to hear.

Rising Star sounded like an amateur talent show, but with all color leaching from the captain's wind-blown features, the term must designate something more serious than a dancer with a sprained ankle. He, too, quickly glanced at Zack and me before turning back to Xavier and asking, "Where?"

"Deck Five, portside. Outside the Smoky Quartz Pub."

"Is the area secured?"

"Crew is working on it now, sir."

"Tell them I'm on my way." He shot Zack and me a look. "You two come with me."

"What's going on?" asked Zack.

"Your killer may have already struck."

SIX

I couldn't move. Terrible images of my sons, Mama, Sophie, and Shane bombarded my brain. I squeezed my eyes shut and concentrated on keeping my limbs from shaking, my lungs from hyperventilating.

Zack grabbed me by the shoulders and shook me out of my stupor. "They're okay."

I opened my eyes and nodded, willing it to be so. Then he laced his fingers through mine, and we raced to keep up with the captain's long strides.

Once inside the elevator, I found the courage to look directly up into the captain's eyes and ask, "Do you know the identity of the victim?"

He shook his head. "Unknown at this time beyond an older male."

Relief washed over me—for a split-second. Until I thought of Shane. His earlier life working construction out west had aged him well beyond his mid-thirties. When we'd first met, I'd pegged the craggy, weathered composite of Daniel Craig and Hugh Laurie as at least fifty.

I glanced at Zack and realized the same thoughts filled his head. "Let's not jump to conclusions," he whispered.

As we descended, an announcement came over the ship-wide public address system. "Operation Rising Star. Port promenade Five SQP."

"Rising Star is code for a murder?" I asked, the irony not lost on me.

"A death," said the captain. "Not necessarily a murder. Euphemisms keep from spoiling the cruise for the majority of our passengers."

Zack squeezed my hand. "Meaning the victim may have died from a stroke or heart attack?"

"Meaning anything," said the captain.

"Shipboard deaths are common enough for a code phrase?" I asked.

"Unfortunately. Many of our passengers are retirees in their seventies, eighties, and even nineties. An older demographic results in a higher death rate."

Was it bad Karma to wish the victim on the Deck Five promenade was an extremely elderly person whose heart had finally given out after a long life? I hoped not. I had had enough bad Karma the past year to last a lifetime.

The elevator came to a stop. Once we exited, we made our way toward the promenade entrance situated near the Smoky Quartz Pub. A uniformed crewmember stood at the sliding glass doors, preventing any passengers from exiting onto the promenade. He unlocked the doors and stepped aside as the captain approached.

The promenade was empty except for various crewmembers

huddled in front of a large white plastic tent, lit from within. The tent covered the width of the promenade. Tent poles were positioned to provide a canopy that extended out over the lifeboat opposite the tent.

One of the crew pulled aside a tent flap for us to enter. Inside we found several other crewmembers. Two stood to the side next to a gurney with an empty body bag laid out on it. The plastic on the opposite side of the tent was pulled back to offer access to the lifeboat. Three additional crewmembers stood facing the lifeboat, blocking our view of the victim.

The captain spoke. "What can you tell me, Doctor?"

One of the three turned to face the captain. "Appears he either fell, jumped, or was pushed from one of the balconies, Captain."

The captain motioned the doctor and the other two crewmembers to step aside and turned to Zack. "Is this your father or a member of your party, Mr. Barnes?"

Even with a partially blocked view of the body, I immediately recognized the victim by the cartoon monkeys scampering across his shirt.

~*~

After Zack identified Orson Gilbert's body, the captain made arrangements for him to view the passenger manifest photos first thing tomorrow morning. As anxious as I was to have Emerson Dawes secured in the brig, I understood the captain had more pressing matters at the moment, and they probably included some of his crew going over security footage to figure out what had happened to Orson Gilbert.

Hand-in-hand, Zack and I walked back to the suite. I couldn't scrub the gruesome battered image of Orson's body from my mind. Did he die on impact, or were his last moments horrifically frightening and painful? I hoped for the former and shuddered at the thought of the latter.

"You okay?" asked Zack.

"Not really. I had trepidations about this cruise from the moment Ira surprised us with tickets, but that had everything to do with spending a week with him and his kids. In my wildest imagination I never could have predicted the last twelve hours."

"Yeah, first, my father shows up. Now, the death of one our dinner companions? One would have been unusual enough, but both within hours of each other defies the laws of probability."

"Fell, jumped, or pushed." I mulled over the doctor's assessment as we entered the corridor to our suite.

"You have a preference?" asked Zack.

"It doesn't take a degree in psychology to have noticed Orson's forced cheerfulness when we first arrived at dinner, not to mention the tension on his side of the dinner table as he introduced his family."

"Especially after his *hands-on* interaction with Lenore," he said before adding, "So, Dr. Freud, are you suggesting Orson jumped, or do you think he was pushed?"

"Maybe he suffered from depression or had a terminal illness. However, I can think of less painful ways to commit suicide."

"Not to mention the difficulty of such a large man hoisting himself over a four-foot high protective glass balcony wall."

Orson had been a portly man with muscular arms and a barrel chest, but I couldn't picture him easily hauling himself over his balcony. Given the telltale signs of alcoholism, more than likely his death was the result of a freak accident.

We had arrived back at our suite. Upon entering Zack once again swept the room for bugs.

"You think someone bugged the room in the short time we were gone?" I whispered.

"I think it's best to make sure no one has."

I glanced across the room to the sliders leading to our balcony. When Zack finished and indicated it was safe to talk, I asked, "How much do you think Orson weighed?"

He thought for a moment. "Given his height? Somewhere between two seventy-five and three hundred pounds. Why?"

"If he'd stood on a deck chair to boost himself up and over the edge of the balcony, would the seat have held his weight long enough for him to succeed?"

"Possibly. Or the concentrated load might stress the fabric enough that it would tear."

"Sounds likely. And if so, then he fell or was pushed." But neither of those scenarios seemed to hold up, either. I walked across the room and pulled open the slider drapes to look out onto the balcony. "How do you push such a large man over a four-foot wall?"

Zack joined me, looping his arm around my waist. "You'd need a much larger man, more than one person, or a crane."

"So we're left with falling, which could have happened if the railing gave way from his weight. Maybe he tripped and fell into it, shattering the glass or breaking the bolts holding the glass in place."

"In which case, there'd be evidence that fell along with him. I didn't see any broken glass or pieces of metal strewn on the decking or the lifeboat, did you?"

"No, but what if someone tampered with the balcony to make his death appear an accident?"

"I suspect a part of the balcony still would have fallen with him.

Now that the captain knows who his dead passenger is, he'll have the Gilbert's balcony examined."

"And check the security footage to see if anyone else had entered the cabin."

"Except the cameras in the cabin hallways don't capture every doorway. Neither do any of the others throughout the ship. Contrary to what the captain said earlier, there are quite a few blind spots."

That information threw me for such a loop that I turned to face Zack. "How do you know that?"

"As a photographer, I'm trained to notice what others might miss."

So are spies. But I bit my tongue. Zack had enough drama to contend with right now. Instead I voiced another thought that had occurred to me. "What if Orson didn't fall from his balcony? Or any balcony? The upper decks have metal railings along parts of the ship's perimeter. He could have climbed over the railing and jumped."

"Or someone might have knocked him out from behind and flipped his body over the railing," said Zack. "Even if one of the security cameras captured an attack, identifying the perpetrator in the dark will be difficult."

"If not impossible." We were back to Orson either jumping or having been pushed. "I wonder how often murders and suicides occur on a cruise ship."

Zack grabbed his laptop. "Let's find out." He tapped a few keys, then began reading. After several minutes he asked, "You want the good news or the bad news first?"

"The good news. I've had enough bad news for one day."

"The odds of dying on a cruise ship are about one in six million.

That's from a combination of both natural and unnatural causes."

"And the bad news?"

"There's an average of nearly twenty disappearances from cruise ships every year."

"Disappearances? How do you disappear on a cruise ship?"

"Overboards. Most are labeled suicides by the cruise industry, even when murder is suspected. There are dozens of cases listed."

"Orson didn't go overboard, and his body isn't missing."

Zack grimaced as he continued to read. After another minute or two, he pulled his attention from the screen. "According to this website, he's not the first to land on a lifeboat instead of in the ocean."

He shifted his concentration back to the computer screen and continued to read. "Apparently, sexual assaults are also on the rise, a spike of nearly seventy percent over last year according to one source. Non-sexual assaults and thefts have also increased. Other than the thefts, one industry insider attributes many of the incidents to passengers imbibing copious amounts of alcohol."

"In other words, blame the victims?"

"Exactly. From what I'm reading, there seems to be a concerted effort to cover up much of the crime that takes place aboard cruise ships, especially when the incidents occur in international waters out of the jurisdiction of any nation."

Less than twenty-four hours into a weeklong cruise, and we already had one dead body. And that didn't even take into account whatever vengeful plan currently percolated in the devious mind of Emerson Dawes. If the day's events weren't enough to keep Mr. Sandman at bay tonight, Zack's research into deaths on cruise ships ensured Mr. Sandman would skip out altogether on his nightly visit.

I hugged my chest. "Is it paranoid of me to want to round up my family?"

Zack pulled out his phone. "Why don't I text them and ask that they return to the suite as soon as possible?"

"Shane and Sophie, too. They need to know what's happened."

"On it."

~*~

Zack's phone chimed a moment later. "Alex wants to know if they can wait until the movie ends."

As much as I needed eyes on my kids for my own sanity, I didn't want to panic them. I reluctantly agreed.

Zack's phone pinged a second time. "Your mother says she's on a streak and has no intention of leaving the casino right now."

Great! I was certain the only *streak* Mama was on was a losing one, and she'd continue playing until she maxed out her credit cards. Of course, that assumed she was playing with her own money. If Ira Moneybags Pollack had given her carte blanche on his American Express, she'd devote her entire time on the ship to various games of chance.

Shane arrived a few minutes later. Zack opened the door and stepped aside to allow him entry, but Shane hesitated, first glancing questioningly toward where I still sat on the sectional sofa, then shifting his attention back to Zack before stepping into the suite. "Everything okay?"

"Sure," I said. "As long as you don't mind a non-stop cruise down the River Styx, on a one-way trip to Hades."

Shane froze. "Sophie? The boys—"

"Are fine." Zack placed a hand on Shane's shoulder and ushered him inside. "They're still at the movie and will join us afterwards."

"Flora?"

"Is busy losing money at the casino."

Shane's brow furrowed. "He pointed toward my left hand. "If the kids and Flora are okay, and Anastasia is still wearing her engagement ring, whatever's going on can't be that bad."

I reflexively glanced down at my ring. "Yes, well it is, and it isn't." I patted the sofa cushion at a right angle to where I sat. "Have a seat, Shane. You won't believe all that's happened since we left you at the theater."

He eyed the bar as he made his way across the room. "Is this a conversation that requires fortification?"

"Couldn't hurt." Zack motioned toward the array of liquor. "What are you having?"

"Depends. How serious are we talking?"

Zack stepped over to the bar and poured two fingers of Scotch into an old-fashion glass. "At least a double serious."

Shane joined me on the sofa. Zack brought him his Scotch and took the seat next to me. Shane stared into the drink for a moment before downing it, then set the glass on the coffee table. "Okay, hit me."

Zack explained most of what he'd already told me about Emerson, but in typical guy-to-guy conversation, he kept to the facts, leaving out all emotion. When he'd finished, Shane shook his head and let loose a whistle.

"Man," he said, adding a few choice four-letter words under his breath. "Now what?"

"That's not the half of it," I said.

Shane shifted his attention to me, worry lines creasing his brow. "There's more?"

I nodded as Zack continued, "We decided to tell the captain

he has a killer on his ship."

"Which must have thrilled him no end," said Shane.

Zack proceeded to relate our conversation with the captain and how it was interrupted by the discovery of Orson Gilbert's body.

Shane's jaw dropped. "The guy from dinner?"

"None other," said Zack.

"I'm assuming he didn't climb up on top of the lifeboat and have a heart attack," said Shane.

"Definitely not," I said. "The ship's doctor said he was either pushed, jumped, or accidentally fell from one of the upper decks."

Shane reached for his empty glass and rose from the sofa. He strode over to the bar and helped himself to another shot of Scotch. However, this time he sipped at the alcohol, growing thoughtful. Finally, he said, "What if Emerson saw all of us at dinner and assumed the others at our table were part of our group?"

SEVEN

My jaw dropped. "Are you suggesting Zack's father killed Orson Gilbert? Why?"

"To toy with me." Zack nodded in agreement with Shane. "Show me how powerful he is, that he can hurt me more by targeting the people I care about than going after me directly."

"But we first met Orson at dinner this evening," I said.

"Emerson wouldn't know that," said Shane. "If he has the connections Zack is suggesting, he knew we were a group of twelve traveling together."

"He wouldn't have known Ira canceled at the very last minute," I said.

"Exactly." Zack took a hefty swig of Scotch.

If they were correct, we all had targets on our backs. I jumped up. "I can't sit here and wait for the kids and Mama to return."

"Agreed," said Zack. "You head to the casino to keep an eye on your mother. Shane and I will make our way down to the Crown Jewels Theater to check on Sophie and the boys."

"And if we see Emerson?" I asked.

"We notify the captain immediately," said Shane.

Easier said than done. The captain had his hands full with a dead body that could be the result of a murder. For all I knew, he'd relegated our recent conversation with him to a back burner of his brain. We needed to give him added incentive to round up Emerson as quickly as possible. "We should notify the captain that Emerson might be connected to Orson's death."

"Not a bad idea," said Zack. He turned to Shane. "You head to the theater. I'll track down the captain."

~*~

A cacophony of bells, beeps, whistles, and disco music assaulted my eardrums as I entered the casino. People shouted above the noise. Bright lights flashed overhead, as well as from the four walls and the dozens of games that filled nearly every square inch of floor space.

The total effect induced flashbacks to the video arcade where Zack and I had recently discovered Ira's son Isaac one night after he'd climbed out his bedroom window and run off. The only difference? The casino was filled with an older crowd with more adult addictions.

I found Mama seated on a stool in front of a slot machine off to one side of the casino. As Zack had indicated, technology had amputated the arm of the one-armed bandit. I watched from a distance as Mama methodically removed a coin from a large plastic cup she held in her lap and inserted it into a slot on the side of the machine. She then pushed a button that set a row of wheels at the top of the machine spinning. When they came to a stop, she frowned, grabbed another coin, and repeated the process.

I expected to find Lenore Rosedale seated next to Mama. They had headed to the casino together. However, after a quick scan of the surrounding area, I failed to locate Lenore. Mama was flanked on one side by a woman close to my age and on the other side by a man easily pushing ninety. Each also methodically fed coins into the hungry metal beasts in front of them.

Before I approached Mama, I slowly sauntered up and down the aisles of slot machines and around the roulette, craps, blackjack, and poker tables, checking for Emerson Dawes. When I didn't find him lurking anywhere in the casino, I made my way back to Mama and sidled up beside her. "You don't look like you're having much fun."

She acknowledged my arrival by frowning at the machine in front of her. "I'll have fun when this machine stops giving me grief. Maybe it's time to switch seats." She glanced around, but every other slot machine in sight was already occupied.

I decided not to mention how she'd told Zack she was on a streak. As I had suspected, it was a losing streak. I wondered how much she'd already lost but bit my tongue. No sense sowing discord. Her foray into the casino was between her and the rich guy footing her bills. Instead, I asked, "What happened to your gambling buddy?"

Mama fed another coin into the machine and pushed the button to start the wheels spinning once more. Without so much as a glance in my direction, she said, "Lenore? She begged off with a headache not long after we arrived."

"I think you should call it a night before you get a headache, Mama." I'd been in the casino less than five minutes and already felt the start of one creeping up on me.

She muttered something under her breath when the wheels came to a stop and grabbed another coin from her cup. "Nonsense.

Lenore drank too much this evening." She waved toward the half-empty glass sitting on the shelf in front of her. "This is only my second frozen daiquiri."

"Plus the two glasses of wine you had with dinner."

"I'm perfectly fine."

And I wanted to keep her that way. I grabbed the cup of coins from her lap. "We have to be up early tomorrow morning for our first land excursion. Let's call it a night, Mama."

I expected an argument from her, but she only offered me a heavy sigh before pushing herself off the stool and grabbing her drink. This confirmed my suspicions. If the one-armed bandit minus the arm had been kind to Mama this evening, she wouldn't give in so quickly. I looped my arm through hers and led her back to the suite.

Upon our return, I found Shane and the teens had already arrived. "Zack's not back yet," Shane said. "I've caught the kids up on everything. They haven't seen Emerson. At least Sophie hasn't. The boys haven't had any interaction with anyone fitting his description."

Since Alex and Nick hadn't observed any of our encounters with Emerson, they hadn't gotten a look at him and had no way of knowing if he was stalking them. "No elderly man has approached either of you?" I asked them.

"Nope," said Nick.

"Ditto," said Alex.

"What's going on?" asked Mama. "Who's Emerson?"

"A scary creep," said Sophie. "He killed Zack's mom years ago."

"And he's on this ship," added Nick.

Mama shifted her gaze back and forth from Sophie, to Nick, then to me. "But, but..." Her jaw flapped several times before words finally flowed. "How is that possible? Why isn't he in prison?"

"Good question," I said. "He should be. Zack is trying to find out why he isn't."

"He's the guy who approached Mom and Sophie," said Alex, "And he probably killed Orson Gilbert."

Mama's eyes grew wide. She placed her hand over her heart and collapsed onto a corner of the sectional. "That obnoxious man from dinner? Why would Zack's father kill a total stranger?"

"We don't know that he did," I said, "but Orson Gilbert is dead."

"My head is spinning," said Mama. She gulped the remainder of her drink and set the glass on the coffee table. "And it's definitely not from my daiquiri. What in the world is going on, Anastasia?"

I explained everything to her, once again giving her a description of Emerson. I ended by asking, "Have you come in contact with any man on the ship who looks like that?"

She grew thoughtful for a moment before shaking her head. "The only man who struck up a conversation with me this evening wasn't clean-shaven, and his hair was more salt-and-pepper gray, not white."

Was it possible Emerson had an accomplice onboard? "What did he say to you?"

"Nothing out of the ordinary, just friendly chitchat that lasted no more than a minute or two. He seemed more interested in Lenore, so I settled in at the slots and gave them some space."

"Did he hang around?"

"No, he wandered off a few minutes later."

"You didn't see him again?"

Mama grew thoughtful. "No, but now that I think about it, Lenore begged off with a headache moments later." Mama grinned. "I wonder if *headache* was code for something else. Maybe she felt guilty deserting me."

"Maybe, but do me a favor, Mama."

"What's that, dear?"

"Until Emerson is apprehended, stay clear of any men who fit his description. Whatever he's planning can't be good."

"I will, dear." She let loose a huge yawn. "Now if you'll all forgive me, I think it's time I turned in for some beauty sleep. Suddenly I'm quite exhausted."

We all bid her goodnight. The boys and Sophie went off to watch a video in the boys' bedroom. I figured with Nick as chaperone, Shane and I didn't have to worry about Alex and Sophie camped out on one of the beds.

~*~

Nearly an hour later, Zack finally returned to the suite. "What took you so long?" I asked.

"When I told the captain of our suspicions regarding Orson's death, he asked me to join in viewing the security video they were pulling."

"Did you see Emerson in any of them?" asked Shane.

Zack shook his head. "Unfortunately, none of the cameras are situated in such a way as to capture the Gilbert cabin door. However, each time a key card is used to access a cabin, a record is made. The key log shows no one entering the Gilbert cabin after the cabin steward performed evening turndown while the Gilberts were at dinner.

"What about the Marwood cabin?"

"The Marwoods are in the cabin directly next door. No one

other than the cabin steward has entered that cabin since dinner, either."

"Then where are they?" I asked. "Do they know what happened to Orson?"

"They do now. The captain had them paged after we identified the body. Birdie and Bunny had gone to the Emerald Lounge to listen to a Harry Connick, Jr. impersonator. Dennis and Orson opted for watching a football game in the Onyx Pub."

How odd that the captain broke the news of Orson's death to Birdie and the Marwoods in front of a virtual stranger. "You were with the captain when he told them about Orson?"

"Not exactly. I was viewing the surveillance video on the bridge and overheard snatches of his conversation with them."

I frowned. "Under the circumstances, the captain should have chosen a more private location to speak with Birdie and the Marwoods." He needed a refresher course in grief counseling, assuming it was part of his training. And if not, it certainly should be, given the statistics I'd learned from Zack's Internet search of deaths on cruise ships.

"From what I could gather," said Zack, "once all three had arrived on the bridge, the captain tried to lead them to his office. Birdie refused to move, demanding to know why they were summoned."

I shook my head. "Poor Birdie. No matter what was going on between Orson and her at dinner, she must be devastated."

"She shut down," said Zack. "Went almost catatonic. While Bunny comforted her, Dennis pulled the captain aside. I don't know what he said, but a few minutes later the doctor arrived and administered what I assume was a sedative. Then Dennis and Bunny escorted Birdie from the bridge."

Shane leaned back against the sofa cushions and stared up at the ceiling. I could almost see the gears whirling. Finally, he said, "So if Orson and Dennis were watching football in the pub, how did Orson wind up dead on the lifeboat?"

"Dennis said at one point Orson left to use the men's room," said Zack. "He never returned to the pub."

"And that didn't concern Dennis?" I asked.

"Apparently not. He said Orson had consumed quite a few beers. Dennis figured he decided to watch the remainder of the game sacked out on the bed in his cabin."

"But he never made it back to the cabin," said Shane.

"Not according to the keycard logs," said Zack.

"Where is the Onyx Pub situated?" I asked.

"Deck Five," said Zack, "but on the starboard side of the ship. Orson was found portside."

"What about the cameras on the upper decks above the lifeboat?" I asked.

"They showed several couples strolling on the deck and a few people standing along the railings," he said. "However, the cameras don't completely capture the entire deck area above the lifeboats. One of the blind spots is on Deck Fifteen directly above the lifeboat where Orson was found. Also, the images are very dark. There's no moon this evening, and clouds have rolled in, blocking most of the stars. In addition, lighting is subdued around the upper deck promenades."

"Doesn't sound very safe," I said.

"I suppose it's the cruise line's attempt to facilitate romantic strolls." .

"But one of those people could have been Orson," said Shane.

"Possibly," said Zack. "I noticed a few passengers with similar builds. Whether one of them was Orson, is anyone's guess. Bottom line, though, none of the cameras captured anyone going over the railing, either on his own or as the result of an attack."

"There are no alarm systems to detect passengers going overboard?" asked Shane. "No cameras on the hull?"

"You'd think that would be a no-brainer," said Zack. "However, the crewmember viewing the video with me said the technology isn't perfected yet, resulting in too many false alarms. So the cruise industry hasn't embraced it."

"Flawed technology is better than none," I said, "given the number of passengers that go missing or overboard each year."

"Meanwhile," said Shane, "we still don't know if Orson jumped or was pushed."

"And if he was pushed," I said, "we don't know if Emerson had a hand in it."

"That about sums it up," said Zack.

Shane stood and stretched. "Since we're at an impasse, there's nothing left to do but retrieve my daughter and call it a night." He ducked into the boys' bedroom, returning a minute later with Sophie.

The ship was scheduled to dock in Nassau at six the next morning. Before Sophie and Shane left, we made plans to meet up for breakfast prior to disembarking for our tour of Nassau.

~*~

I woke the next morning to find we weren't docked in Nassau. Worse yet, we seemed to be anchored out at sea with no land in sight.

EIGHT

Our suite was situated on the starboard side of the ship. Perhaps the port side faced the dock. Or the ship had nosed in or backed into its assigned berth. If so, shouldn't I at least have a view of other cruise ships docked alongside us? After all, we were at the height of the winter cruise season in the Caribbean.

Zack had already risen. When I entered the bathroom, I found a note on the counter next to the sink: *Woke early. Went up to the bridge to view the passport photos from the manifest. Will meet you in the dining room for breakfast. Z.*

The evening before, the cabin steward had left us a copy of *GemEvents* when he brought fresh towels and turned down the beds. Along with listing the day's shipboard activities, various available shore excursions, and Nassau shops featuring the best prices on anything a tourist might desire, the newsletter included a weather report. We could look forward to a sunny day with a mild breeze and a high in the mid-seventies.

Once I showered, I slathered on sunscreen. Even with

relatively cool temperatures, I knew I needed to protect my skin from the harsh rays of the Caribbean sun. I dressed in a pair of black jeans, a scooped-neck pink T-shirt, and my Mets ball cap for additional sun protection.

By the time I finished dressing, Mama and the boys were also awake and dressed. Or in Mama's case, overdressed. She wore a yellow, peach, and orange floral tea-length sundress, better suited for the annual Westfield Garden Club luncheon than a morning of walking on cobblestone streets. A yellow-dyed straw hat with a floral band in the same patterned fabric as her dress sat perched on her head. Strappy yellow sandals with a kitten heel finished off the outfit.

"Mama, part of our tour involves walking around Nassau's historic district. Maybe you should rethink your choice of footwear."

"Oh, I'm not going with you this morning, dear."

"You're not?"

"I decided to switch to the wine and dine food tour with Lenore and a few of the seniors I met at the social yesterday. We'll be transported around the city in a jitney. I'm sure I mentioned it to you last night."

I was certain she hadn't. "I don't think that's such a good idea, Mama, not until Emerson is apprehended."

"Nonsense, Anastasia. You worry too much. I'll be in a group with a tour guide. Nothing is going to happen to me."

I couldn't do much beyond sigh. Mama was an adult. It's not like I could ground her. "Promise me you'll be careful?"

"Of course, dear. Now let's go to breakfast. I'm famished."

~*~

We arrived in the dining room to find Shane and Sophie waiting for us. Although the teens had decided at dinner last night to ditch us at mealtime in the future, I had insisted we all dine together this morning. I knew I couldn't keep tabs on them twenty-four/seven, but after the events of last night, this mother hen wanted her chicks snug under her wing for as long as possible. Under protest, they had agreed to join us for breakfast.

• "But that's it," said Nick.

"We'll see," I said, knowing I'd have to give in eventually. However, I hoped I could stretch out *eventually* to more than one meal.

To my surprise, Birdie Gilbert and the Marwoods were also at the table and already eating breakfast. They gave no signs of Orson's horrific demise the night before. No dark circles, red eyes, or puffy faces indicated any of them had spent a sleepless, tear-filled night. I glanced questioningly at Shane. He offered a nearly imperceptible shrug of one shoulder.

What does one say in a situation like this? Should I even acknowledge their loss, or was it best to ignore the pachyderm in the dining room? I suddenly understood the responses—or lack of them—from many of our friends and neighbors when Karl died suddenly in Las Vegas.

As I grappled with whether or not to mention Orson's death, Mama took control of the situation. Sometimes having served as the social secretary of the local Daughters of the American Revolution chapter had its advantages. "Please accept our condolences on your loss," she said.

I probably would have verbally tripped and stumbled as I searched for the perfect words.

Birdie paused, a forkful of scrambled eggs halfway to her mouth. "Thank you," she said, her eyes flat and her voice completely devoid of emotion.

Dennis and Bunny looked up from their plates to acknowledge Mama with a nod of their heads but said nothing. Then all three turned their attention back to their breakfasts.

How odd! Perhaps they'd all self-medicated prior to arriving in the dining room this morning.

I glanced out the wide expanse of dining room windows, again seeing nothing but water. "Are we in port yet?" I asked Shane.

"Doesn't appear so. I wonder what's going on."

The waiter handed menus to Mama, the boys, and me. Alex and Nick both ordered cream cheese and blueberry stuffed French toast with a side of sausage links. Mama chose a Belgian waffle with fresh berries and whipped cream.

I frowned behind my menu. Oh, to have my mother's metabolism! But since I didn't and never would, I opted for an egg white omelet with spinach, mushrooms, and feta cheese, along with a fresh fruit cocktail.

Shortly after we placed our orders, Lenore arrived. She wore a blue and lavender floral sundress so similar in style and pattern to Mama's that I had to wonder if they'd coordinated their outfits this morning. Lenore had forsaken her tight bun for an equally tight ponytail threaded through an opening at the back of her lavender-dyed straw sunhat.

She greeted all of us and took the seat next to Mama. "Well?" asked Mama. "How'd it go last night?"

"With what?" asked Lenore.

"Your...*headache?*" Mama ended her question with a wink, then added, "I wasn't born yesterday, dear."

Lenore feigned ignorance. "I have no idea what you mean."

Mama glanced over at the teens. "I'm sure the evening will

come back to you once we're alone. And when it does, I want details of your rendezvous with that good-looking gentleman we met in the casino."

"Really, Flora, my only rendezvous last night was with two aspirins and a glass of water. Besides, do you think I'm the kind of woman who would kiss and tell?"

"I guess I'll soon find out, won't I?"

I wondered how recently Lenore's husband had died. Last night at dinner she grew teary-eyed when she mentioned this was her first cruise since his passing. Yet it now sounded like less than an hour after that emotional performance, she'd hooked up with a complete stranger for a bit of senior hanky-panky—unless Mama's imagination had run wild, and Lenore really did have a headache last night.

Mama then leaned over and whispered in Lenore's ear. When Lenore glanced sideways at Birdie and the Marwoods, I knew Mama had told her about Orson's death.

As soon as Mama stopped whispering, Lenore turned to Birdie and said, "My sympathies on your loss."

With tightly pursed lips, Birdie stared at her without saying a word.

Zack finally joined us about five minutes later. "Sorry," he said as he settled into the empty chair next to me. He nodded across the table to Birdie and the Marwoods but said nothing. I suppose he'd already offered his condolences at some point after they had arrived on the bridge last night.

The waiter swooped in and handed Zack a menu. With the menu raised to cover his face, he spoke under his breath so that only I heard him. "Things are a bit chaotic upstairs."

"Have you decided, sir?" asked the waiter, stepping between us.

Zack quickly scanned the menu, choosing a Western omelet with a side of hash browns and a rasher of bacon.

"Did you find Emerson?" I whispered after the waiter took Zack's menu and hurried off to place his order.

"I'll tell you later. There's something else going on."

"Does it have anything to do with our not being docked in Nassau?"

"It does. I believe the captain will be making an announcement shortly."

Sure enough, almost before Zack had finished his sentence, the bells sounded, alerting us to an impending message.

"Ladies and gentleman, good morning. This is Captain Halvorson," he said. "Some of you may have noticed we're not docked in Nassau."

Around the room many passengers shifted in their seats to stare out the windows. I wondered how they hadn't previously noticed we were still at sea, especially since many of the shore excursions were scheduled to depart within the next hour.

The captain continued, "This is due to a forced change of plans. One of our crewmembers came down with a case of measles last night. He was immediately placed in quarantine. Because his duties don't include interfacing with passengers, he poses minimal risk to any of you who have not had the measles or the measles vaccine."

A buzz of angry voices now filled the dining room.

"As mandated by law, we have notified the CDC and the Ministry of Health in Nassau, which is presently rounding up doses of vaccine to tender out to our ship. I've been informed that administering the vaccine within seventy-two hours of exposure should provide protection to those unvaccinated passengers who may have been exposed, even though, as I said, exposure is highly unlikely. I will make another announcement once we have the vaccine onboard."

He cleared his throat before continuing. "Meanwhile, I regret to inform you that due to the highly infectious nature of this disease, the Bahamian Health Minister has denied us docking and disembarkation at any of our ports of call in The Bahamas."

At this, the angry buzz within the dining room grew into a loud roar of objection, the rising decibel level nearly blocking out the sound of the captain's voice.

"So now what?" I asked Zack.

The captain answered for him. "Once we have the vaccine, we'll move beyond the twelve-mile limit, enabling us to open the casino. We'll then begin a leisurely sail around the various islands of The Bahamas until it's time to make our way back to Bayonne, New Jersey. Meanwhile, our cruise director and her assistants will schedule additional onboard activities for all of you."

At the table next to us a man stood abruptly, knocking his chair over backwards. "We should all go up to the bridge and demand our money back," he shouted above the noise in the dining room.

Others immediately agreed, jumping to their feet. As the man stormed out of the dining room, dozens of other passengers followed him.

The captain finished by saying, "I apologize for the change of plans, but my crew and I will endeavor to make your stay onboard the Gemstone Empress as enjoyable as possible."

"Why won't they allow the ship to dock in Nassau and let those of us who aren't sick onto the island?" asked Sophie.

"Because measles is highly contagious," I said. "Worst of all, if you're infected, you're spreading the virus for several days before you even know you're ill."

"So you have measles before you know you have measles?" asked Alex.

"That's right, but you don't have to worry. Both you and your brother were vaccinated, as was I, and your grandmother had measles as a child." I turned to Zack. "I'm assuming you were also vaccinated as a kid?"

"With all the traveling I do? I'm vaccinated for everything, including viruses you've never heard of."

"What about you and me?" Sophie asked Shane.

"Totally protected," he assured her.

"Then why do we have to stay on the ship?" she asked.

"Because we don't carry around proof of vaccination with our passports," I said. "The authorities in the Bahamas are not going to take our word that we pose no risk to any of their citizens."

"And they shouldn't," added Zack. "Too many people would lie, putting the island's population at risk."

"And to think," said Nick, "we could be skiing in Vermont right now."

"Hey Dad," said Sophie. "Any chance you'd like to take us up to Stowe for spring break?" She held her breath, her hands clasped in front of her in the universal gesture of teenage begging. "Please?"

Shane studied his daughter for a moment before glancing over at Alex and Nick, both of whom held their breaths awaiting his answer. Then he turned to me and said, "The ball's in your court."

"Mom, you have to say yes," said Nick.

I shot him a Mom Look. "Really, Nick? I *have* to?"

"Way to go, bro," said Alex, landing a punch on Nick's bicep.

"You better hope you didn't just blow it for us."

Nick hung his head and eyed me sideways. "I'm sorry, Mom. That came out all wrong."

I raised an eyebrow. "You think?"

"Can we still go?"

The way I saw it, I had several options. I could outright deny the trip, hands-down capturing the Worst Mother Ever Award. In addition, Alex and Nick would probably remind me of my fall from grace for the next several decades, if not the remainder of my life.

I could keep them in suspense, stating I'd have to think about it, but what would be the point of setting myself up for a barrage of nonstop nagging?

Then there was my third option, the one that would garner my sons' undying gratitude now, plus hopefully ensure they'd pick out a decent nursing home for me when the time came.

I turned my head to find Zack watching me as I performed a mental Eenie-Meenie-Miney-Mo. The boys might be worried about my answer, but from the slight smile playing on Zack's lips and the twinkle in his eye, I knew he knew the choice I'd make.

And why shouldn't I give in and let them go skiing? They'd suffered enough over the last year, thanks to their father's betrayal. What purpose did it serve to deny them a fun trip, especially since I knew it wouldn't cost me anything? There was no way Shane would ever allow me to pay the boys' expenses, not after saving Sophie from a kidnapper and clearing him of murder charges.

"Okay," I finally said, "as long as Shane doesn't mind dealing with you on his own."

To my surprise, both boys jumped out of their seats and sandwiched me in a bear hug. "You're the best," said Nick, planting a kiss on my cheek.

"Ditto," said Alex, adding a kiss to my other cheek.

As the boys returned to their seats, I noticed Birdie and Bunny sporting identical tight-jawed frowns. Although they kept their heads bowed over their plates, I realized they had turned their attention to the conversation going on across the table, observing us through dark, hooded eyes. However, I couldn't tell if their expressions telegraphed disapproval or some other emotion. Envy, perhaps?

I wondered if either of them had children or grandchildren, but both women had made it clear, even before Orson's death, they had no desire to converse with us. Such a question would have been met with a blank stare yesterday. Asking now would be completely inappropriate.

When they realized I was aware of them watching us, they both turned their attention back to finishing their breakfasts. Shortly thereafter they and Dennis rose from the table and left just as the waiter delivered our meals.

"Strange people," said Mama, staring at the trio's backs. "They didn't even say goodbye. Up and left as if they were the only ones seated at the table."

"Maybe they're in shock," I said. "People handle grief in different ways."

"They were strange before Orson's death," she reminded me.

I couldn't argue with her on that point. If Ralph were on the cruise with us, he'd squawk about something being rotten in Denmark, even though we were sailing in the Caribbean.

Lenore cocked her head toward Mama. "I'll second that. Although I suppose I can't blame Birdie for giving me the evil eye. I know it's not right to speak ill of the dead, but did you notice how her husband pawed me last night? And right in front of her, no less!"

"You handled the situation with admirable restraint," said Mama.

"I saw no point in making a scene," said Lenore.

"Speaking of dead bodies," said Alex, "what do they do with them when someone dies on a ship? Do they hold burials at sea like in olden times?"

"They probably store the corpses in the refrigerator," said Nick.

"With our food?" asked Mama. Her eyes grew wide as her hand flew to her heart. "I certainly hope not."

"Relax, Flora," said Shane. "I did a little research last night. All cruise ships are outfitted with morgues. The bodies are nowhere near our food."

"Well, that's a relief!" said Mama, fanning herself with her napkin.

~*~

With shore excursions canceled, after breakfast the teens opted for the gym while Mama took Lenore to check out the spa facilities. "Stick together," I told Sophie and the boys as they stood to leave. "No one goes off alone, and I want a text if you see Emerson, even if he doesn't approach you."

"And text us when you leave the gym to go somewhere else," added Shane.

Nick opened his mouth to object, but before he could say anything, Alex beat him to the punch. "No problem. We'll check in hourly if you want." He waved as the three of them raced from the dining room.

At least one of my sons was progressing toward becoming a

mature adult. At fifteen, Nick still needed time to learn a thing or three—or three hundred.

I turned to my mother. "Same directions for you, Mama."

"Really, Anastasia, how am I supposed to be aware of a man I've never seen? Have you any idea how many men on this ship fit the general description you gave me last night?"

Zack had pulled out his phone. "I'm texting his passport photo to everyone right now, Flora."

"Who's Emerson?" asked Lenore.

Mama rose from the table. "A murderer who is supposed to be in prison."

Lenore's mouth dropped open, and her eyes widened. "And he's on this ship?"

Mama placed her hand on Lenore's arm. "I'll tell you all about him on our way to the spa."

Lenore turned to Zack. "Maybe I should have his photo as well."

"That's not a bad idea," said Zack. "What's your cell number?"

Lenore rattled off the digits. A moment later her phone pinged. "Got it." She stared down at the image on her screen and frowned.

"Have you seen him?" asked Zack.

"No." She shook her head and emitted a long sigh. "But what a shame!"

"What do you mean?" I asked.

Lenore continued to fixate on the image on her phone. "He's rather handsome, isn't he?"

"So are jaguars," said Zack, "but trust me, you don't want to get up close and personal with either a jaguar or Emerson Dawes."

Lenore pulled her attention from her phone and shuddered.

"Noted." She waved the cell toward Zack. "Thanks for the warning."

Mama and Lenore looped arms. Acting like they'd known each other forever, the two women started toward the dining room exit, but after taking three steps Lenore stopped and turned to face Mama.

"Something wrong?" asked Mama.

"Just thinking," said Lenore, "since our excursion was canceled and we're confined to the ship, we should change into something more comfortable. Why don't we meet at the spa in half an hour?"

Mama nodded in agreement, and the two women resumed their side-by-side strut through the dining room.

"I'm glad Mama has found someone to hang with during the cruise," I said to Zack. "I just hope they stay out of trouble—and away from strange men."

"We are talking about your mother, right?"

I sighed. "Point taken."

Zack glanced over at Shane, then back toward me. "We need to talk."

"I'm listening," said Shane.

Zack cocked his head to indicate the buzz of activity going on around us. Dozens of wait-staff scurried about, clearing dishes and resetting tables as passengers finished their breakfasts and left the dining room. "Not here. Somewhere private."

"Our suite?" I asked.

Zack shook his head. "It's probably being cleaned or will be shortly. Let's find an empty corner of the ship where we're out of earshot from everyone."

Easier said than done, since we were all stuck on the ship. After strolling around several decks, we finally found a vacant outdoor patio attached to one of the celebrity chef restaurants. We chose a table hidden from the deck promenade by oversized, brightly colored glazed pots filled with fragrant flowering shrubbery.

Since the restaurant didn't open until dinnertime, chances were good that we could talk freely without fear of any eavesdroppers. Even so, before taking a seat, Zack pulled out his phone and checked the area for listening devices.

Shane's brows knit together as he watched Zack scan the area. "You think Emerson's bugged the ship?"

"Not personally," said Zack, "but someone is helping him, and I have no idea how deeply that help runs, including having paid off crewmembers."

"But still..." said Shane.

"Seems paranoid to you?" asked Zack.

"Slightly."

Zack shrugged. "Never hurts to control what you can. Especially when there's so much in life you can't."

"I see your point," said Shane.

I was more bothered by the fact that checking for bugs meant Emerson Dawes still had the run of the ship. Had Emerson been picked up after Zack identified him through the passport photo on the ship's manifest, we wouldn't still need to worry about bugs—or Emerson.

Once Zack was satisfied no listening devices were hidden around the patio, he shoved his phone back in his pocket and joined Shane and me at the table. "Emerson is traveling with a Canadian passport under the name Desmond Rutledge."

"I'm sensing a huge *but*," I said.

Zack grimaced. "The captain circulated his photo to the crew. No one admits having seen him."

"Not even his cabin steward?" asked Shane.

"No."

"How is that possible?" I asked. "We know he was in the Pearl of the Sea Buffet yesterday before we sailed and later in the jewelry shop where he approached Sophie and me."

"Plus, when he accosted Zack outside the restrooms by the theater," said Shane.

"It's easy to get lost in a crowd when you don't stand out for any obvious physical reason," said Zack.

"You two nearly came to blows last night," I said. "Surely someone noticed."

"Probably, but apparently none of the ship's security officers or other crewmembers were nearby at the time," said Zack.

"So what happens now?" I asked. "Will the captain have Emerson's cabin staked out?"

Zack shook his head. "Doubtful. The captain has his hands full right now, both with Orson's death and the measles case. Emerson has become a low priority."

"Why?" I asked. "He's a killer."

"A *paroled* killer who hasn't committed any crime on this ship."

"Other than using a fake passport," I said.

Zack sniggered. "The captain actually suggested I had no proof that Emerson hadn't legally changed his name and become a Canadian citizen."

I rolled my eyes. "Seriously?"

"Seriously. Security is aware of the situation and will remain on the lookout, but the captain isn't devoting any additional resources toward apprehending him."

Until Emerson succeeds in pulling off whatever he has

planned, moving him back to the top of the priority list. Of course, at that point it might be too late. "What about Orson?" I asked. "Does the captain have proof Emerson wasn't involved in his death?"

"No, but according to what he told me this morning, he thinks it's a long shot. All indications are that Orson jumped."

"How can he be sure?" I asked.

"From his discussion with Orson's wife, her sister, and the brother-in-law. They told him Orson suffered from dementia. They suspected he had chronic traumatic encephalopathy."

"The brain injury football players and other athletes sometimes get?" I asked. As the mother of two sons who played sports, I constantly worried about them sustaining concussions that could eventually lead to CTE. To my immense relief, so far both had remained free from head injuries.

"Many CTE sufferers wind up committing suicide," said Shane.

"Exactly," said Zack. "And since the captain said his crew found no evidence of a struggle or tampering of railings or balconies on any deck above the lifeboat where Orson was found, he considers the case closed."

"How convenient," I said.

"There's one more thing," said Zack.

His brow furrowed and his face grew dark. I was certain I wouldn't like what he was about to say. "What?"

"Emerson's key card hasn't been used to enter his cabin since shortly after he arrived onboard yesterday afternoon."

NINE

"And the captain doesn't consider that suspicious?" I asked. "Where did Emerson sleep last night?"

"Maybe he hooked up with someone," said Shane.

"That's what the captain suggested," said Zack.

I immediately thought of Lenore's breakfast confession to Mama. With so many seniors onboard the Gemstone Empress, I doubted Lenore was the only passenger on the prowl for a shipboard romance. After all, Mama had met Lou Beaumont on a cruise. And knowing my mother, I was certain their high seas interlude had been anything but platonic. After all, she came home engaged to the man.

"He'd still need to return to his cabin to change clothes this morning," I said.

"He could have slipped into the cabin while the steward had the door propped open for cleaning," said Zack.

"Is it possible Emerson hacked into the system?" asked Shane. "Maybe he did spend the night in his cabin."

"And found a way to keep his card from registering when it's used?" I asked.

"Not by himself," said Zack. "He's been locked up for thirty-five years. He'd have no way of acquiring the necessary computer skills for something that technically sophisticated, not in the short time since his release."

"But he could be working with a skilled accomplice," I said, "someone either on the ship or operating from a remote location. Anyone with the money and connections to pull off Emerson's release would have no problem hiring an expert computer hacker."

Zack grimaced at the possibility.

Then another thought occurred to me. "Where is Emerson's cabin located?"

"Deck Seven," said Zack, "Why?"

"I'm assuming in an area of the hallway that's a dead zone for camera surveillance?"

His grimace deepened as he nodded once. "I already checked before meeting you in the dining room."

"I wonder if that was by coincidence or by design on Emerson's part."

"Or by the person responsible for him being here," said Shane.

"Either way," I said, "I think we need to speak with his cabin steward."

Zack tilted his head toward me. "Again, why?"

"To find out if Emerson Dawes is actually staying in that cabin," I said. "If he has an accomplice onboard, they may have switched cabins."

"Then wouldn't the accomplice have used the key card to enter the room?" asked Shane.

"Not if the accomplice has been in the cabin ever since entering yesterday," I said.

At that, both men locked eyes with me. My head spun with possible scenarios. I began to tick them off on my fingers. "One, Accomplice X stuck a Do Not Disturb sign on his door."

"What about meals?" asked Shane.

"Emerson is bringing him food." I held up another finger. "Two, the cabin is a decoy, and Emerson is sharing a cabin with Accomplice X."

They both continued to stare intently at me as I continued. "Three, there is no Accomplice X onboard, and as Shane suggested, the hacker remotely engineered Emerson's key card not to record when it's used."

"Which makes locating him much more difficult," said Shane.

"But there's a fourth possibility," I said. "Accomplice X is in Emerson's cabin but hasn't left since first entering yesterday because he can't."

Zack let out a slow whistle under his breath. "So, you're suggesting...?"

"A man who's killed once would have no qualms killing again." After all, one possible motive for Emerson being on the ship was to exact revenge on Zack. Isn't murder the ultimate revenge? "Don't you think that's a plausible explanation?"

"Plausible but unlikely."

"Why?"

Zack wrinkled his nose. "I wouldn't want to be holed up in a cabin with a putrefying corpse."

"He wouldn't have to, not if he switched cabins with his accomplice."

"But why kill his accomplice?" asked Shane.

"To get rid of a witness once he'd served his purpose." Zack smacked both hands on the table, pushed his chair back, and rose. Then he reached for my hand. "Let's go."

"Where?"

"To stop speculating and get some answers. We need to speak to his cabin steward."

Once inside the ship, we found dozens of passengers cramming the area in front of the double bank of elevator. Instead of waiting, we pivoted toward the staircase.

Halfway down the second flight of steps Zack's phone rang. He checked the screen, answered by saying, "Hold on a sec," then diverted to a quiet alcove at the next landing.

"I'm guessing that's his lawyer," I whispered to Shane as we waited a few steps away from Zack, allowing him some privacy.

Even with Zack's back to us, I noticed the tension consuming his body. From the white-knuckled grip with which he held the phone to his ear, to the stiff stance of his torso and legs, and the way he curled his free hand into a fist and pounded the side of his thigh, Zack was wound tighter than a cobra about to spring.

The call lasted less than a minute. Grim-faced, he strode across the short expanse to where Shane and I waited. I laced my fingers through his, tilting my head to meet his gaze. He squeezed my hand, and shook his head. "It's as bad as I feared."

"Meaning?" I held my breath, anticipating the worst.

"Several people on the parole board recently came into unexplained windfalls of cash wired from offshore accounts. Someone big is definitely behind Emerson's release."

"How was your lawyer able to find that out so quickly?" asked Shane.

Zack turned to him. "Connections in high places." He didn't explain further.

Had Zack really been speaking with his lawyer or had he called someone else last night? We locked eyes. I knew this was not the time to suggest those connections involved him and any one of a number of unnamed alphabet agencies. Right now I was grateful for any connection that helped him put Emerson Dawes back behind bars. "What now?" I asked.

"Interviews are taking place as we speak."

Shane's eyebrows darted toward his hairline. "Interviews or interrogations?"

"Yes," said Zack. "Someone will cave and talk. Hopefully sooner rather than later."

But it would take more than someone spilling the beans on bribery. I'd seen enough of the underbelly of society this past year to know the person who orchestrated Emerson's release most likely hadn't done so directly. Anyone with that kind of power would have employed at least one intermediary—possibly several—in order to give himself plausible deniability.

Even if the parole board members admitted to taking bribes, it was highly unlikely they knew the name of the person at the top. They probably didn't even know the real identity of the person who had paid them to vote for Emerson's release.

In addition, Emerson's benefactor hadn't sprung him from prison out of the goodness of his heart. He'd want something in return, something that led directly to us. Otherwise, why would Emerson be on this cruise?

One person came to mind—Lawrence Tuttnauer. However, Zack thought Lawrence was a highly unlikely suspect. But if not Lawrence, then whom? And if so, why?

I thought back to the killers who had crossed my path over the last year. All now cooled their heels in various prisons, thanks in part to me. Some had close connections to organized crime. Perhaps I needed to let go of my Lawrence obsession and concentrate my sights elsewhere.

Ricardo the Bookie and Dirk Silver, AKA assassin Dante Silvestri, both came to mind. However, neither had any connection to Zack, at least as far as I knew. It seemed more than a stretch to connect the dots from Emerson to either Ricardo or Dirk.

That led me to wonder if perhaps Emerson's *assignment* from his benefactor had nothing to do with my involvement in any recent murder investigations. I glanced over at Zack as we continued down to Deck Seven. Had he lied to me from nearly the first day we'd met? When he'd recounted his tale of having inadvertently stumbled across marijuana growers in rural Guatemala, was he really on assignment shooting a photo essay on indigenous villagers for *National Geographic*? Or was that assignment cover for a different sort of assignment from a more covert D.C. based organization?

We had arrived on Deck Seven. Knowing the cabin number, Zack led the way. Sure enough, a magnetic Do Not Disturb sign was attached to the door. Zack zeroed in on a laundry cart sitting in the hallway several doors down from the cabin. The cabin door was propped open, and we could hear a vacuum cleaner running from within the room. "Follow my lead," said Zack, rushing down the hall.

Shane and I hurried to keep up with him.

Zack knocked on the open door, shouting into the room to be heard above the noise of the vacuum. "Hello?"

The steward jumped. When he turned toward the doorway, his round baby-face and startled expression made him appear more boy than man, although I assumed anyone working on a cruise ship had to be at least twenty-one years of age. His name badge identified him as Afu from Samoa.

"Sorry to startle you," said Zack.

The steward turned off the vacuum. "Not a problem, sir. How may I help you?"

"We're concerned about my fiancée's uncle. He's down the hall in Cabin 7548. We haven't seen or heard from him since yesterday."

I'm by no means an actress. I've always had trouble lying with a straight face. So I had my doubts my lack of thespian talent would fool this young man. Still, I had to try. I placed my hand over my mouth to stifle a sob, sniffled twice, then forced a quiver into my voice as I said, "I'm so worried. Uncle missed breakfast this morning and isn't answering his phone."

"We've tried knocking," said Shane, joining in the ruse. "He's not answering."

"Perhaps the gentleman is sleeping in and has turned his phone off?" suggested Afu. "Or could he have risen early for a swim or a visit to the gym and lost track of the time?"

I shook my head. "No, he doesn't know how to swim, and he isn't able to exercise. We had plans to meet this morning. He wouldn't forget."

"He's always the first to arrive anywhere," said Shane. "Punctuality is his middle name."

Zack pointed to the passkey dangling from Afu's waist. "Would you mind if we use your passkey to check on him?"

Afu fingered the passkey and bit down on his lower lip, hesitating before saying, "I am not allowed to do that, sir. I will have to call my supervisor."

I let loose a fake sob. "He's elderly and suffers from diabetes. I'm afraid he may have gone into diabetic shock or even a coma. Please, Afu! You have to help us. Every second may count."

"What if you unlock the door for us?" asked Zack.

Afu shifted his gaze back and forth from Zack to me to Shane. Then he glanced over at the open door and reluctantly said, "I suppose there is no harm in that. I do have to clean the room."

The three of us headed back toward Emerson's room with Afu following. However, when we reached the cabin, Afu stopped short. "I am sorry. I will have to call my supervisor after all."

"Why?" I asked.

"I am not allowed to enter a room with a Do Not Disturb sign on the door."

"Sorry, Afu," said Zack, "but we can't wait." With one swift move, he whipped the passkey from Afu's waist, tapped it against the locking mechanism, and swung the door open. The three of us rushed into the room with a panicky Afu following.

I scanned the cabin. No Emerson Dawes. No dead body. "He's not here."

Zack stuck his head into the bathroom. I opened the closet door, then pulled aside the drapes to check the balcony. Shane got down on his hands and knees and checked under the bed. Not only was the cabin empty, there were no signs that anyone had recently checked into the room. No suitcase stored under the bed, no clothes in the closet, no toiletries in the bathroom.

"Please, sirs and lady!" Afu's voice filled with fear. "You must return my passkey and leave immediately. I will get fired."

Zack handed the passkey back to Afu. The cabin steward's fingers trembled as he reattached it onto his uniform. I placed my hand on his arm. "No one will ever know, Afu. I promise."

His frightened eyes told me he didn't believe me. Zack stepped closer to him and asked, "Have you seen the gentleman who's supposed to be staying in this cabin?"

Afu shook his head. "No, sir, I am supposed to introduce myself to each of my passengers, but I have not yet seen Mr. Rutledge."

Shane held his phone up to Afu. "Have you seen this man?"

Afu glanced at the photo. "No, sir. Is that Mr. Rutledge?"

Zack nodded. He reached into his pocket, then extended his hand to Afu. The cabin steward stared for a moment, hesitating at the sight of the fifty-dollar bill Zack held between his fingers. Afu tentatively raised his hand but wavered, his fingers poised in the air inches above the money. He pulled his eyes from the bill and stared up at Zack. With his free hand, Zack took hold of Afu's hand, placed the money in his palm, and closed his fingers over the bill. "Thank you for your help, Afu."

On our way out, Zack removed the Do Not Disturb sign from the outside of the door and slapped it onto the inside.

~*~

"At least we know he didn't kill his accomplice," I said as the three of us made our way back upstairs. "Assuming he has an accomplice onboard."

"Do we?" asked Shane. "He could have killed him in his cabin late last night and tossed the body overboard. No one would ever know the guy was missing until he failed to show up after the cruise. Emerson could be staying in the accomplice's room and using his key card."

"Assuming he's killed the accomplice," said Zack. "We don't know whether he has, what he's up to, who's aiding him, and whether the accomplice—if there is one—is also onboard the ship or operating remotely."

"Or both," said Shane.

I hadn't thought about that. "He may have more than one accomplice, one on the ship and one located somewhere on the mainland."

"We're operating blind in a feedback loop," said Shane. "How do we break through?"

"What if we ask Guest Services to page Desmond Rutledge?" I said.

"And do what?" asked Zack. "Have security march him to the brig? The captain made it perfectly clear to me this morning that he's had a change of heart. He'd rather ignore the problem for now."

"I wonder why," I said. "Aren't captains trained to deal with all sorts of unexpected emergencies? He admitted deaths on cruise ships are not uncommon, and I'm sure he's had to deal with at least one Norovirus outbreak on his ship in recent years. Having half your passengers and crew down with all sorts of awful intestinal symptoms has to be worse than dealing with one case of measles."

"You're suggesting someone got to him," said Zack.

"I don't think we can rule it out."

Cruise ship captains probably make good money, but that didn't mean they couldn't be bought. Some people have enormous expenses, legitimate or otherwise. Maybe the captain had fathered quadruplets, currently all attending Ivy League colleges. Or his wife suffers from a debilitating illness that has eaten up all their savings. Or like Karl, Lady Luck stuck her talons into his bank account.

Then there are the Bernie Madoffs of the world, those people who are just plain greedy. Enough is never enough for them.

Zack paused, ruminating over my suggestion for a moment before he said, "You might be on to something. Captain Halvorson certainly executed quite an about-face in a very short period of time."

"Perhaps your lawyer could have his people look into the captain's finances," I said, forcing myself not to put any additional emphasis on the word *lawyer*.

Not for a minute did I believe Zack's lawyer had the forensic resources or subpoena power to dig into the finances of parole board members, but what did I know? Maybe the guy knew a guy who knew a guy. After all, we did live in New Jersey.

Then again, come to think of it, *we* knew a guy.

TEN

Maybe Zack had contacted our very own personal hacker extraordinaire—Tino Martinelli. I'd assumed the call he received was from his lawyer since he'd spoken with him last night and was expecting a return call. But what if he'd also reached out to at least one other person while I sulked on the balcony? Tino had the skills to find information quicker than anyone forced to deal with the red tape of going through legal channels.

However, Zack had mentioned the parole board members were being questioned. That would rule out Tino, indicating the state's attorney general had opened an investigation. So maybe his lawyer did have more pull than I assumed. Then again, whichever alphabet agency Zack swore he didn't work for might have contacted the attorney general. I wasn't going to open my mouth and stick my tongue into that volatile topic.

Mentioning Tino was a more neutral topic. "Do you think Tino might be able to do some cyber-sleuthing into the captain's finances for us?"

"Tino?" Shane turned to Zack. "Did he discover the payments to the parole board members?"

Zack stopped momentarily and glanced between Shane and me as we entered the corridor that led to our suite. His eyes narrowed slightly, and his lips tightened before he faced forward again. As he strode down the hallway, he said, "Everything has to be done by the book. Otherwise evidence will be tossed out of court, and both Emerson and his benefactor walk."

I noticed he hadn't answered Shane's question or mine.

We arrived at our suite to find two white envelopes emblazoned with the gold and silver Gemstones of the Seven Seas cruise line logo sitting in the message slot alongside our door. One addressed to me, the other to Zack.

"Should we be concerned about fingerprints?" I asked. "We already know Emerson is on the ship."

"But we don't know about a possible accomplice," said Zack. "We have no idea who delivered these envelopes." Using the tips of his thumb and forefinger, he gingerly lifted the envelopes by their corners.

"Don't tell me you carry a fingerprint kit and have access to NGI," said Shane.

"What's NGI?" I asked.

"Next Generation Identification. It's an FBI database that contains fingerprints and biographical information of not only criminals but anyone ever fingerprinted for a background check."

"Like teachers?" Shane had gone to school part-time at night while working construction for years, eventually receiving a degree in education. His recent arrest for murder had come as a result of a fingerprint match.

He nodded before turning back to Zack. "Well, do you?"

Instead of answering, Zack raised one eyebrow in my direction. "Have you been feeding our friend here your conspiracy theories?"

I opened my mouth in denial, but before I could answer, Shane asked, "What conspiracy theories?"

Zack laughed and rolled his eyes. "Never mind. Not only don't I travel with a fingerprint kit, I wouldn't have a clue how to use one."

"Then what's the point?" I asked, opening the door with my keycard.

"Shh," said Zack as we stepped inside the suite. He dropped the envelopes onto the coffee table and removed his phone to sweep for bugs. Satisfied the room was free of listening devices, he pocketed his phone. "Do you have a tweezers with your toiletries?" he asked me.

What woman doesn't? "You want it?"

He grinned. "It is why I asked."

Smart Aleck! I answered back in kind. "Odd time to pluck your brows," I said, heading for the bedroom. When I returned a minute later and handed Zack the tweezers, he finally answered my question. "If this letter contains an accomplice's fingerprints, it could be used to identify and track him down at some point once we're off the ship."

That made sense, whether or not we arrived back in New Jersey with Emerson secure in the brig. If he had an accomplice onboard, and that accomplice remained at large, the envelope and its contents might identify him and lead to his apprehension.

Zack settled onto the sofa. I sat on one side of him, Shane on the other. But as Zack reached for the first envelope, I grabbed his wrist. "Wait!"

"What's the matter?"

"I know this sounds completely paranoid, but what if the envelope contains anthrax or some other deadly poison?"

"I don't think we need to worry," said Zack. "Neither envelope is sealed."

"That makes a difference?"

"If you wanted to poison someone with a toxic powder, would you leave it in an unsealed envelope and place the envelope in a message holder where the powder might spill out before your victim had a chance to remove and open the envelope?"

"Only if I were a really dumb killer."

"Right," said Zack. "Given what we know so far, we have to assume we're dealing with pros, not bumbling amateurs." He waited while I digested that theory. "You good with that, Nancy Drew?"

I couldn't disagree with his logic. I released my grip on his wrist, hoping Agatha Christie was watching over us from up in Heaven. After inhaling a deep breath—which in hindsight probably wasn't the brightest move if anthrax was present—I said, "Go ahead."

Using the tip of the tweezers, Zack grabbed the point of one envelope flap and lifted the envelope off the table. With his other hand, he pulled back the envelope pocket with the edge of his index fingernail and glanced inside. "No anthrax," he said. "Nothing but a card inviting you to a special luncheon this afternoon.

He dropped the envelope onto the coffee table and repeated the process with the second envelope. "And an invite for me."

All three of us exhaled our relief in unison.

Zack carefully removed both invitations to avoid adding his fingerprints to the cards and placed them on the table for us to read. Lily, the ship's cruise director, had invited us to join her at Diamante, one of the celebrity chef restaurants. "I suppose this is a perk of staying in the best suite on the ship," I said, "but I wonder why Mama wasn't also invited."

"You don't know that she wasn't," said Zack. "She may have already picked up her invitation."

Shane stood. "I'll let you two get ready for your exclusive soiree. I think I'll hit the jogging track, then do some laps in the pool."

"You may have received an invitation as well," I said. "Perhaps they were sent to all passengers who booked suites."

"I hope not. I didn't pack a tux."

I laughed. "Horrors! How gauche of you!"

He shrugged his shoulders. "What do I know? I'm from the plains of North Dakota."

"Not to worry, cowboy. The invite doesn't mention black tie."

"In that case, I may see you at lunch." He waved as he headed for the door. "Otherwise, later."

Once Shane closed the door behind him, Zack said, "I need to make a few phone calls."

I deliberately didn't ask for details. Instead, I played it cool. "Since we have time before we need to meet for lunch, I think I'll grab a cup of coffee and take a leisurely stroll around the ship."

"Stay out of trouble."

"Always."

Zack didn't even bother to answer. He simply cocked his head, arched an eyebrow, and stared at me.

"Well, at least I try!"

~*~

I arrived at the Pearl of the Seas Buffet to find hordes of people crowding around the various food and beverage stations.

Passengers filled every available table while others circled, plates in hand, searching for a place to sit. I executed an immediate about-face and descended several decks to one of the gourmet coffee shops on the Atrium level.

Less than five minutes later, with a large vanilla latte in hand, I settled into a deck chair in front of the railing. As I sipped my coffee, I gazed out at the calm waters of the Caribbean and watched a school of dolphins frolicking in the distance.

The peaceful moment was soon interrupted by the sounds of bickering coming from somewhere behind me. From their vantage point the two women must not have seen me lounging in the chair in front of them when they arrived. They obviously felt free to talk without fear of being overheard, and I wasn't about to disabuse them of that notion.

"I don't think it's appropriate," said one woman.

"I don't care," said the other. "I'm not going into mourning for an alley cat of a man who cheated on me for years."

"People will talk," said the first woman.

"Ask me if I care? They've always talked. What difference does it make?"

"Because now he's dead."

"So? I didn't kill him. Do I look like I have the strength to toss anyone overboard, let alone a man who weighed close to three hundred pounds?"

"Of course not. No one would accuse you of that, Birdie, especially in your condition."

"I should think not. But I don't believe for one moment that he jumped. What ever possessed you and Dennis to tell the captain Orson had dementia?"

"We both felt you didn't need the stress of undue scrutiny, not in your condition. It was the easiest way to make the problem go away."

"I do appreciate that. Your motives were pure and thoughtful. Still..."

"No one ever needs to know otherwise. Dennis said Orson had quite a bit to drink at the bar after dinner."

"On top of what he drank before and during dinner."

"He may have lost his footing. Accidents do happen."

"Accident, my bony derriere. I'll tell you what probably happened. This time the drunken fool made a pass at the wrong woman. Her husband confronted him, and now I'm finally free of the philandering dog."

"Could be. I'm sure the couple will never come forward, and since there doesn't seem to be any other witnesses, who's the wiser?"

"True. We'll probably never know what really happened, but I don't care."

"Are you saying it wouldn't bother you if someone had murdered Orson?"

"If someone killed Orson, either deliberately or accidentally, he did me a huge favor. I'm glad he's dead."

"I know. I just don't think you should broadcast your feelings. It might raise doubts about whether or not the death really was an accident or suicide."

Birdie let loose a Lucille-type harrumph. "You know my one regret?"

"What?"

"That it didn't happen years ago. It's not like I have much time left to enjoy my golden years."

"Don't talk like that, Birdie. You're going to beat this, but you need a more positive attitude."

"Really?" Birdie laughed. "You think a positive attitude cures cancer? Don't be a fool, Bunny. You know the odds are extremely low for surviving what I have."

"I know, but people do survive. I keep hoping you'll be one of the lucky ones."

Birdie sighed. "So do I."

"You look tired. Let's get you back to the cabin where you can lie down before lunch."

"I think that's probably a good idea."

A moment later the chairs scraped against the deck, and I heard their voices fade away as the door behind us swooshed open. I waited several minutes before daring to leave. Not wanting to risk running into the twins by leaving through the door I'd previously used and they had just exited, I walked along the deck toward the opposite end of the ship.

My path took me through the pool area into an outdoor bar near a group of round Jacuzzis, each large enough to hold up to eight people. Mama, Lenore, and two men lounged within the steamy bubbles of one of them. In-between chatting and laughing, they sipped from pastel-colored frozen drinks, complete with paper parasols and skewers of tropical fruits.

I walked over to the edge of the spa pool, eyeing the man giving my mother his rapt attention. From the affectionate way Mama gazed into his eyes, I suspected she might already consider him the next candidate in the long line of my short-lived stepfathers.

I forced a light-heartedness I didn't feel into my voice. "Don't you look like you're having fun!"

Mama pulled her attention from her smitten suitor. "Oh, hello, dear."

I squatted to eye level, quirking my head toward the man whose arm draped possessively across her bare shoulders. He had a full head of wavy midnight black hair, too perfect for anything but hair plugs or a toupee, and a matching bushy walrus mustache. "Care to introduce me?" I asked.

Before Mama could speak, the man held out a dripping wet hand. "Basil Chatsworth," he said in a thick upper crust British accent. "And you must be Flora's daughter Anastasia."

I accepted his hand, expecting him to shake mine. Instead he planted his sticky alcohol-drenched lips on the back of my hand. "Charmed to make your acquaintance," he added, accentuating his words with a full teeth-baring grin.

Was this guy for real? He sounded and acted like he belonged in a nineteen-thirties British period piece. *Featuring Basil Chatsworth, playing the role of the minor aristocrat sipping a brandy in the drawing room of Dunbury Castle.* The needle of my skept-o-meter moved sharply into the red zone.

Mama claimed she had a sixth sense for Lotharios on the prowl, but I had my doubts. When I glanced over at her and raised an eyebrow, she said, "Don't you just love his accent, dear?"

"Indeed." I pulled my hand from his and forced myself not to wipe it against my jeans. "Nice to meet you, Mr. Chatsworth." *Not!*

"Please call me Basil. I have a feeling we're going to be seeing quite a bit of each other."

Not if I can help it.

Instead of answering, I offered a tight smile and turned my attention to the man canoodling with Lenore. Given the comb-over to disguise his balding head and the lack of facial hair, I assumed Lenore had moved on from her hookup of last night—

assuming there was an actual hookup and not a figment of Mama's overactive imagination. "And you are?"

Since he was on the opposite side of the Jacuzzi, he didn't bother extending his hand. Instead, he raised his seafoam green drink in greeting and said, "Harvey Kreider," before returning his undivided attention to Lenore.

I returned my attention to Mama. "I thought you and Lenore were having a spa morning."

"No, dear, you misunderstood. I took Lenore to check out the facilities. We booked appointments for tomorrow."

I couldn't wait to leave. Luckily, I had an excuse. "If you'll excuse me, I have an appointment." I stood and offered the foursome a wave, adding, "You kids behave yourselves. Don't do anything I wouldn't do."

As I scurried off, I heard Mama say, "You'll have to excuse my daughter. She can be a bit of a stick-in-the-mud."

Behind me I heard Basil and Harvey roaring with laughter. I wondered how many of those umbrella drinks they'd each already consumed. It wasn't even noon yet.

I also hoped Mama didn't wind up so blotto that she forgot to use protection. Knowing my mother, I had no doubt what she and Basil had planned for an afternoon activity, and although she might be too old to get pregnant, STDs contained no age restrictions.

I just hoped the two lovebirds scheduled their cavorting in his cabin and not in our suite where my sons might stumble upon them. Inadvertently coming across your parents having sex is bad enough. *But a grandparent?* That's an image I doubt Alex and Nick would ever be able to scrub from their minds.

On that disturbing thought I made my way back to the suite.

Zack glanced up from his laptop as I entered. "Get your calls made?" I asked.

"All taken care of."

"Anything I need to know?"

"Nothing new."

"So we don't know if the captain is on the take?"

"We do not."

"Is anyone checking into that?"

"Hopefully."

Sometimes getting news out of Zack was like coaxing a raw T-bone from a lion—not that I'd ever done so or ever would, but I could imagine it was much the same. If he were more open, maybe I'd believe his I'm-not-a-spy claims.

"Well, I have news." I plopped onto the sofa cushion at a right angle to him.

He closed his laptop and turned to face me. "What kind of news?"

"Bad news and odd news. Which would you like first?"

"Let's get the bad news out of the way. It's not another dead body, is it?"

"Not unless I strangle my mother."

Zack blew air from his lungs. "What's she done now?"

"Looks like she's found herself another shipboard romance."

"She doesn't waste any time, does she?"

"Hey, she waited an entire twenty-four hours. That's probably a record for her. Anyway, at the moment the two lovebirds are sharing a hot tub and getting soused with Lenore and her next hookup-in-waiting."

Zack rolled his eyes as I provided him with the details of my encounter with the swinging seniors. "He strikes me as totally fake, from his too perfect head of hair to his too British accent that has Mama swooning with lust."

Zack screwed up his face. "Let's file that one under Way Too Much Information. What's the odd news?"

"Orson wasn't suffering from dementia."

ELEVEN

"How do you know that?" asked Zack.

I related the conversation I'd overheard between Birdie and Bunny. "Apparently the only thing Orson suffered from was serial philandering."

"That certainly explains his wife's sour disposition."

"That's not the half of it."

"There's more?"

"Birdie is dying. She said if she discovered someone had killed Orson, whether accidentally or on purpose, she'd thank him for setting her free, that she only wished it had happened years ago."

Zack let loose a slow, sustained whistle. "That's some bombshell."

"Do you think we should tell the captain?"

"Tell him what, exactly?"

"That Birdie and the Marwoods lied to him about Orson having dementia."

Zack pondered for moment. "I don't see what purpose it

would serve."

"Really?"

"Put yourself in the captain's position," said Zack. "He's got a dead body, no witnesses, and no video surveillance of how Orson died. The crew found no tampering or damage to any balconies or railings. The captain wants the incident dealt with as swiftly as possible. Suicide is the most logical conclusion. Case closed."

"But wouldn't learning that Orson didn't have dementia reopen the case?"

"Not necessarily. I suspect the captain might suggest Orson had suffered from depression over his wife's impending demise."

I snorted. "After the way he treated her all those years?"

"Especially because of the way he had treated her. He was consumed with regret. Stranger things have happened."

I shook my head. "I'm not buying it. I think Birdie's scenario of Orson hitting on the wrong woman sounds more likely."

"True, but since there is no evidence to prove that's what happened, the captain will still opt for suicide as the most likely cause of death."

"Because it makes his life a heck of a lot easier?"

Zack nodded. "From what I've been reading online, it's common practice for cruise lines to use suicide as a cover-up to a possible murder."

"I suppose you're right." I stood. "I'll go change for lunch. By the way, Mama didn't mention receiving an invitation."

"Did you ask her?"

I shook my head. "Frankly, I was in too much of a rush to escape the sight of my bikini-clad mother getting up close and personal with a Speedo-wearing septuagenarian."

"She may have received one and decided she prefers the

company of Mr. Speedo to that of Lily the Cruise Director."

"No doubt."

~*~

Twenty minutes later we stepped into Diamante. As with the main dining room, the décor included an homage to Valentine's Day but decidedly more upscale. There were no balloons, and instead of carnations in faux crystal bud vases, each table held an elegant floral arrangement of roses in varying shades of reds and pinks with white baby's breath and greenery.

After a host checked off our names, a waiter escorted us to a private room at the back of the restaurant. About two-dozen people had already gathered, some standing in small groups and chatting, others already seated at the half dozen tables, each set for six people. We were directed to a table with three empty seats.

I offered a quick greeting to the three women of retirement age already seated, then leaned over and whispered to Zack, "I don't think this is a gathering for suite passengers. The room is too small."

"Unless only premier suite passengers were invited," he said.

"Don't Shane and Sophie have a premier suite?" I craned my neck to get a better view of the room. "I don't see Shane anywhere."

Before Zack had a chance to answer, a spotlight flipped on at the front of the room. A moment later a petite woman of no more than thirty with medium-length bouncy blonde curls stepped into the light. She wore a navy pencil skirt and white military style short-sleeved shirt with the silver and gold cruise logo embroidered on a breast pocket.

After offering us a wide smile, blue eyes twinkling, she said, "Good afternoon, ladies and gentlemen." She sang her words, as if speaking to a group of toddlers. "For those of you who haven't met me yet, allow me to introduce myself. I'm Lily Moreau, your cruise director."

A smattering of polite applause broke out among some of the passengers, along with a shrill two-fingered wolf whistle, followed by vociferous clapping coming from behind us. The man plopped into the empty seat to Zack's left. I forced myself not to glare at the Neanderthal, an obvious holdover from the *Mad Men* decade of the nineteen-fifties.

Zack leaned over and whispered in my ear. "That's Victor Hogan."

"Seriously?" This time I couldn't help staring. I wondered how much Mama knew about Victor Hogan, other than having seen his author photo on the jackets of his books. She obviously had no idea that the object of her pursuit didn't rise to her usual Junior League and D.A.R. standards. Even ignoring his crass behavior—something Mama would never condone in any man—the guy was a slob. He certainly hadn't dressed for an invitation-only luncheon in the ship's most upscale restaurant. He had arrived wearing a frayed ball cap, which he hadn't removed before taking his seat, and a wrinkled novelty T-shirt, easily a decade old. The shirt was so faded I couldn't make out the wording sprawled across his barrel chest.

Lily blushed, waiting for the clapping to die down before continuing. "Well, aren't you all too sweet for words!"

This produced another round of clapping, as well as a second two-finger wolf whistle from Victor Hogan, after which she continued, "I want to thank you all for coming this afternoon. If those of you still standing will settle into your seats, the waiters will come around to take your lunch orders. Afterwards, I'll explain why I've invited you all here today."

I picked up the menu card from my place setting and scanned the luncheon selections—shrimp cocktail or Insalata Caprese as an appetizer; lobster, filet mignon, or broiled Chilean sea bass with truffle fries and grilled asparagus for an entrée; and chocolate soufflé, raspberry crème brûlée, or Bananas Foster for dessert. While I tried to decide between the lobster and sea bass, a sommelier moved around our table, filling champagne glasses.

"They've certainly spared no expense," I said to Zack. "Why do you think we were singled out for such an elegant lunch?"

"It's obvious," said Victor Hogan, who had overheard me. He pointed a chubby index finger toward Lily. She was chatting up a couple at the table in front of us. "She wants something."

"From us?" I asked. "Like what?"

"Beats me, doll. All I know is there's no such thing as a free lunch."

I gritted my teeth to keep from telling the guy off. Zack placed his hand on my thigh. I wasn't sure whether he meant it as support or to keep me from exploding. I assured him with an almost imperceptible shake of my head, that I wouldn't let Victor Hogan get to me. I saw no point in engaging in a sparring match with the chauvinist.

Hogan continued, "Dinners at Diamante go for a hundred bucks a pop, and that doesn't include the tip or drinks."

"So this isn't a perk of staying in one of the premier suites?" asked Zack.

He snorted. "Buddy, I've cruised on this ship at least four times a year for the last decade. Always stay in a premier suite. I've never been treated to a meal at Diamante before today. There's no way the cruise line is shelling out for this little gathering without wanting something in return."

He leaned around Zack and winked at me. Then he picked up his flute and quickly guzzled the champagne. After smacking his lips, he held the glass aloft and yelled, "Garçon!" The sommelier immediately rushed over to refill his glass.

"If they're paying," he said, winking at me a second time, "I'm drinking the bubbly for as long as they're pouring it."

Easily somewhere north of seventy, Victor Hogan reminded me of an older version of Archie Bunker from *All in the Family*. I hoped that was where the similarity ended, and he wouldn't go off on a political rant during lunch. There are few things worse than becoming a forced captive audience to a boorish total stranger.

Lucky for me, at that moment the waiter approached to take my order, giving me a reason to ignore Victor Hogan. I decided on the salad, lobster, and raspberry crème brûlée for dessert, thanks to my well-established lack of willpower.

Once all the waiters headed off to the kitchen to place our orders, Lily stepped back up to the mic. "So why have I invited all of you to lunch today?" She clasped her hands together at chest level, pausing for dramatic effect before saying, "The truth is, I need your help."

Hogan elbowed Zack in the side. "See? Didn't I tell you?" Then in a booming voice, loud enough for the entire room to hear, he called to Lily, "Spill it, doll."

The guy definitely hadn't gotten the #MeToo memo. Lily's smile tightened, but she kept her cool as she zeroed in on him. Her voice lost much of its lilt, and the twinkle disappeared from her eyes, but she remained smiling as she said, "I was getting to that, Victor."

Around the room, heads turned as people focused on the

obnoxious passenger at our table. Since it appeared Lily and Victor Hogan had history, and he obviously made her uncomfortable, I had to wonder why she'd included him on the invitation list.

Lily refocused her attention onto the room at large and continued, "As I'm sure you realize, our plans for your cruise were turned upside down when all shore leaves were cancelled."

An undercurrent of buzzing voices began to fill the room, forcing Lily to speak louder. "Normally, we have a limited number of shipboard activities planned for the days when we're in port because so few passengers stay on the ship."

"The natives getting restless already, doll?" asked Victor.

Lily sighed. "They are indeed. That's where all of you come in. Everyone invited here today, according to the information you filled out when you booked your cruise, has a special talent or interesting profession. For example, we have a poetry professor, a retired three-star general, several musicians and singers, a photojournalist, an art historian, a women's magazine crafts editor, an archeologist, a yoga instructor, and a romance author, to name just a few."

She waved toward Victor. "For those of you who don't recognize him from his appearances on morning and late-night talk-shows or in the tabloids, Victor here is *New York Times* bestselling author Victor Hogan. Some of you may have read one or more of his..." She paused for effect before continuing, "...salacious...biographies."

All heads once again pivoted toward our table. A buzz filled the room. Victor Hogan stood. He flipped the ball cap off his head, waved it in the air, and took a bow. When he turned to face the tables behind us and take a second bow, I realized he was wearing a pair of plaid swim trunks. At least he wasn't in a Speedo.

"*Unauthorized* celebrity biographies," said the woman to my right, speaking under her breath. "I can't imagine any celebrity voluntarily divulging some of the details that make their way into his books."

"You've read them?" asked one of the other women.

"Definitely not! My sister has, though, and she talks nonstop about them each time he releases a new book."

"Sounds like my mother," I said.

Before taking his seat, Hogan segued into a sales pitch. "For those of you who haven't already purchased my latest bestseller detailing the secret life of America's newest troubled pop princess, a limited number of signed copies are available for the bargain price of $29.99 at Gems Between the Covers on the Atrium Deck. Trust me, you're not going to want to miss this one."

He then turned back to Lily. "So, let me guess your motive for this little soiree, doll. You want me to give a few lectures, spilling all the juicy beans on the hoity-toity glitterati?"

Before Lily could answer, he grabbed his menu and waved it over his head. "For what? In exchange for a steak and champagne lunch?" He snorted. "I don't know about the rest of the folks here, but it's going to cost you more than that if you want me entertaining your bored passengers."

Lily's cheeks flushed. "But of course, Victor. Anyone who agrees to help us out will be compensated by the cruise line at the going rate we pay our guest entertainers, lecturers, and instructors."

Hogan cocked his head. "Huh! Well, that's a horse of a different color. You can count me in." He dropped into his seat and smacked both hands on the table, resulting in everyone at the table swiftly grabbing their glasses to avert a tsunami of spilled champagne.

"After all," he continued, "a guy can only spend so much time lolling in a hot tub with bikini-clad babes before he turns into a prune."

One look at Victor Hogan's flaccid, wrinkled flesh told me he didn't need a hot tub to transform into a prune. He was already there. I doubted many bikini-clad babes would ever want to share a hot tub or anything else with him, but I supposed some women will do anything for money. I hoped Mama wasn't one of them.

Hogan roared as if he'd just told the greatest joke ever written, but Lily brightened. She let loose a huge sigh of relief, then said, "Thank you, Victor. I had a feeling I could count on you. I know how much you enjoy an audience."

Oh yeah. Those two definitely had history.

Hogan shrugged. "What gifted raconteur doesn't?" He raised his empty flute. "Now, do me a favor, doll. Send over the guy with the magnum."

Lily turned to the sommelier and tipped her head in Hogan's direction. The man rushed over to fill Victor's glass for a third time. I wondered if Lily was under orders to indulge Hogan, given how often he sailed with the cruise line. Then again, maybe she'd played him. After all, she did get what she wanted from him.

She grabbed a stack of cards from the nearby table and fanned herself with them. "I'm going to pass out questionnaires. If you're interested in giving a lecture, a performance, or teaching a class, please fill out your information, and I'll schedule sit-downs with you for later in the day. Meanwhile, enjoy your lunch."

She began walking around each table, handing out cards, stopping to chat briefly with various passengers.

"I guess we know who the photojournalist and magazine editor are," I whispered to avoid Victor Hogan's superhero power of hearing.

"What do you think?" asked Zack. "Should we help out?"

"We? I'm sure people would be interested in hearing about your adventures in Madagascar and other exotic places, but who's going to want to hear what it's like to work at a third-rate women's magazine sold at supermarket checkout counters? Unless..."

"Unless what?"

I hated to pass up an opportunity to whittle down my massive debt, which vied with the GNP of several third world nations. Ideally, I could offer my services to teach crafts classes, but where would I get supplies while we're floating around the Caribbean, unable to dock at any port of call?

"Unless I talk about morphing from a mild-mannered crafts editor into a reluctant Jessica Fletcher."

Zack shook his head. "With a killer onboard? Not one of your better ideas."

"Really?" I glanced around the room. "I wonder where it went."

"Where what went?"

"You're sense of humor."

Zack responded with a snort.

A few minutes later, as the waiters began serving the first course, Lily finally made her way to our table. When she handed me a card, she asked my name. "I'm Anastasia Pollack, the magazine crafts editor."

"Wonderful," she said. "I'd love for you to teach a few craft classes."

"With what? I didn't see a shop onboard that sells craft supplies."

"Not to worry. I have a huge stash of supplies for emergencies such as this."

"You often have emergencies that keep you from docking at various ports?"

"Not usually, but occasionally an instructor or guest lecturer cancels at the last minute, usually due to illness. Craft classes are one way I fill the void. There's often someone on the ship willing to step in to teach a class, and if all else fails, I hold beading classes. Anyone can string beads, right?"

"Unless they're all thumbs."

"Luckily, I haven't come across any of them."

"In that case, I'd be delighted to teach a few classes."

Since Karl's death, I'd taken on assorted moonlighting jobs to stave off the bill collectors. I had no idea what the going rate was for paid instructors on cruise lines, but Victor Hogan didn't strike me as someone who would work for pennies.

I'd begun my career as an art teacher. Last summer I picked up extra cash subbing for the arts and crafts instructor at Sunnyside, the assisted living and rehabilitation center where Lucille had convalesced after suffering a minor stroke.

Of course, I hadn't expected to wind up dealing with murder along with pottery wheels and watercolor paints, but then again, who does?

TWELVE

I had agreed to meet with Lily directly after lunch to discuss logistics, payment details, and figuring out what classes I could offer based on an inventory of her crafts supplies. When I arrived at her office, situated through a door and down a corridor behind the Guest Services desk, she first led me to a small storeroom beyond her office. "Feel free to use anything," she said, swinging the door open and flipping on the light switch.

Floor-to-ceiling shelving units along three sides of the small room held labeled clear plastic storage tubs containing not only various arts and crafts supplies but materials for floral arranging, cake decorating, cookie and cupcake baking, origami, toys and games for children ranging from toddlers to teens, adult games, sheet music, and more. "I believe in being prepared for any emergency," she said.

She wasn't kidding. My old classroom held fewer arts and crafts supplies.

A closer inspection of some of the larger tubs revealed an

overabundance of cotton print fabrics and felt squares. A slightly smaller bin contained an assortment of notions, including scissors, needles, and straight pins. Another was filled with spools of thread. There were bins that held assorted ribbons and trims, others with yarns and embroidery supplies, and one with various types of glues as well as hot and low-temp glue guns. One large tub was filled with plastic zip bags of buttons and decorative beads in various styles, colors, and sizes.

I suggested a series of fabric crafts that wouldn't require a sewing machine and could be tailored to passengers from beginners to those with advanced skills. "I'll need access to a copy machine to print out patterns and instructions."

Lily beamed. "Of course. I can take care of that for you. As for a stipend, I can offer you a hundred dollars for a one-hour class."

"That seems fair." More than fair, actually, but I tamped down my excitement.

"I'd like you to teach a minimum of four classes," she continued, "one a day, possibly more, depending on the passenger response."

"Not a problem." If teaching had paid this well, I might still be in the classroom. Or not. The salary hadn't driven me from the profession as much as dealing with hormonal middle school kids, not to mention administrators with Napoleonic complexes.

"When would you be ready to teach the first class?" she asked.

"As soon as I work up some samples."

"Tomorrow morning?"

"I can be ready by then. Just let me know where I should be and when."

Lily pulled a canvas tote with the cruise line logo from one of the bins and helped me fill it with the supplies I'd need to create the samples. Before we left the supply closet, she asked, "Would you mind working up the samples in one of the larger lounges?"

"Why?"

"So passengers can see you working. I'm hoping it will generate interest in the classes. I'll make up a sign. Just let me know when you're ready, and we'll pick a spot."

"Sure." I could understand Lily wanting to get her money's worth from my classes. She'd have a hard time justifying paying me a Benjamin an hour if only three or four passengers showed up for each class.

Besides, if the classes were a success, she might ask me to teach additional ones. It was going to be a long cruise otherwise, especially for someone who didn't gamble and was reluctant to don a bathing suit, exposing her forty-something body to a ship of fifty-five hundred passengers and crewmembers. I'd leave that to my uninhibited mother and her Size Two figure.

After we'd returned to Lily's office to dot every "i" and cross every "t" in the cruise line's standard contract, she said, "I assume you have a laptop with you?"

"I do."

She opened her desk drawer, removed a jump drive, and handed it to me. "If you bring me the patterns and instructions you need as soon as you have them, I'll make sure everything is ready for you before your first class tomorrow."

"I can have the jump drive to you in about fifteen minutes."

Surprise filled Lily's face. "That soon?"

"I won't have to create new designs from scratch," I explained. "I can pull projects from various back issues of *American Woman*. Everything I need is already on my work computer, which I can access from my laptop."

"And the samples? How soon do you think you'll have those made?"

"By dinner. When I bring you the jump drive, let me know in which lounge you'd like me to work up the samples."

"Wonderful! I'll get busy making a sign and see you shortly." She stood, thanking me once again as she walked me from her office.

As I strolled through the Atrium on my way back to the suite, I mulled over which projects to choose for my prospective students. Once I'd settled on an appropriate assortment, I could begin constructing samples in one of the lounges.

However, the aroma of freshly roasted java drifting out from one of the coffee shops waylaid me. I quickly made an executive decision to detour for a hit of caffeine.

As I stood at the counter, waiting for the barista to make my vanilla latte, I noticed Lenore Rosedale sitting alone at a table toward the back of the café. No Mama. No Harvey Kreider. She sat drinking a cup of coffee while staring out the window at the sparkling turquoise blue Caribbean Sea.

Lenore had replaced her sundress from breakfast with a pair of white linen slacks and a pastel silk T-shirt reminiscent of Monet's *Water Lilies*. Her lithe figure and regal posture made me wonder if she'd once danced in a ballet company. However, right now she reminded me of a queen surveying her aquatic realm. She'd released her hair from the confines of the tight ponytail and allowed her chestnut hair to cascade in soft waves that fell below her shoulders.

Latte in hand, I headed toward her, even though I was pressed for time. "Am I interrupting?" I asked when I arrived at the table.

She pulled herself away from her sea gazing and with an elegant sweeping gesture waved toward the chair opposite her. "Join me. I was just enjoying the view."

"Did you need a break from my mother?" I asked, settling into the chair.

Lenore smiled. "Not at all."

I couldn't decide whether she was telling me the truth or simply being polite. She was a woman of few words, at least during those times we'd shared a table in the dining room, and she hadn't spoken a word when I saw her earlier in the hot tub. I decided to press. "I hope she's not monopolizing your time on the ship."

Lenore took a sip of her coffee before responding. "Actually, I'm enjoying her company. In some ways I wish I could be more like her. She's so full of *joie de vivre*."

I chuckled. "That's Mama. She'd never admit it, but I suspect her first words as a toddler were *carpe diem*."

Lenore chuckled. "More like *carpe vita*. Flora seizes life, not just the day."

"True." I made a show of glancing around the café. "So where is she?"

"Having a little alone time with Basil."

I rolled my eyes and shook my head. I really didn't want that man becoming my next stepfather. "What do you know about Basil?"

"Not much. I know your mother met him at the seniors social yesterday afternoon. We were supposed to go on that cancelled land excursion with him, Harvey, and several others this morning."

I frowned.

Lenore waved away my concern. "Don't worry, dear. He's merely a shipboard fling. Let your mother have her fun. It's harmless."

"Is it? The last time Mama entered into a shipboard fling, she came home with a fiancé." I paused for a moment, remembering how Mama's romance nearly led to my death, but all I added was, "It didn't end well."

"Lou Beaumont."

"She told you?"

"She's told me quite a bit about herself. Your poor mother hasn't had such a great track record since your father died, has she?"

"Definitely not."

"You needn't worry about, Basil."

"Why is that?"

"Flora simply needs to exorcize Lawrence."

"You know about Lawrence, too?" Had Mama spilled her entire life's history in the short time she'd spent with Lenore? How much had she blabbed about me?

She nodded. "Think of Basil as nothing more than a palate cleanser."

I took a sip of my latte and raised my eyebrows over the rim of my coffee cup. Now that I sat inches from her, I realized Lenore was older than I'd originally thought. The tight bun she'd worn at dinner last night had definitely acted as a non-medical facelift, pulling back the slightly sagging skin and age lines now evident on her face. Like Mama, she probably had a standing monthly color appointment at her local salon to further disguise her years. However, letting her hair down—literally—had softened Lenore's features, giving a hint of the beauty she'd obviously been back in the day.

"Is this you speaking, or did my mother actually say that?" I asked.

"Not in so many words but it was definitely the gist of our conversation about Basil when we were alone."

I sighed.

"Was that a sigh of resignation or relief?"

"Relief. Is it me, or does Basil strike you as a little bit of a phony?"

Lenore laughed. "Oh, much more than a little bit. I wouldn't be surprised to find he's never stepped foot on British soil. That accent of his is as phony as his hair. If Basil Chatsworth is from London, it's London, Arkansas, not London, England."

"I wonder if that's even his real name. I suspect he may be trying to scam Mama."

Lenore shrugged. "And what if he is? We both know she might claim to descend from Russian nobility, but she's certainly not carrying around the Romanov crown jewels or any Faberge eggs in her purse."

It was my turn to laugh. "You do realize that lineage link she claims is far more fabrication than speculation, right?"

"Of course! But you don't give your mother enough credit, Anastasia. She's extremely perceptive, more than you realize."

Were we talking about the same woman? What did Lenore know about Mama that I didn't? "I'll admit, she did mention she has great gigolo radar, but Mama has always been prone to hyperbole."

Lenore shook her head. "I've come to learn quite a bit about your mother in a very short amount of time. Trust me, she knows when someone is trying to con her."

I snorted. "Really? I have two words for you: Lawrence Tuttnauer. None of us saw that coming, not even Mama. She fell for every line he fed her."

Lenore shifted her gaze back out to sea briefly. Was she weighing her words? Deciding how much of her conversations with Mama to divulge to me? Finally, she focused back on me and said, "Lawrence isn't a gigolo, and he wasn't conning her in any way. He truly loves your mother."

My mouth flapped open. "How on earth would you know that?"

"Even the most despicable monsters are capable of love. Think about it. If Lawrence didn't love Flora, wouldn't he go after you out of revenge?"

So Lenore knew about my role in Lawrence's arrest and conviction, as well. Was there anything Mama hadn't told this woman she'd met less than twenty-four hours ago? "I'll admit, I've thought he tried to go after me on more than one occasion. I don't doubt he's still pulling strings from behind bars. The man has connections that don't disappear just because he now resides on a cellblock."

She lifted one of her eyebrows. "But?"

"I was wrong about the other times."

"Because even though he blames you for his arrest, he knows harming you or your sons would kill your mother. He won't do anything to hurt Flora. Even though he knows he'll spend the remainder of his life behind bars and their marriage is over, he's still begged your mother to forgive him, as well as having sworn to her he'll never seek any retaliation against you."

My jaw nearly plummeted to the café floor. "How would you know that? She swore she hasn't accepted any of his calls. Are you telling me my mother's been lying to me?"

Lenore shook her head. "No, she hasn't spoken to him, but she does read his letters."

Red warning flags began wildly whipping around inside my brain. My voice climbed several octaves and an equal number of decibels, and I nearly jumped out of my seat. "He writes to her?"

Lenore's eyebrows shot up. "You didn't know?"

"I certainly did not!" With mounting trepidation I asked, "Does she write back?"

Lenore didn't answer my question, which only increased my anxiety. I hoped it was because she didn't know the answer, but with everything else Mama had told her, it seemed odd she wouldn't know whether or not Mama was answering Lawrence's letters.

Instead, she said, "Flora is much smarter than you realize, Anastasia, in many ways. As for Basil, trust me. She sees him for what he is."

Obviously, she'd said all she intended to say on the subject of Mama and Lawrence. So I decided to do a bit of prying of my own. "What about you and Harvey? If I'm not being too presumptuous, that is."

Lenore waved a hand in dismissal. "I gave him the heave-ho shortly after you saw us together."

"Oh? You two seemed quite close in the Jacuzzi."

She glanced down at the table for a moment before raising her chin to meet my gaze. "My mistake. Second and last."

"Oh?"

"I tried a palate cleanser of my own last night to move on from my grief. I believe it's what Millennials call a hook-up?"

So Mama was right after all. "If you mean what I think you mean, then yes."

Lenore continued. "In retrospect, I'd had way too much to

drink and wasn't thinking clearly."

"Not a good experience?"

She shuddered. "Awful! The guy was a real Dr. Jekyll/Mr. Hyde, a perfect gentleman until he morphed into a creep. I quickly let him know what I thought of him."

Creep covered a broad field, but further details would definitely fall into TMI territory. I certainly didn't want Lenore going there. "So your *headache* was a ruse to rush off with the man you met in the casino?"

"Let's just say the entire evening wound up rather headache inducing."

She paused, as if waiting for me to say something, but I wasn't sure how to respond. When I cocked my head to indicate she should continue, she heaved a huge sigh and said, "I can't be someone I'm not. And I'm woefully out of practice when it comes to dating, as evidenced by my near-transgression last night."

Too bad Mama didn't share Lenore's need for emotional commitment before plunging between the sheets. Her *joie de vivre*, as Lenore put it, could use a heaping dose of circumspection.

I moved the conversation away from sex with strangers by asking, "How long were you married?"

Her eyes grew misty as they took on a faraway look. "Thirty-five wonderful years."

I wondered if Lenore was opening up to me the way Mama had opened up to her. Sometimes people just need to let it all hang out, and a stranger's ear is often a safer bet than anyone close to you. Isn't that why people pay huge sums of money to spill their guts to psychologists and psychiatrists?

I didn't want to appear nosey, but I couldn't resist asking, "So Harvey struck out as Bachelor Number Two this morning?"

She glanced up toward the ceiling, shook her head, rolled her eyes, and chuckled. "Harvey Kreider! Ugh! I had to take a shower after ditching him at the hot tub shortly after you left. When I agreed to join him in the Jacuzzi, he took that as an invitation to foreplay."

"Why didn't you stop him?"

"Same reason I didn't stop Orson Gilbert last night. I don't believe in making a scene in public. Harvey had just started getting overly friendly right before you arrived. As soon as you walked away, I politely excused myself."

"Maybe Mama is a bad influence on you."

"Perhaps, but she's also fun to be around." She winked at me. "However, even if Harvey had turned out to be perfect in every other way, things could never have worked out between us."

"Why is that?"

"When he tried to kiss me, he slobbered."

"Oh, no! Few things worse in a relationship than a bad kisser," I said.

"Indeed!"

Then suddenly she grew melancholy as she stared into her coffee cup. "Actually, I was doing a bit more than enjoying the scenery before you arrived. I was doing some thinking. I'm not your mother. Palate cleansers won't work for me. The truth is, I'm not ready for another man in my life, especially anyone who pales in comparison to my dear husband." She offered me a slight smile. "I may never be."

"I'm sorry things didn't work out for you with either man, but that doesn't mean you won't find someone eventually."

She patted my hand, and the sorrow evaporated from her eyes. Lenore seemed capable of flipping her emotions on and off with the practiced ease of someone used to spending time on the stage or in front of a movie camera.

"Don't be," she said. "I'm not. My standards are quite high. I doubt any man will ever come close to living up to my husband. What point is there to sullying wonderful memories with pale imitations?"

"Sounds like your husband was quite a guy."

"Much more than that. He was my soul mate." She studied me for a moment, then segued into another topic of conversation. "From what I understand, you've found your soul mate as well."

A surge of heat rose up my neck and onto my cheeks. "Is there anything my mother hasn't told you?"

She grew thoughtful for a moment before offering me a wide grin with a shake of her head. "Doubtful."

"Karl?"

Lenore nodded.

"Lucille?"

"Indeed! She and your mother could star in a remake of *The Odd Couple*."

"Commie vs. D.A.R. Edition?"

Lenore chuckled. "A surefire hit."

"What about Ira?"

She nodded again. "As well as his rather difficult children."

I crossed my arms over my chest. "My mother has a big mouth."

"Your mother has a big heart. She's been worried about you."

"Still, that's quite a bit of personal family history to share with a total stranger."

"I often have that effect on people."

Certainly not as a former prima ballerina or thespian, but

perhaps those were careers of her youth. "You're a therapist?"

"I like to think of myself as more of a people problem solver."

"In that case, want to solve a problem for me? Off the clock, of course. With everything else Mama has told you, I assume you know about the financial quagmire Karl left me."

She tilted her head. "Go on."

"I'm worried about Zack."

"Because of his father showing up on the cruise?"

"I think he has an agenda."

"I'm sure he must. Otherwise, why would he be on this ship?"

"Exactly."

Lenore's voice grew tight. Her eyes narrowed. "I'm afraid too often our judicial system lacks justice for many of society's victims. In my experience, justice isn't blind; it's looking for a payoff. Corruption runs deep."

Now she sounded like a defense attorney. "It certainly seems that way lately."

"However," she continued, both her face and voice taking on a softer tone, "from what Flora tells me, your Zachary Barnes is quite capable of handling anything that comes his way, including his father." She reached over and patted my hand again. "Don't worry. I'm sure everything will work out for the best."

"How can you be sure?"

She winked. "Call it women's intuition."

I certainly hoped her women's intuition worked better than mine. If I'd had better intuition, I might have suspected Dead Louse of a Spouse was pulling a fast one on me and stopped him before he gambled away everything we owned and then some.

Out of the corner of my eye I noticed a woman storm into the café and approach two teenage girls seated several tables away from us. "What are you doing here?" she demanded. "Your father and I have been waiting for you. We're late for Family Karaoke."

Late! I'd promised Lily I'd return with the jump drive in fifteen minutes. I pulled out my phone and scowled at the screen. That was twenty minutes ago, and I hadn't even made it back to my suite yet.

"Am I keeping you from something?" asked Lenore.

I rose to leave. "I'm sorry. I was supposed to be somewhere five minutes ago. Thanks for the chat, Lenore. You've certainly enlightened me. I'll let you get back to enjoying the view."

She eyed me suspiciously. "I hope you don't plan to interrogate your mother. I wouldn't want her to think I was telling tales out of school."

"Don't worry. It will be our secret." I grabbed the tote of craft supplies I'd placed on the floor beside my chair when I arrived at her table.

She eyed the bag as I hitched it onto my shoulder. "A successful shopping trip?"

"Hardly." I quickly explained about the craft classes I'd agreed to teach.

"Sounds like fun. Maybe I'll take a break from Bingo and the casino to join you for one or two of them."

"See if you can convince Mama to tag along. She won't admit it, but I don't think Lady Luck has been very kind to her so far on this trip."

"I'll do my best. And, Anastasia?"

"Yes?"

She stood and reached for my hand, giving it a squeeze. "Try not to worry so much."

Easier said than done.

THIRTEEN

When I headed to my initial meeting with Lily, Zack had indicated he had some business to attend to and would meet me back in the suite later. I expected to find him glued to his laptop upon my return. Instead, I entered an empty suite and found no note indicating where he'd gone. Not that it mattered. I had work of my own to do. I knew Zack's meeting with Lily was scheduled after mine, although I didn't remember exactly when.

I spent the next ten minutes downloading a few files. Once I'd finished, I hurried back to Lily's office as fast as my exercise-averse legs would carry me—*fast* being somewhat of a stretch. I found her alone in her office. As I struggled to catch my breath, I handed her the jump drive. "Sorry," I said in-between panting gulps of air. "I was held up by a latte and a quick chat that turned out to be anything but."

Lily glanced at her watch. "Heavens! I was beginning to worry you'd changed your mind. How's this?" She held up a poster she'd printed up that touted me as the Queen of Crafts. I was certainly no Martha Stewart, but who was I to argue with her? The poster went on to state that passengers should check their daily issues of *GemEvents* for specific projects offered as well as times and locations of my classes.

"The Diamond Lounge gets the most traffic," she continued. "We'll set you up there to make the sample crafts. I've had one of the staff reserve a table in a prime location near the entrance."

She rose from her desk and headed toward the door. "I'll take you there now." Still winded, I struggled to catch up with her.

Once inside the Diamond Lounge, she deposited me at a high-bar table that normally sat six. "This should give you plenty of room to work," she said, "and passengers will spot you as they enter the lounge."

After she arranged the poster on an easel beside the table, she said, "When you've finished the models, drop them off at my office. I'll have them, along with the sign, placed in the glass display case at the entrance to the lounge." She then scurried off to meet with another volunteer.

Over the next two hours I worked up four sample projects ranging in skill levels from Can't-Even-Sew-on-a-Button to Been-Crafting-Since-I-was-in-Diapers. To my surprise, dozens of passengers—men included—stopped by to watch, ask questions, and grow enthusiastic over the upcoming classes. Some even stated they'd show up for all four classes. I certainly didn't expect to draw the crowds of someone like gossipmonger celebrity biographer Victor Hogan, but I no longer worried about Lily canning me for lack of passenger interest.

In the back of my mind I was already going over my various outstanding debts and debating where best to apply the funds I'd receive for teaching the classes. As much as I hated to admit it, I suppose I had Ira to thank—as well as the measles-quarantined Gemstone Empress crewmember—for this serendipitous windfall of cash.

I knew that once we were married, no matter how much I'd protest, Zack would insist on assuming my outstanding debts. He'd argue that he could certainly afford to do so, and that was true. He hadn't rented the apartment above my garage due to a lack of finances. He'd done so for the privacy, which in hindsight is quite ironic.

But Zack wasn't responsible for Karl's irresponsibility. I was— for being blind to it for so long. I'd made halfway decent headway the last year, thanks to moonlighting, my latent sleuthing skills, and a half-brother-in-law who made me a deal I couldn't refuse when my junker of a Hyundai died. I also no longer had to worry about Alex's impending college tuition, thanks to Shane's undying gratitude regarding those aforementioned Jessica Fletcheresque skills.

However, I was under no delusions that I was anywhere near zeroing out that enormous debit column anytime soon. Still, I wanted to pare it down as much as possible before I said "I do" to Zack. I knew he knew I wasn't marrying him for his money but still...I had my pride.

I was finishing the last sample project, a hanging felt heart pocket embellished with simple embroidery stitches and buttons, when I noticed Victor Hogan, still dressed in swimming trunks, ball cap, and ratty T-shirt, approaching the entrance to the lounge. The brighter light of the lounge made it possible to read the crude, sexist statement printed on his T-shirt.

Victor stopped a few feet away, arms on hips and feet spread apart like a barbarian surveying his kingdom. After studying the sign on the easel, he sauntered over to the table.

"So you're the Queen of Crafts?" As if his tone alone didn't convey enough condescension, he picked up one of my finished projects, examined it as if it were moldy cheese, then tossed it back on the table. With a sneer he asked, "Who's going to waste time on this trash?"

I looked him right in the eye, offered him a sweet smile, and in a voice that would melt an iceberg said, "Probably all the people who don't want to listen to a blowhard who writes trash."

Dumbfounded, Victor Hogan stared at me for a split second before erupting in a series of loud hoots and guffaws that had people throughout the lounge turning in our direction. When he finally stopped laughing, he said, "I'll say this for you, doll, you've got spunk. I like a woman who gives as good as she gets." He then reached behind me and patted my derriere.

Stunned, my mouth dropped open. Before my brain had time to process what had happened, Victor Hogan executed an about-face and lumbered off, waving his cap over his head as he called out one final insult. "Just don't be surprised when no one shows up for your crappy classes."

"Someone needs to put that man in his place, no?"

I spun around to find one of the lounge waitresses glaring at Victor's departing back. Her nametag identified her as Bianca from Portugal.

"He certainly is full of himself," I muttered, angry with myself for freezing rather than immediately calling him out on his inappropriate behavior.

"The cruise line should ban him," she continued.

"Unfortunately, there's no law against inflated egos."

"But there are laws against sexual harassment and assault, are there not? I saw the way he touched you."

She spoke as if she had firsthand experience with Victor Hogan. "Has he touched you inappropriately?"

She snorted. "Me and just about every other female crewmember on this ship—from the cruise director on down. That man does not keep his hands to himself."

That explained the tension I sensed between Lily and Victor at lunch.

"I have never seen him assault a passenger before, though," she said. "Not that he has to. He is rich and famous. You would not believe how many women passengers throw themselves at him."

"Have any of you reported him to the captain?"

"Many of us have."

"And?"

She snorted again. "He did nothing. Several of us even filed a complaint directly with the cruise line management. They never even acknowledged our letter."

"Have you considered going to the press?"

She screwed up her face. "Like they would care? We are not celebrities." Then she shrugged. "A famous writer gets fresh with a cocktail waitress? Comes with the job as far as they are concerned."

I was beginning to sense a general pattern of cover-ups on this ship. "But—"

She cut me off. "We have two choices. We either put up with men like Victor Hogan, or we leave. The most the cruise line will do is let us out of our contracts. Most of us can't afford to do that. We are expendable. Mr. Hogan is not. He is a Super Gem."

"A Super Gem?"

"A passenger with the most elite status. He practically lives on this ship. I could buy a house on the outskirts of Lisbon with just what he spends in the bar each year."

"Doesn't he get unlimited bar privileges due to his elite status?" Our premier suite came with that particular perk.

"There is a limit. Mr. Hogan exceeds his after a day or two. All additional drinks go on his cruise card tab."

That explained why Lily put up with Victor. She had no choice. "Is his behavior a problem unique to this particular cruise line?"

"Hardly. It is pervasive throughout the industry. If you do a Google search, you will find dozens of stories posted online from former crewmembers."

Someone called out from a table to our right, "Can we get some refills here?"

Bianca turned to acknowledge a table of two couples, all having raised their empty glasses. She waved to them. "On my way." She then rushed off to the bar without another word to me.

I finished packing up everything, then headed to Lily's office to drop off the models. On my return to the suite, I ruminated over my encounter with Victor Hogan, debating whether or not to tell Zack what had happened.

We still hadn't found Emerson or uncovered his motive for showing up on the ship. Zack had enough on his plate without adding an additional heaping dose of stress to the mix.

I'd experienced my share of men and their wandering hands over the years. Males of a certain age had never shed their caveman mentality. As inappropriate as a pat on the tush was, it ranked fairly low on the assault scale. Victor Hogan's hand hadn't lingered; his fingers hadn't caressed or pinched. I'm sure he did it for shock value and as his way of showing me who was in control.

The man was in for a rude awakening. I could handle the Neanderthal. If he hadn't dashed off so quickly, I wouldn't have hesitated to tell him off, but I didn't see the point in making a scene by shouting after him in public. I suppose that consigned me to the same category as Lenore.

However, should I cross paths with Victor Hogan again, I'd definitely put him in his place. If words didn't work and he laid a hand on me again, a swift knee to the groin would do the trick. I didn't need a white knight stepping in to defend my honor.

~*~

Five minutes later I rounded the hallway toward our suite to find Zack being escorted down the corridor by two officers on either side of him. As they marched toward me, I recognized the man on the left as Xavier, the ship's First Officer. I stopped short, blocking their path. "Where are you going?" I asked Zack.

"Step aside, please, miss," ordered the other crewmember before Zack had a chance to answer. His tone left no question that he was issuing an order rather than making a request.

"I don't think so." Ignoring him, I turned to Xavier. I knew little about military rank, but as the ship's First Officer, serving directly under the captain, it stood to reason that he outranked the other crewmember. "Where are you taking my fiancé?"

Zack answered for him. "The captain wants to see me."

"And he sent a contingent?" I glared at Xavier. "Are the ship's phones no longer working?"

"I'm sorry, ma'am, but this is serious," he said.

"More serious than a killer roaming the ship? Your captain seemed perfectly content to disregard the very thought."

Two red spots sprouted on his cheeks, indicating Xavier wasn't exactly thrilled with his current assignment and possibly agreed with my assessment of his captain. "Please don't interfere with ship's business." His voice and eyes both pleading with me. "I really need you to allow us to pass, Mrs. Pollack."

Then it suddenly hit me. Emerson had carried out his plan.

My knees grew weak. I began to sway. As three pairs of arms reached out to steady me, I lost hold of the tote. Supplies spilled around our feet.

Zack immediately read my mind. "They're okay," he said, grasping both my upper arms to steady me. The two crewmembers had grabbed my lower arms, one on each side of me.

"Everyone?" Panic had constricted my throat. I had trouble forcing out the words. "The boys? Mama? Shane? Sophie?"

"All accounted for."

"Then who?"

"I'm about to find out."

"I'm going with you," I said, recovering both my voice and my equilibrium. I stared down at the fabric and notions strewn across the floor of the corridor. Xavier knelt to scoop everything back into the tote bag.

"Our orders are to bring only Mr. Barnes," said the second crewmember, dropping his hand from my arm.

I checked his nametag. "You and what army, Gustav?"

He exchanged a questioning glance with Xavier who shrugged as he handed the tote back to me. I took that to mean I was welcome to accompany them.

"I'm not taking the blame for defying captain's orders," Gustav told Xavier.

"No need," said Xavier.

This time Gustav shrugged. "It's your funeral, sir."

I hitched the tote onto my shoulder as the four of us walked to the elevators. However, once at the elevator bank, instead of hitting the button to go up to the bridge, Gustav pressed the down button. "The captain isn't on the bridge?" I asked.

"No, ma'am," said Xavier.

Once inside, he pressed the button for Deck Seven. I exchanged a glance with Zack. Were we headed to Emerson's empty cabin? Earlier we'd found no evidence that he'd ever set foot inside Cabin 7548.

However, Xavier and Gustav marched us to the opposite side of the ship, stopping in front of an exterior cabin mid-section. An officer stood guard in front of the door. Xavier rapped once. When the door swung open, we were quickly ushered inside.

The captain zeroed in on me from his towering height. His mouth tightened into a thin line as he shifted his gaze to glare at his officers, but he said nothing. He didn't have to. I got the message loud and clear. I suspected so did Xavier and Gustav as evidenced by how their eyes now seemed inordinately preoccupied with their feet.

The captain and the ship's doctor stood alongside the unmade bed, partially blocking our view of what appeared to be the prone body of an elderly naked man, his exposed legs covered in wrinkled, leathery skin dotted with patches of brown age spots.

The captain stepped back and motioned for the doctor to join him, allowing us a view of the torso and head. The man's face was turned toward us, his eyes staring out blankly. He had shaggy gray hair, a goatee, and a thin wire wound tightly around his neck.

Was this Emerson's accomplice?

FOURTEEN

"Who is it?" I asked.

"The cabin is booked to a Mr. Colton Brown," said the captain.

"That man is not Colton Brown," said Zack.

"No, it's not," said the captain," nodding in agreement.

My head whipped from Zack to the captain, then back to Zack. "How do you know that?"

Instead of answering me, Zack addressed the doctor and captain. "May I approach the body?"

They both shifted position, allowing Zack to move closer to the bed. He studied the victim's face for a moment before glancing toward the captain and doctor. "With your permission?" he asked.

Permission to do what?

The captain waved his hand, giving Zack the go-ahead to proceed with whatever he had in mind.

To my astonishment, Zack reached down and peeled the goatee from the dead man's face. Then he flipped back a wig covering the head.

I gasped at the sight of Emerson Dawes. "How did you know?" I asked Zack.

He tipped his head in the direction of the wall opposite the foot of the bed. I hadn't given the room so much as a cursory glance when we walked in, my attention having immediately been pulled to the body on the bed. I now noticed the built-in dresser and desk. Three wig stands lined the dresser top. Two held men's wigs of differing lengths and styles, one grayer than the other.

Since no one made any effort to stop me, I crossed the room to take a better look at the other contents strewn across the surface of the dresser and desk.

"Don't touch anything," warned the captain.

"I won't." Although it bothered me that he had given Zack permission to touch the body of a murder victim but felt it necessary to warn me not to touch any items on the dresser. After all, this wasn't my first crime scene. It wasn't even my first crime scene aboard this ship.

A tray holding an assortment of facial hair in a variety of styles—mustaches, beards, sideburns, and eyebrows, in three different shades of gray—lay alongside the wig stands. An open case revealed a large selection of theatrical makeup and a bottle of spirit gum. Back in my high school days, I'd worked behind the scenes in enough plays and musicals to know spirit gum was used to attach false facial hair.

No wonder we hadn't found Emerson since he approached us outside the theater last evening. The man had enough disguises to alter his appearance in dozens of different ways. It wasn't inconceivable to think he may have shadowed us continually from the moment we boarded the ship, even eavesdropping clandestinely on some of our conversations.

A lump the size of Gibraltar landed in my stomach. Was Basil Chatsworth really Emerson Dawes? Basil had wavy black hair and a matching walrus mustache. The disguises on the dresser were shades of gray, but that didn't mean there weren't additional pieces in the case or a drawer.

Mama had already unwittingly married one killer. How would she deal with learning that Emerson had posed as Basil? I turned to the doctor. "Do you know when he was killed?"

As the doctor began to answer, the captain interrupted him. "Why do you ask?"

"My mother has been keeping company with a man who sports a hairpiece and speaks with what I believe is a phony English accent. I met him briefly this morning. He introduced himself as Basil Chatsworth."

The captain tipped his head for the doctor to continue. "Desmond Rutledge—or Emerson Dawes—was killed sometime between last night and this morning."

"Do you think Basil was Emerson?" asked Zack.

"No, according to Lenore, Mama was with Basil this afternoon."

Zack turned to the doctor. "You can't be more specific about time of death?"

The doctor shook his head. "I'm a general practitioner, not a medical examiner. My calculation is merely a preliminary assessment based entirely on my observations of lividity and rigor mortis. I have no means of narrowing the time of death beyond that."

"Under the circumstances," said the captain, "I'm going to need you to account for your whereabouts last night and this morning, Mr. Barnes."

"Are you serious?" I asked, my voice pitching several octaves higher as I confronted the captain. "You should be tracking down Colton Brown, not interrogating the one person who tried to warn you about a convicted killer roaming your ship. But no, you dismissed his concerns, and now you have another murder on your hands."

"If you're referring to Mr. Gilbert, we have every reason to believe he took his own life," said the captain.

I had every reason to believe otherwise, but anticipating I was about to refute the captain's claim, Zack placed his arm around me and said, "Captain Halvorson is only doing his job, sweetheart."

"Well, from what I can see, he's not doing it very well."

This drew another glare from the captain, but I didn't care.

Zack squeezed my shoulders as he again spoke to the captain. "I have nothing to hide. You already know my whereabouts for much of last evening and earlier this morning, Captain Halvorson, and I'm confident your security cameras and my keycard data will attest to everything else."

When the captain nodded, Zack continued. "Have you located Colton Brown, assuming he's still on the ship?"

"Not yet. I have crewmembers viewing surveillance video. Why would you suggest he's no longer on the ship? Where would he be?"

"I have a theory if you're interested," I said.

"You?" said the captain. He practically laughed in my face. I half expected him to pat me on the head as if humoring a child. "What would you know about solving a murder, Mrs. Pollack?"

"As it turns out," said Zack, stepping up to defend me, "she knows plenty. My fiancée is responsible for helping solve several recent crimes in the New York metropolitan area."

I offered Captain Halvorson a knowing smile as I watched the telltale signs of a man struggling to swallow his pride and ask a woman for help. Finally, he gave in, albeit, reluctantly. Crossing his arms over his chest, and in a voice that suggested he had already made up his mind before I uttered a single word, he said, "So tell me about this theory of yours, Mrs. Pollack."

"I wouldn't be surprised to learn you can't locate Colton Brown on the ship."

"Why is that?"

"I suspect Emerson Dawes killed him."

"And his motive for killing a total stranger?" asked the doctor.

"If I'm correct, Colton Brown wasn't a stranger."

"Then what was he?" asked the captain.

"An accomplice."

The captain's eyebrows knit together in an expression of skepticism. "That's quite a leap."

"Not really. I believe Dawes hired Brown for the purpose of securing a second cabin in a different name. Colton Brown may even be an alias. Odds are, he's a former convict who served time with Dawes."

"Interesting theory," said the captain, not sounding all that convinced.

"Why kill his accomplice?" asked the doctor.

"To eliminate a witness," I said. "Once onboard, Dawes didn't need Brown. He became a liability. So Dawes killed him, dumped his body overboard after dark, and began using his room."

"Which would explain why there's no record of Dawes using his keycard after he boarded the ship yesterday," said Zack.

"If you check his room, you'll find it hasn't been occupied," I added.

The muscles around the captain's jaw tightened, and his eyes narrowed. "How would you know that?"

"We checked with his cabin steward this morning," said Zack, jumping in to answer. I shot him a side-eye. Did he really think I might slip and implicate Afu in our morning sleuthing, costing him his job?

The captain appeared to mull over my theory for a while before finally saying, "Then who killed Mr. Dawes if not Mr. Barnes?"

I exhaled a rush of exasperation as I quirked an eyebrow. "Really? We're back to that?"

"Emerson Dawes might have more than one accomplice onboard," said Zack, remaining exceedingly calm, given the captain's insinuation. "We still have no idea who pulled the strings that got him out of prison and onto this particular cruise."

"Or why," I added.

The captain nodded to Zack, then turned and spoke directly to me. "You make a compelling case, Mrs. Pollack. Whether it has any merit, is yet to be seen, but I will take your theory under advisement as I continue to investigate."

I found his tone exceedingly patronizing and had little hope that he meant what he said, especially when I spotted the smirk plastered on Gustav's face.

However, the captain had seemed satisfied that an investigation into Zack's whereabouts would prove his alibis for last night and this morning. After all, Zack had spent a good deal of that time on the bridge in full view of the captain and other officers.

Emerson's death didn't remove the threat for us, though. His plan may not have died with him. There was still a killer onboard the ship. Why had he killed Emerson, and were any of us still in danger? Not wanting to risk being overheard as we left the cabin and walked through the ship, I held off voicing my concerns until Zack and I had returned to our suite.

Zack, on the other hand, had no qualms about bringing up another subject as we waited for the elevator. "You really let loose on the captain and his crew," he said.

"They had it coming."

"Maybe, but I'm quite capable of fighting my own battles."

Earlier Lenore had suggested much the same thing. "I know."

"So why the tirade?"

I huffed out my frustration. "Chalk it up to stress and too much chauvinism."

"Present company excluded, I hope."

"Of course," I offered him an adoring smile. "You're the embodiment of what every man should strive to become. That's one of the reasons I love you. However, I've encountered too many men on this ship who act like we're still living in the nineteen-fifties and not the twenty-first century. It's depressing."

Zack laughed. "You are woman. Hear you roar!"

"It's not funny." When he raised an eyebrow, I couldn't help myself and laughed. "Okay, maybe I did overreact a little."

"Who besides the captain is responsible for your one-woman war on clueless men?"

I screwed up my face. "Victor Hogan."

"Over his drunken performance at lunch?"

"No." I told Zack about my encounter with the blowhard in the Diamond Lounge, although I deliberately omitted the part where he patted me on the tush. I hardly expected Zack to get physical with Hogan, but even a verbal confrontation between the two might raise suspicion that Zack was in some way connected to his father's death. I didn't want that getting back to the captain.

We arrived at the suite to find it empty. The boys, true to their word, had kept me apprised via text messages of their whereabouts throughout the day. They and Sophie planned to have burgers and shakes this evening at a diner-themed restaurant on the Promenade Deck, taking in another movie afterwards.

I had no idea where Mama was—hopefully not in the casino gambling away her Social Security check or hooking up for some whoopee with a gigolo. Contrary to Lenore's professional assessment of Mama, I had a far more intimate knowledge of my mother than her new cruise buddy. Ever since my father had died, I'd witnessed Mama's continual lack of financial responsibility as well as her often hasty, short-lived serial marriages.

Zack pulled out his phone and proceeded with another bug sweep. Even with Emerson dead, I knew he'd continue checking for listening devices throughout the remainder of the cruise, if for no other reason than it's better to be safe than sorry. Just because he hadn't found any eavesdropping devices yet didn't mean one wouldn't appear at some point, courtesy of either Emerson's killer or a remote hacker who might somehow access one of the computer-driven devices in the suite.

I dropped my tote on the coffee table and myself onto the sectional. Exhaustion had seeped into every molecule of my body. I couldn't wait for the day to end. "What now?" I asked.

"I think we'd better gather everyone back here to let them know Emerson was murdered."

As he began to send a text, I said, "Tell my mother I don't care how big a streak she's on or with whom she's canoodling. She needs to drop everything and return immediately."

Zack pulled his attention from his phone. His lips twitched. "*Canoodling?*"

"My brain doesn't want to imagine more explicit details, especially if she's with that sleazy British imposter Basil or Victor Hogan." I wasn't sure which man bothered me more.

"Understood. Any further instructions before I hit *send*?"

I thought for a moment. "I suppose if she's with Lenore, she should bring her along."

"Probably not a bad idea since the two of them seem joined at the hip."

"You don't know the half of it." While we waited for everyone to arrive, I related my earlier conversation with Mama's new BFF.

~*~

Fifteen minutes later our entire party, plus Lenore, had gathered in the suite's spacious living room. Zack stood as everyone else spread out on either the sectional or the two upholstered chairs on the opposite side of the coffee table.

Once he had their attention, he got right to the point. His voice devoid of emotion, he said, "Emerson Dawes is dead."

Shane glanced over to where the teens sat on the opposite end of the sectional. Sophie, sandwiched between Nick and Alex, gripped one of Alex's hands with both of hers and inhaled sharply.

Still eyeing his daughter, Shane said, "Natural causes, I hope?"

Zack's jaw tightened. He offered a nearly imperceptible shake of his head as he muttered, "Afraid not."

Sophie's eyes grew wide. "You mean he was murdered?"

"By whom?" asked Lenore.

"We don't know," I said. "However, even though Emerson no longer poses a threat to us, there's still a killer onboard this ship. We don't know why he killed Emerson. Everyone needs to stay vigilant." I spoke directly to the teens. "You're to continue sticking together and letting us know where you are."

"And don't talk to any strangers," added Shane.

"I hate this ship," said Sophie, her lower lip trembling slightly. "I wish we'd never come."

She wasn't the only one. I turned to my mother. "That goes for you, too, Mama. I want to know where you are and with whom at all times."

She opened her mouth to protest but apparently had second thoughts and instead only offered a deep sigh of resignation.

"Can we still have dinner tonight without you guys?" asked Nick. "And go to the movie afterwards?"

As much as I now wanted eyes on my kids at all times, I knew I had to allow them some space. If I cinched the apron strings too tightly, they'd resent me and rebel. I glanced over at Shane.

"We can't sit on them," he said.

"We can try."

"Mom!" said Nick.

"We'll be careful," said Alex.

I studied both boys and Sophie. Their eyes begged me. They were good kids, but still kids with not yet fully developed higher reasoning and decision-making skills. I trusted them—to a point—but we were dealing with too many unknowns right now.

Finally, I ceased my inner debate and gave in, sending up a silent prayer to whichever deity watches over unaccompanied teenagers roaming around a cruise ship with a killer on the loose. "All right. As long as you continue to text us your whereabouts." Then I added an ultimatum, "Break the rules, and you're grounded for the remainder of the cruise."

When all three agreed, I said, "If it's okay with Shane, you can leave now." I didn't want them hearing the lurid details of Emerson's murder.

Sophie turned to her father. "Dad?"

"Text when you arrive at the restaurant," he said.

Before dashing out, Sophie hugged her father, and the boys each planted a kiss on my cheek.

"You're the best, Mom," said Alex.

"Ditto," said Nick.

I sighed. "Don't make me regret my decision."

As soon as the door closed behind them, Shane asked Zack, "I assume you have details?"

Zack headed to the bar. "We do," he said. "What are you drinking?"

"Bourbon," said Shane. "Straight up."

Mama, and I opted for glasses of Chablis. Lenore requested a club soda with a twist of lime. Once Zack poured and distributed the drinks, he joined us on the sectional.

"How was Emerson killed?" asked Shane.

"Garroted with a wire."

"Like in *The Godfather*?" asked Lenore. She shuddered. "How awful!"

"What's awful is that the captain actually suspected Zack," I said.

"No! How could he?" asked Mama.

"I think it was more wishful thinking in the hope of wrapping up this latest incident as quickly as possible," said Zack.

"What made him change his mind?" asked Lenore.

"I reminded him that much of last night and this morning I was either with him or on the bridge in sight of other crewmembers."

"So, he didn't suggest you sneaked out of the suite in the middle of the night to kill Emerson?" asked Shane.

"I didn't give him the chance," said Zack. "I quickly offered that both the ship's surveillance cameras and my keycard data would verify my whereabouts at all times."

Shane took a sip of his bourbon. "I suppose he had to ask."

"He wouldn't have been doing his job otherwise," said Zack.

"Too little, too late," I said. "Now that Emerson is dead, we'll never know who bribed the parole board members or why Emerson was on this ship."

"We may not have ever found that out anyway," said Zack.

"I'd like to think otherwise," I said. "And I'm still not convinced Lawrence isn't somehow behind all this."

Mama frowned at the mention of her ex-husband's name, then said, "But with Emerson dead, there's no longer a threat to any of us. I don't understand your need to keep such tight tabs on us, dear."

"We don't know if there's no longer a threat," said Zack, "because we don't know who killed Emerson or why. His murder may or may not have something to do with me."

Mama stood. "Well, we have to keep living, and Lenore and I have dinner plans. We need to get going."

"What sort of dinner plans?" I asked. "Maybe we'll join you."

"None you'd be interested in," she said.

Lenore was a bit more forthcoming. "The Emerald Lounge is hosting a supper club for seniors this evening." She glanced at her watch. "Flora is right. We should get going if we want to grab a good table."

"You're not changing?" I asked. Lenore still wore her linen slacks and silk T-shirt from earlier, while Mama was dressed in a pair of orchid print Capri pants with a pink Lily Pulitzer sweater set.

"It's a casual affair," said Mama. She hooked arms with Lenore, offered a royal wave with her other hand, and said, "Don't wait up, dear."

"Before you go, Mama—"

She stopped short at the door and spun around. "What is it now, Anastasia?"

"I was wondering if you'd had a chance to bump into Victor Hogan yet."

"No, why?"

"Zack and I wound up seated at lunch with him today."

Her face lit up. "You did? So, he is on the ship."

"Don't get too excited, Mama. He's not your type."

"Really, Anastasia!"

"Really, Mama. The man is a pig with a reputation for sexually harassing women."

She waved a hand in dismissal. "I'm sure you must be mistaken. He's a famous author."

"The two are not mutually exclusive, Mama."

My mother huffed an admonition. "You should know not to believe everything you read in the tabloids, dear."

"I don't read the tabloids, Mama. You do."

"And I don't believe a word of what I read."

So why did she read them? "All I'm saying is if you do run into Victor Hogan, be forewarned he's not what you're expecting."

She turned to Lenore. "How would she know what I'm expecting?" Without saying another word to me, Mama opened the door and exited the suite.

After a moment of silence, during which Zack and I simply

stared at each other as we shook our heads, Shane said, "Speaking of dinner..."

Given our three-course lunch at Diamante, I hadn't expected to want more than a salad for dinner this evening. Surprisingly, though, the rumblings of hunger began to stir within me at the mere mention of dinner. "What are the chances we can get a reservation at one of the celebrity chef restaurants tonight?" I asked.

"Doubtful," said Shane, "unless one of them has had a cancellation. Why?"

I sighed. "I'd really like to have dinner this evening without suffering the silent slings and arrows of Birdie and the Marwoods."

"Sounds good to me," said Zack, whipping out his cell phone. "I'll check the ship's app." After scrolling for a minute, he said, "How about Italian? Gemme del Mare has an available table at seven-thirty."

"Fine with me," said Shane.

"Book it," I said, walking over to the refrigerator. Along with a well-stocked bar of potent and non-potent beverages, the suite had come with an assortment of fruits, cheeses, crackers, dips, and crudités. I piled a selection, along with utensils, plates, and napkins, onto a tray and brought everything over to the coffee table. "This should tide us over until dinner," I said.

~*~

Shortly before seven-thirty, having changed into appropriate dinner attire, Zack, Shane, and I made our way along the Atrium Deck toward Gemme del Mare. The restaurant was situated portside near the bow and beyond the arcade of shops that ran down the middle of much of the Atrium. As we walked toward our destination, I couldn't help eyeing every man we passed, silently asking each, "Did you kill Emerson Dawes?"

Unfortunately, none of them silently answered back. So much for my mind-reading skills.

I had hoped Zack would open up about his father's murder once we were alone. He hadn't, remaining tight-lipped when I gingerly attempted to broach the subject after Shane had gone back to his suite to change. Not that I was surprised, given Zack's reluctance to speak about Emerson from the moment I learned of his existence. I decided not to press, affording him some mental and emotional space. In due time I hoped he'd work through the demons that still haunted him.

As we neared the restaurant, I heard lively chatter and classic rock and roll spilling out from the Emerald Lounge. I stopped at the entrance and glanced inside. Every table was filled. Weighted heart-shaped gold mylar and red latex balloons floated above each table.

A huge buffet ran along the back of the lounge in front of the ocean-facing windows decorated with heart decals and a *Happy Valentine's Day* sign. In between the tables and buffet, a dance floor was packed with dozens of seniors gyrating up and down and round and round as they twisted to the sounds of Chubby Checker.

I scanned the passengers on the dance floor and spied Mama with Imposter to the United Kingdom Basil Chatsworth, more confirmation that he and Emerson weren't the same person. A few feet away, Lenore danced with someone who wasn't Harvey Kreider.

"They look like they're having fun," said Shane.

"Mama's in her element," I said. "As long as she's got a man paying attention to her, she's a happy camper."

We were about to move on when a loud commotion off to the side of the room caught our attention—as well as the attention of everyone else in the lounge. The room grew silent except for Chubby Checker, still singing about twisting the night away, and the woman causing the uproar. One of the cocktail waitresses whipped out her cell phone and began filming the altercation.

Heads turned in time to see the woman splash her drink in the face of her dinner companion—Victor Hogan. Although at least twenty years his junior, she was more middle-aged schoolteacher or administrative assistant than *bikini-clad babe*. Judging from her indignation, I suspect she hadn't known Hogan more than a nanosecond before agreeing to dine with him.

As Victor sputtered, she stood, deliberately tipping the wooden table toward him. Dishes, utensils, and glasses flew into his lap, the table coming to rest across his chest.

Before she stormed off, the woman grabbed the wine bucket, removed the bottle, and dumped the ice over his head. Wildly waving the bottle in Victor's apoplectic face, she screamed, "I'd smash this over your head, except the wine is too good to waste on a sleazy alley cat like you."

She then threw back her shoulders, raised her chin, and with bottle in hand, marched toward the exit. As she crossed the lounge, one person began clapping loudly. Another quickly joined in, then another and another until every waitress in the lounge clapped in solidarity.

One by one many of the female passengers began joining in. Those sitting rose to their feet. The applause swelled with even some men adding to the ovation.

Those who weren't applauding had whipped out their cell phones to capture as much of the incident as possible. I doubted it would take more than five minutes before social media had its latest viral video.

As the woman strode past me, I added my applause to her chorus of supporters.

FIFTEEN

Victor Hogan hurled the table off his chest with such force it flipped over backwards, crashing onto the floor and toppling his departed dinner partner's chair in the process. Then he knocked over his own chair in the opposite direction as he stood. The food, dishes, and utensils that had remained in his lap clattered and shattered onto the floor, joining those items already scattered across the terra cotta tiles.

The applause petered out as Hogan leveled a glare at the roomful of people staring at him, some with their mouths hanging open, Mama included. He smacked his hands against each other, wiping away the pasta that clung to his fingers. "Crazy menopausal dame," he said, his voice loud enough to carry over the music. He then added an expletive to show exactly what he thought of not only his former dinner date but all women of a certain age, which begged the question: If that's how he felt about older women, why was he dining with one?

After he kicked the detritus from his path, he plastered a

smarmy grin on his face and bowed to the dumbstruck lounge patrons before turning his back on them and wending his way toward the exit.

Chubby Checker ceased twisting. The DJ immediately chose to offer up an editorial comment by way of the next dance number, inviting the crowd to do The Jerk. Most of the people still on the dance floor continued to stand and stare rather than resume dancing. Mama wasn't one of them. Spying me, she began zigzagging her way around groups of people and tables to reach us.

A buzz of comments filled the room, competing with the music as Victor Hogan, mumbling under his breath, also stumbled toward us. Along the way he bumped into nearly every table he passed.

At one point he lost his balance, and moving to steady himself, his hand landed in the mashed potatoes on a shocked diner's plate. Hogan reached over to swipe the mess from his hand onto her blouse, lost his balance again, and nearly landed in her lap. She pushed him away with such force he bounced off another table before righting himself.

People watched transfixed. No one offered him any assistance. As soon as he regained his balance, he resumed his staggering departure.

That's when I realized Mama wasn't making her way toward me. She had her sights focused on Victor Hogan. They met up directly in front of us. Mama held out her arms to Hogan and said, "Let me help you."

Hogan abruptly stopped, stared at her for a moment, then cursed as he stiff-armed her out of his way. Luckily, Zack and Shane were there to catch her before she sprawled backwards onto the tile floor.

The crowd gasped. Someone screamed. I think it may have been me. Even though Zack and Shane had broken Mama's fall, she appeared dazed and confused. As she stared after Victor Hogan's departing back, she whimpered, "I only wanted to help."

Poor Mama. I'd tried to warn her about the man, but some lessons can only be learned through personal experience. At least only her pride had sustained injury. She could have broken a hip. Or worse.

Lenore, her date, and Basil rushed to Mama's side. "Flora, are you all right?" asked Lenore, placing her hand on Mama's arm.

"I think so." She graced Zack and Shane with a grateful smile. "Thanks to my knights in shining armor."

"Let's get you to a chair," I said.

Lenore and the men led us across the room to a table at the opposite end of the dance floor. Zack and Shane remained on either side of Mama, guiding her along. They didn't release her until they'd settled her into a chair.

One of the cocktail waitresses rushed over and offered Mama a glass of water. I realized it was Bianca, the waitress I'd met earlier in the day. She glanced between Mama and me, her eyes growing wide, then she said, "You know this woman?"

"She's my mother."

Bianca shook her head. "Odd coincidence, no? I told you someone needs to do something about that man. No one listens to us, but now after this and what happened to you earlier? Maybe if you speak to the captain?"

"I will," I said. Victor Hogan was out of control. Had Zack and Shane not broken Mama's fall, Hogan might have seriously harmed her or worse. Sexual harassment was bad enough. Physical attacks took his offenses to an entirely different level.

"What was that about, dear?" asked Mama, looking up at me.

I patted her shoulder. "Nothing, Mama."

She turned her attention back to the glass of water and sipped gingerly until she'd regained her composure. Finally, she placed the glass on the table, took a deep breath, and said, "I'm fine now, really. No need for any of you to continue fussing over me."

"Are you sure, Mama?" I knelt down so that I was at eye level with her. Even though she hadn't hit her head, I studied her pupils for signs of concussion but found no dilation. "You didn't twist an ankle or anything? Your chest doesn't hurt where he shoved you?"

She patted my cheek. "A bit shaken but nothing more, dear."

"Maybe we should have the ship's doctor check you out anyway."

"Nonsense. It will take more than a shove to knock me out of commission." Then she offered me a sheepish grin. "I suppose you were right about Victor Hogan. The man has definitely lost one of his biggest fans."

"After that drunken demonstration," said Lenore, "I think he's lost more than one fan tonight. According to this evening's copy of *GemEvents*, he's giving a talk tomorrow. We should stage a boycott."

"That sounds like a wonderful idea," I said. I glanced up at Bianca.

She tipped her head in agreement. "I'll make sure any staff not on duty joins you."

Mama sighed. She glanced around at the chaos Victor Hogan had left in his wake. Several crewmembers had begun cleaning up the mess while most passengers either returned to their dinners or dancing. Several exited the lounge.

"Who would have thought that a man who writes such fun

books would be such a mean, nasty creep?" asked Mama.

Fun books? From what I knew of Victor Hogan's unauthorized biographies, they were anything but fun for the victims of his poison pen. I stood and over Mama's head exchanged a look with Zack. I might not have a talent for reading minds, but I could definitely tell he was thinking the same thing at that moment. I stifled a grin.

Bianca still hovered near Mama. "Is there anything else I can get for you, ma'am?"

"I'd love a drink," said Mama. "Something frozen and fruity with lots of rum."

"I'll have the bartender whip up one of his specialties for you," said Bianca.

Mama smiled at her. "Thank you, dear."

As Bianca made her way to the bar, Mama turned to me, Zack, and Shane and waved a hand in dismissal. "The three of you can leave now. As you can see, I'm perfectly fine and don't need babysitters."

When I hesitated, Lenore said, "We'll take good care of her, Anastasia. I'm sure you have plans for the evening."

"Yes," said Mama, wrinkling her forehead and narrowing her eyes at me. "What were the three of you doing here anyway? Spying on me?"

"Of course not!" I said. "We have dinner reservations next door."

Lenore came to my defense. "Really, Flora, if not for Zack and Shane being in the right place at the right time, you could be in the ship's infirmary right now."

Mama grew thoughtful. "Well, there is that. And I am grateful." She looked up at both men. "Thank you again. Now shoo, all three of you."

I opened my mouth to say something but thought better of it.

Zack linked an arm through mine and nodded to Mama and her friends. "Enjoy the remainder of your evening." He then nudged me toward the exit.

~*~

Gemme del Mare was filled with classic Italian décor. Tufted red pleather semi-circular banquettes, each paired with a round table, ran along two walls. Square tables with bentwood chairs filled the remainder of the floor space, which was tiled in retro-style black and white hexagons. Red and white checkered tablecloths draped the tables. A Chianti bottle with a faux flickering candle sat in the center of each. The lighting was subdued, conveying an aura of intimacy.

Framed movie posters from the fifties and sixties featuring Sophia Loren, Gina Lollobrigida, and Claudia Cardinale lined the walls. Like the other restaurants and lounges on the ship, Gemme del Mare hadn't forgotten the upcoming holiday, adding heart-shaped red paper doilies interspersed between the movie posters.

A strolling violinist played what I assumed was a traditional Italian love song, perhaps something from a Verdi or Puccini opera. Although the tune sounded familiar, I couldn't place it, my knowledge of Italian love songs limited to the standard pizza parlor background music of Dean Martin singing *That's Amore* and *O Solo Mio*. The melody mingled with the muted sounds of conversation and the soft clinking of cutlery.

After the maître d' seated us at one of the banquettes and handed us menus, a waiter arrived with a complimentary basket of bread, a dish of seasoned olive oil for dipping, and an antipasto platter filled with various cheeses, meats, and olives. The sommelier followed with the wine list.

The atmosphere was perfect for a romantic dinner, but I was seated between two men, one of them not my fiancé, and the three of us had two—if not three—murders on our minds, not to mention the attack on my mother.

There was no mystery surrounding Victor Hogan's behavior. The guy was a drunken cretin. But as I drizzled olive oil onto a slice of ciabatta, I tried to connect the ever-increasing number of dots that made up a deadlier puzzle.

We'd speculated on various scenarios concerning Orson Gilbert's death and whether or not it was murder. But what if Gilbert's death and Emerson's death were connected? What if Gilbert died, not by suicide, accidentally, or because he hit on some guy's wife or girlfriend? What if Orson Gilbert was killed because he saw Emerson Dawes dump Colton Brown's body overboard?

After the sommelier returned with the bottle of wine we'd ordered, poured three glasses, and departed, Zack asked, "How long do you plan to stare at that slice of bread before you eat it?"

I pulled my focus from the bread, looking first right toward Zack, then left toward Shane. Both men stared at me, the slice of bread hovering halfway between my plate and mouth. I had no idea how long I'd zoned out, but from their expressions, it was definitely more than a few seconds. "Sorry. It's been a long day."

"And?" asked Zack.

I wish I could read minds as well as he does. "We need to get hold of Colton Brown's passport photo," I said. "Either Emerson killed him, and he's no longer on the ship, or he's lurking somewhere."

"Waiting to carry out Emerson's plan?" asked Shane.

"It's a theory. We need to know what he looks like."

"Already on it," said Zack.

I had no idea when he'd set that particular wheel in motion unless it was while I was getting ready for dinner. Zack had finished dressing first and waited for me in the living room.

"The captain is allowing you to search the ship's manifest again?" Even under these unusual circumstances, Zack's continued access of ship records raised questions I had promised myself I wouldn't ask. Not with our lives in jeopardy.

Zack shook his head as he lifted the wine glass to his lips. After taking a sip, he said, "I decided to use a different source."

Now it was my turn to wrinkle my forehead. "What happened to doing things by the book?" He'd previously refused to ask Tino for help, having cited that obtaining information in such a manner might compromise any case against Emerson.

Over the rim of his glass he offered me a sexy smile. "Different book."

"How so?"

"Emerson is dead. We no longer need to worry about some crafty lawyer getting the case tossed on a technicality."

"So, you *did* contact Tino?" asked Shane.

Zack nodded. "After receiving Brown's passport photo."

"Wait," I said, "When did that happen? And why haven't you passed the photo on to all of us?"

"While you were dressing, I texted the officer on the bridge who had helped me search for Emerson. On captain's orders, Ensign McGuire was already going through the video feeds, trying to locate Brown. I received the passport photo as the drama broke out in the Empress Lounge."

My jaw dropped open. "You just happened to have his cell

phone number?"

Zack shrugged. "He's a she, and she's no fan of her captain. She said to contact her if I needed further assistance." He chose a black olive from the antipasto platter. As he took a bite, he winked at me. "You'd like her."

I knew he was baiting me. I took a pass on the wiggly little worm at the end of his hook and responded without a trace of sarcasm in my voice, which took Herculean effort. Smiling back, I said, "I'm sure I would."

Maybe. Although, probably not. Scratch that. Definitely not.

Seriously, what woman in her right mind would *like* a stranger who offered her phone number to another woman's fiancé? Besides, I knew the effect Zack had on women. I'm certain Ensign McGuire had something else in mind when she offered him her contact information.

Zack chuckled. "Moving on..." He pulled out his phone, tapped a message, and shot off a text. "Photo on the way to the two of you, the kids, Flora, and Lenore."

Shane's phone and mine dinged simultaneously. "Does he look familiar?" asked Zack after we both checked the image.

The man in the photo scowled at me. He looked to be somewhere in his late thirties or early forties with closely cropped light brown hair, five o'clock shadow, and the thick neck of someone who either works out excessively, pops muscle-enhancing steroids, or both. The top edge of an indiscernible tattoo peeked out above his crew neck T-shirt. Other than that, he had no unique features that would set him apart from thousands of other men.

"No," I said.

"Doesn't look familiar to me, either," agreed Shane.

"It will take Ensign McGuire hours to go through all those feeds," said Zack. "Meanwhile, Tino can run the passport photo through facial recognition software to see if Colton Brown is an alias. He said he'd get on it as soon as he puts Ira's hellions down for the night."

"Maybe by the end of this evening we'll have a few answers," I said.

"Let's have some now," said Zack. He speared me with one of those looks that told me he was on to me about something.

I had a pretty good idea exactly what that something was, but I played dumb. "I had another thought."

Zack raised an eyebrow. "About?"

"A connection between Orson Gilbert's death and Emerson's death." I offered my theory about Gilbert being in the wrong place at the wrong time."

"I don't think anything can be ruled out at this point," said Zack, "but I'm more interested in another topic right now."

Again, I played dumb. "And that would be?"

His tone grew serious. "How long are you going to wait before you tell me what really happened between you and Victor Hogan earlier today?"

Shane's eyes grew wide as he joined Zack to gang up on me. "He didn't attack you, too, did he?"

"No, it was nothing like what happened in the Emerald Lounge just now."

Zack grabbed a breadstick and snapped it in half. I'm sure it was a metaphor for what he'd like to do to Victor Hogan's neck. "I didn't ask you what *didn't* happen."

I shot a side-eye toward Shane. Did we really have to go into this right now? "It was nothing. Hogan's a holdover from another era. I handled it." Or I would have, if I hadn't frozen from sheer shock at the man's audacity, but Zack didn't need to know that.

"I overheard your conversation with the cocktail waitress," he said. "Do I need to ask her what happened?"

The look he leveled at me told me in no uncertain terms that he'd do just that if I didn't come clean. I heaved a forceful sigh as I threw my arms up in the air. "Fine. He got fresh with me."

Anger filled Zack's voice. "Physically?"

"Sort of."

His eyes grew wide. "Are you telling me Victor Hogan assaulted you?"

"Calm down, please." I placed my hand over his and glanced around the room to see if any heads had turned in our direction. Thankfully, none had. "This is why I didn't want to tell you."

Zack leaned back and crossed his arms over his chest. "Well, how about telling me now?"

"Only if you drop the caveman act."

He uncrossed his arms and held his hands up in surrender. "A bit over the top?"

"Slightly. I know it comes from a place of love, but you're overreacting, Tarzan."

"I'm sorry." He leaned over and planted a kiss on my temple. "This Tarzan is worried, though. He loves his Jane and doesn't want anyone messing with her."

"I know."

I glanced between him and Shane. Zack grew up without sisters or a mother. Shane was raising a daughter on his own. #MeToo aside, there were things neither man could truly understand. Shane, especially, needed an education because Sophie would soon be dealing with these issues, assuming she hadn't already.

As much as I preferred not going into what had happened between me and Victor Hogan, I owed it to Sophie to speak up. I took a fortifying sip of liquid courage. "You men have no idea what it's like to be a woman. I've been dealing with men like Victor Hogan since puberty."

Worry filled Shane's face. "Puberty?"

I nodded. It couldn't be easy, raising Sophie from infancy after his wife walked out on them. The worry in his eyes told me he hadn't considered his daughter may have already experienced sexual harassment—or worse. "Yes, puberty. Adolescent boys mimic the macho mentality they see around them from other males in their lives, on TV, and in the movies. Sometimes it's verbal innuendo. Sometimes it's someone getting handsy. And sometimes it's a lot worse."

"You're telling me Sophie has probably experienced some of this behavior already?"

"Most likely."

Stunned disbelief filled his face. "She's never said a word."

"She's probably afraid of what you might do. She knows how protective you are of her."

"Do you think I should broach the subject with her?"

I gave his question careful thought before answering. "I wouldn't come right out and ask."

"Then what?"

"Open a dialogue by telling her about Victor Hogan. Allow her some space to open up to you about any experiences she's had, but don't press if she doesn't. As long as she knows she can talk to you about anything, she will. In her own time."

Zack turned the conversation back to the current situation.

"Which was it with Hogan? Handsy or worse?"

I frowned, then mumbled, "Handsy."

"In what way?"

"An inappropriate pat."

"Where?"

"My tush. Bianca observed it."

"Who's Bianca?" asked Shane.

"The cocktail waitress." I explained what had happened that afternoon in the Diamond Lounge. "Turns out Hogan has a reputation for sexually harassing female crewmembers."

"And no one has done anything about him?" asked Shane. "Why hasn't that man been banned from the cruise line?"

"Bianca said many crewmembers have complained, both to the captain and the cruise line. But apparently when it comes to *he said/she said*, the powers that be side with the *he's*—especially the *he's* with Super Gem status."

"Meaning?" asked Zack.

"Hogan is responsible for a boatload of cash landing in the cruise line's coffers every year. Bianca said he practically lives on this ship, which might explain Ensign McGuire's disdain for Captain Halvorson. She might be one of Hogan's victims."

"Makes sense," said Zack. "But that doesn't give him the right to molest women."

"Of course not." But did a quick pat on the backside, no matter how inappropriate, rise to the level of molestation? I knew that many women—and some more enlightened men—now agree that it does.

However, previous generations of women had put up with that sort of behavior and worse for fear of losing their jobs. Thanks to some brave women, men behaving badly is finally becoming no longer the norm.

Victor Hogan either hadn't gotten the memo or had dropped it into his circular file. It was time he suffered the consequences of his behavior. Because putting aside whether a pat on the tush rose to the level of molestation or not, what he'd done to my mother was definitely assault, and I wasn't going to let him get away with that.

Victor Hogan was going to pay for what he'd done, and I had a plan to make it happen.

SIXTEEN

Zack seemed to be waiting for me to say more. Instead I veered off in a different direction. As I helped myself to a slice of buffalo mozzarella from the antipasto platter, I said, "There are cameras throughout all the public areas of the ship, right?"

He executed a doubletake at my odd pivot. "With the exception of a few blind spots, as you already know."

I had no idea how Zack would react to my plan. Stalling, I cut the mozzarella into bite-size pieces and popped one into my mouth before I continued. "So, chances are there are recordings of the incident that occurred in the Emerald Lounge?"

"I would think so." He studied me for a long moment before he finally asked, "Exactly where are you going with this?"

I inhaled a deep breath, letting my words spill out on the exhale. "I want you to contact Ensign McGuire and ask her to send you the footage of Hogan attacking Mama."

"What do you plan to do with it?" asked Shane.

I shrugged. "Nothing much. Just upload it to every passenger on the ship."

"I noticed dozens of passengers recording what went down in the Emerald Lounge," said Zack, "including the attack on Flora. I'm guessing some of those videos have already made their way to various social media sites."

"No doubt," I agreed. "But that's not good enough."

"Why not?" asked Shane.

"Not every passenger on the ship has paid for Internet access," I said. "It's also extremely unlikely that all the ship's passengers are active on social media. I want every passenger on this ship to see that video."

"How do you plan to do that?" asked Shane.

"We enlist Tino's help."

"To do what?" he asked.

Zack answered for me. "Anastasia wants Tino to hack into the ship's app and post the video so that it pops up as a notification on everyone's phone." He looked at me for confirmation. "Isn't that right?"

I nodded. "He can do that, can't he? Without getting caught?"

"I'm sure he can," said Zack.

"That's what I was hoping." From what I had seen of Tino's computer skills, they surpassed those of mere mortal men. Or women. Give the guy a keyboard, and he became superhuman.

"That's diabolically brilliant," said Shane. "Maybe then the cruise line will have no other recourse than to ban Hogan from all their ships."

I grinned at both men before reaching for a thin slice of Asiago. "That's what I'm hoping."

Zack shot off a text to Ensign McGuire. A few minutes later, after our entrees had arrived, his phone dinged with a text alert.

He placed his fork on his plate and picked up the phone he'd earlier placed face-down on the table next to his plate.

After reading the text, he said, "Anastasia was right. The ensign is one of Hogan's victims. When she complained to the captain, he did nothing. She's attached several videos from different cameras in the Emerald Lounge and said together they capture the entire incident, not just the attack on Flora."

"That would include footage of what happened before the other passengers whipped out their phones and started recording," I said.

"Too bad it won't include audio," said Shane.

I tipped my head in agreement. "I'd love to know what Hogan said or did that set off his dinner companion." Not only wouldn't we have audio, but with wall and ceiling-mounted cameras, we wouldn't have video of what might have transpired beneath the table. Had Hogan slipped off his shoe and placed his foot where it didn't belong? Nothing would surprise me.

"I'm forwarding the videos to Tino now," said Zack. "I'll ask him to splice everything together chronologically before he uploads."

"How long do you think it will take him?" I asked.

"Not long. He'll be able to work on it while the facial recognition software is running."

I pulled out my own phone and opened the cruise app. Along with the daily printed copy of *GemEvents* delivered to passengers each evening, the ship posted all scheduled events on the app. "Victor Hogan's talk is taking place in the Diamond Lounge at two o'clock. I wonder how many passengers will bother to show up after they view the video, especially given that his readership is predominantly women."

"I'm assuming wild horses couldn't keep you from checking that out," said Shane.

"If that's the ex-cowpoke in you speaking literally," I said, "this city girl won't mess with wild horses. However, metaphorically speaking? I can't wait to see the look on his smug face."

"My guess," said Zack, before returning to his bowl of cioppino, "is that he's either going to face a room full of empty seats or one filled with extremely angry passengers."

"I'm not sure which I prefer more." Either way, Victor Hogan was going to be one extremely infuriated Neanderthal.

~*~

We were finishing dessert—because I'm genetically incapable of passing up complimentary chocolate chip cannolis, no matter how stuffed I am—when Zack's phone dinged again.

"Tino got a hit on Colton Brown." He scanned the text, then tipped his head in my direction. "Once again Westfield's resident Nancy Drew nails it."

At least he didn't refer to me this time as Miss Marple or Jessica Fletcher. When it came to amateur sleuths, I'd prefer to think of myself as more the driving around in a roadster type than the snoopy old lady type. "What did I nail?"

"Colton Brown is an alias. His real name is Donald "Donny the Duck" Rizzo."

"With a nickname like that," said Shane, "he's got to be involved in organized crime."

"It gets worse." Zack frowned and reached for my hand.

I braced myself. I didn't want to be right about my other theory. "New Jersey Mafia?" I asked.

"Afraid so."

An involuntary shudder coursed up my spine. My hand

trembled under his. "Lawrence?"

"Rizzo was one of Tuttnauer's bagmen before he got caught in a sting several years ago. Like a good soldier, he refused to talk and did his time."

"Where?" I asked.

"Not only the same penitentiary as Emerson but the same cell block. He was released last year."

There are times I hate when I'm right. This was one of them.

I closed my eyes and took several calming breaths before I was able to speak. Finally, I said, "According to what Lenore learned from Mama, Lawrence promised he would never go after me or the boys." I stared into Zack's eyes. My voice trembled. "He said nothing about you."

"At least we now know who greased the parole board palms to get Emerson released and on this ship." Zack sounded incredibly calm for someone who had just received confirmation of a price on his head.

"He won't stop," I said.

He grimaced. "I know."

Emerson's death didn't put an end to the threat on Zack's life. If Lawrence had issued a hit, someone else would now pick up the gun. The only way the threat would end would be if Lawrence either withdrew the hit or was no longer alive to pay out on it.

"How can you inform the authorities without letting on where you came by the information?" asked Shane.

"There are ways," said Zack. "I'll notify my attorney. He'll handle it."

Because the guy is really Zack's handler and not his attorney? I no longer cared. Obviously, prison was no deterrent for Lawrence Tuttnauer. Someone needed to stop him before he succeeded in his vendetta against me. A lump grew in my throat as I blinked back the tears gathering in my eyes.

My appetite having suddenly deserted me, I shoved aside the half-eaten cannoli. For the first time, I also hoped I was right about something else—my suspicion that Zack's real job was that of an alphabet agency operative. I needed to know someone in power had his back.

As the three of us sat in silence for a moment, digesting the ominous news, the strolling violinist was suddenly drowned out by the pinging and dinging of dozens of text alerts going off in rapid succession around the room. Within minutes an increasing crescendo of gasps and murmurs followed. I didn't have to look at my own phone to know Tino had come through for us for the second time tonight.

While the other diners continued to stare at their phones, commenting on the video, Zack, Shane, and I exited Gemme del Mare. All around us throughout the Atrium other passengers were also gasping and gaping at their phone screens as they watched the incident that had occurred in the Emerald Lounge play out before their eyes. Victor Hogan was quickly becoming the talk of the ship—and not in a good way.

Off to my left an older woman held up a shopping bag emblazoned with the Gems Between the Covers logo and exclaim, "I just bought his latest book." She grabbed her companion's arm and said, "Let's go, Marvin."

Marvin shifted several other shopping bags from one hand to the other and glanced at his watch. He heaved a deep sigh. "Where to now, Edna?"

"Back to the bookstore, of course."

"But we were just there."

She yanked on his arm. "And now we're returning to demand a refund. I'll be darned if that horrible man is getting any richer off my Social Security check!"

Edna began scurrying down the Atrium with Marvin in tow.

Zack wrapped his arm around my shoulders. "I think we're seeing the beginnings of a movement."

"I hope so." At least something was going right tonight. I'd like to see every other *Edna* on the ship queue up to return Hogan's book.

Shane's phone dinged. He glanced down at the text message. "The kids are finished watching the movie. They're heading up to Deck Fifteen to play miniature golf. I think I'll join them. See you both at breakfast tomorrow morning."

Once Shane headed off, Zack asked "How about a stroll in the moonlight?"

A moonlight stroll? Really? The man had a target on his back, and the guy formerly known as Colton Brown could be lurking in the shadows around any corner of the ship. My first instinct was to gather my family, head back to the suite, lock the door, and not leave until the ship docked in New Jersey. Was Zack suggesting we ignore the massive elephant on the ship?

As he awaited my reply, I realized the last thing Zack needed right now was for me to turn into a quivering basket case of anxiety. I put on a brave face, smiled, and forced myself to say, "You read my mind."

He cocked an eyebrow. "You sure?"

"Of course," I said, playing the bravery card with forced gusto. "I need to walk off about a gazillion calories from lunch and dinner."

"All right, then." He laced his fingers through mine and led me out onto the Promenade Deck. The elephant followed us, but by mutual silent consent, we both ignored its presence.

A Cheshire moon smiled down on us as we leisurely ambled around the deck. The crescent sliver allowed for a blanket of stars to fill the cloudless night sky. However, the romantic setting was marred by the gossipy buzz of dozens of other passengers also out for an evening stroll around the ship. At least there was safety in numbers. Brown/Rizzo wouldn't strike in front of witnesses.

As we passed other couples and several groups, Victor Hogan's name wafted along on the warm breeze. "I doubt it will take long before word gets back to the captain, and the video disappears from everyone's phones," I said, pulling out my own phone. "We should probably take a look at Tino's handiwork before that happens."

"At this point, it won't matter," said Zack. "The damage is done. Besides, I'm sure at least some people have downloaded it to post elsewhere. I wouldn't be surprised to find it already up on YouTube and other sites."

I still felt the need to see for myself. Zack watched over my shoulder.

Afterward, I walked over to the railing and stared out into the night. A few lights shone miles off on the horizon, delineating what was probably a tiny private island. "I wish our other problem was as easy to fix."

He looped his arm around my waist and drew me into a sideways hug. "Everything will work out for the best."

I sighed. "I wish I had your confidence. Very little has worked out for the best this past year." I turned to face him. "With the exception of you, of course."

He chuckled. "I'm happy to be the exception to your year."

I leaned my head on his shoulder. "Do you realize we've now taken two vacations, and both have resulted in kidnapping or death? I'm beginning to feel like the Typhoid Mary of the travel industry."

"Are you telling me you don't want a honeymoon?"

"We've already had two strikes. I have to admit, I'm beginning to worry about a third."

"Three strikes and you're out?"

"You, me, or both. It's certainly crossed my mind lately."

"But if we're talking in clichés, Madam Pessimist, there's also third time's the charm."

Madam Pessimist? "More like Madam Pragmatist," I said. I saw the glass as neither half-empty nor half-full but simply half a glass. "but I'll try to hang onto your more hopeful metaphor."

"As well you should. I promise you're not getting rid of me that easily."

I hoped not. But no way was this Mama Bear leaving her cubs while she flew off on a honeymoon. What we'd learned tonight proved Lawrence remained a menace. The man was a convicted murderer. His word meant nothing.

"Let's not make any more travel plans, though, not until we know for certain Lawrence is no longer a threat to any of us."

Assuming that was even possible. I couldn't see Lawrence rescinding the hit on Zack, and even if Zack did work for one of the alphabet agencies, realistically, what could the government do short of placing us all in Witness Protection? That left hoping Lawrence succumbed to natural causes, sooner rather than later, but Lawrence Tuttnauer was in excellent health and could live another twenty or thirty years.

Zack planted a kiss on the top of my head. "Deal."

~*~

We arrived back at the suite to find Mama and Lenore sitting side by side on the sectional in the living room. Mama dabbed at her eyes with a wadded tissue. Mascara raccoon rings, evidence of a crying jag, circled her lower lids and streaked her cheeks. Beside her, Lenore patted her other hand, attempting to calm her.

I rushed to my mother's side and sat next to her. "What happened, Mama? Are you hurt?"

She shook her head. "Only my pride, dear."

"She's upset over that video the ship sent out to everyone," said Lenore.

"Why would they embarrass me like that?" asked Mama, her voice trembling.

Uh-oh! Zack and I exchanged a guilty glance. I had never stopped to think how Mama might react to my plan to expose Victor Hogan.

"Mama, you have nothing to feel embarrassed about," I said. "Victor Hogan does. It exposes him for the crude misogynist that he is."

"You don't understand," she said, hiccupping between words. "It makes me look like a fool for rushing over to him."

Well, that was certainly true, but I seriously doubted I should agree with her. "No, it doesn't. It shows a man who is out of control, who shoves a woman out of his way with such force that she could have sustained serious injury if someone hadn't grabbed hold of her to break her fall."

Mama continued to blubber and hiccup. "I was acting like a silly fan girl. I wasn't thinking."

"No one knows that, Mama. There's no audio, and the camera angle doesn't show your face while you were speaking. No one has any way of knowing that you even said anything to him."

She turned her head to face me. "You're sure?"

I nodded with enough vigor to resemble a bobblehead. "I'm positive."

Her features telegraphed her skepticism before she reached for her phone to access the app and check for herself. As she repeatedly stabbed an index finger at the screen, her frown grew deeper and her frustration mounted. Finally, she looked up, her eyes wide with disbelief. "It vanished!"

SEVENTEEN

"What do you mean it vanished?" asked Lenore, grabbing her own phone from the coffee table. "How could a video simply vanish?"

Like Mama, she repeatedly stabbed at her screen, trying to access the video. Finally, she also pulled her eyes from her phone and looked up. "Flora's right. The video is no longer on the app."

That didn't take long.

"Why would the ship post the video, then almost immediately delete it?" asked Lenore, pointedly directing her question toward Zack and me. Did she suspect we knew more than we were letting on? Her expression seemed to suggest she did.

Zack had gone to the bar to pour Mama a brandy. Before he answered Lenore, he walked over to the sectional and handed Mama the glass. "Drink this, Flora."

He then took a seat on one of the chairs opposite the coffee table and responded to Lenore. "I would imagine because the video probably wasn't an authorized upload."

"You mean the ship didn't post it?" asked Mama. Confusion

spread across her features. "Who would do such a thing?"

"Yes, who?" echoed Lenore, again zeroing in on Zack and me.

"One of the crew?" I suggested. Technically, this wasn't a lie, thanks to Ensign McGuire's assistance. Besides, I'd couched my words in a question rather than making a statement.

"Why?" asked Mama.

Was I digging myself deeper into a hole? Coward that I am, I didn't think now was the best time to admit the video had been my idea.

However, at some point I'd have to fess up to Mama. I had a tell—an involuntary smile—that I'd never been able to overcome, no matter how often I'd tried, especially as a teenager. I'd never make it as a poker player. Or a spy. Good thing I'd never considered either as a career choice.

Lucky for me, Mama was currently too wrapped up in her own emotions to concentrate on studying my face for signs of fibbing. In for a penny, in for a pound. At least my next words would be one hundred percent truthful. "A cocktail waitress told me Hogan has a reputation for sexually harassing female crewmembers."

Her forehead furrowed as she narrowed her gaze at me. "She just happened to mention that to you out of the blue? When did this conversation occur?"

"After I had my own little dustup with Hogan earlier today."

"You did?" asked Lenore.

"Yes, shortly after you and I had coffee."

"What happened?" asked Mama.

"He hit on me."

"As well as *hit* her," said Zack.

I grimaced. "It was more of a tap."

"A sexually demeaning tap," he said.

Mama turned her ire on him. "And where were you when this happened to my daughter, Zachary?"

I jumped in before he could respond. "Zack was nowhere nearby." I glared at him. "Which is a good thing for Victor Hogan. Otherwise we would have had another murder on the ship."

Lenore crossed her arms over her chest. "I'd call that justifiable homicide."

"I'm not sure a judge and jury would agree," I said. "Anyway, we should be happy that the video went out to every passenger on this ship."

Mama raised an eyebrow. "Why should I be happy about it?"

"Because," I said, "now everyone is aware of Hogan's offensive behavior and will steer clear of him. Frankly, if I knew who his dinner companion was, I'd send her a dozen roses for standing up to him. The woman has more courage than most of his other victims."

Including me.

~*~

After breakfast the next morning, I headed to Lily's office to pick up the copies of the patterns and directions she'd run off for me and raid her storeroom for the materials I'd need for my morning class. Not knowing the skill levels of the passengers who might attend, I chose to start off my series of classes with a scented felt hot pad, a project that anyone could create with little to no crafting experience.

"Do you have any idea how many passengers will show up?" I asked Lily, given that she hadn't required people to register ahead of time.

"No idea. Could be as few as half a dozen or as many as several dozen."

"That makes it difficult to know how much of everything to bring with me." Did I grab a handful of scissors or the entire plastic bin? A few bottles of fabric glue or a dozen? The entire storage tub of felt squares? A bolt of quilt batting or a yard?

She opened one large bin and began counting out heavy-duty plastic tablecloths. "You're in the Onyx Pub," she said, handing me the stack.

When I stared curiously at the armload, she added, "For the tables in the bar. They're extremely durable, and it's not like you'll be using power tools or anything, but I don't want the hospitality manager giving me any grief."

"Understood."

"Anyway," she continued, "The Onyx Pub holds a maximum of sixty people, four each around fifteen square tables. Plan for a full house."

She pulled a small cardboard carton from one of the shelves and added it to the stack of tablecloths in my arms. "I made enough copies, plus a few extra, of the patterns and directions for each craft. You'll find them all in here."

I frowned at the myriad stacks of plastic tubs and smaller bins filling the supply closet. "In that case, I'd better get started. I'll need to make several trips."

"Don't worry about that," she said. "Pull the tubs and bins with the various supplies you need for today's class. Stack them up in the hallway outside the storeroom. I'll arrange for a crewmember to grab a luggage cart and deliver everything to the pub. That way you'll have enough, no matter how many people show up."

Lily headed back to her office while I got to work pulling tubs of supplies off the shelves. The corridor that housed the storeroom, as well as Lily's office, also contained various other ship's offices and was a beehive of activity this morning. Crewmembers scurried back and forth as I hauled tubs and bins from the storeroom and stacked them along the corridor wall.

As I worked, I caught snatches of conversation, especially from the female crewmembers, with Victor Hogan's name continually mentioned. I didn't realize the video had also popped up on crewmembers' phones last night, which explained how it was deleted so quickly. No doubt, the captain had also received the alert. I hoped he had no way of tracing the clips Zack had sent to Tino back to Ensign McGuire. She may have eyes for my guy, but I didn't want her getting into trouble for helping us.

"Someone should toss the bloody bugger overboard," said one woman with an English accent.

"Without a life vest," added a second woman, this one also sounding English but more Cockney.

"Maybe we should do just that," said a third with a German sounding accent. "You know nothing's going to change when it comes to Victor Hogan, not from the captain and not from the cruise line. All those greedy throwbacks to the Stone Age care about is their bottom line, not our pinched bottoms."

"She's right," said the second woman. "We can expect a continuation of status quo as long as the cruise industry is run entirely by the good old boys' network."

"And it's a sure bet none of them will be adding any women to their boards anytime soon," said the first woman.

The other two grunted in agreement.

"So, what do you say?" asked the first women. "Should we plan a murder tonight after we're off duty?"

"Jolly good idea," said the second woman. "I'll bring the wine."

"I'll bring the arsenic," said the third.

"It's a date, then," said the first woman. "My cabin. Twenty-hundred hours."

I peeked out from the storeroom and watched as the three female crewmembers chortled their way down the hall, around a corner, and out of earshot.

I was adding one of the final plastic tubs to my collection when I heard the unmistakable sound of a luggage cart rolling my way. A moment later, Lily rounded the corner. "I thought you were sending a crewmember to help me," I said.

"No one is available right now." she said.

"No one?" On a ship with a staff of fifteen hundred crewmembers?"

She shrugged. "Apparently, the captain has pulled all available personnel for something."

"Is that normal?"

"Not really, but there hasn't been much normal about this cruise from nearly the moment we set sail."

"You mean the two murders?"

Her eyes grew wide. She quickly glanced up and down the corridor before answering, keeping her voice to a whisper. "Two? We were told the first was a suicide, that the victim suffered from dementia."

"He didn't."

"How do you know that?"

"Long story. I also know that another passenger is missing."

She grabbed my arm, pulled me into the storeroom, and closed the door behind us. "That's why I couldn't find anyone to help you. The captain has everyone searching the ship from top to bottom."

"I doubt they'll find him."

"Why?"

"Because I believe he's dead."

Lily sank down onto one of the plastic tubs still sitting on the storeroom floor. "I think you'd better tell me this long story."

I settled onto another tub and explained my connection to the second murder victim and my theory that Emerson killed the missing passenger.

"You're probably right," said Lily when I had finished. "Rumor has it that a body was found washed up on Fowler Island."

"Fowler Island? I've never heard of it."

"It's a small private island resort that specializes in deep sea fishing excursions."

"In the Bahamas?"

Lily shook her head. "Off the coast of South Carolina."

If the victim was Brown/Rizzo, that would mean Emerson killed him and dumped his body before we arrived in The Bahamas.

"Does the body appear to be the victim of foul play?" I winced at the unintended pun.

"I don't know," she said. "But people who stay at these private island resorts tend to party hard. They drink more than they fish."

"Oh?" I didn't think cruise directors made enough money to take vacations on private islands. "You've been to Fowler Island?"

She laughed. "Heck, no. Fowler Island caters to old dudes living out their Ernest Hemingway fantasies. The only women you'll find on the island are worker bees."

"Like chambermaids?"

"Those, of course, but also cocktail waitresses, hostess, masseuses, and others." She wove her hands in and out to indicate an hourglass shape. "Well-endowed worker bees, if you get my drift."

"So, the body that washed up onshore is definitely male?"

"That's what I'm hearing. Which is why the captain is anxious to find our missing passenger, to eliminate the possibility of another murder on the ship. I think he's hoping the guy had a medical emergency and passed out somewhere."

"I find that highly unlikely."

She snorted. "That makes two of us. Someone would have come across him by now. Besides, it's more likely the dead guy is someone who fell overboard while on one of the Fowler fishing excursions. Booze and boats don't mix well."

"How do you know so much about Fowler Island?" I asked.

A look of disgust crossed her face. "I overheard Victor Hogan bragging to some male passengers about the free-flowing booze, the size of the marlin he caught, and other more carnal perks." She rolled her eyes. "Fowler Island is right up Victor's alley. But between you and me? He was probably too liquored up to catch anything other than a cold. It's a wonder he didn't fall overboard and drown."

Lily's phone dinged an alert. She gave it a quick glance, then said, "We'd better get moving. You don't have much time before your class starts."

As we grabbed the last of the tubs from the storeroom, she said, "Please keep what I said to yourself. The captain doesn't want the passengers panicking."

"Gee," I said, "I don't know why anyone would panic over a killer roaming loose on the ship."

She rolled her eyes again. "Yeah, weird, huh?"

~*~

Even though we arrived at the Onyx Bar nearly half an hour before the start of my class, every chair was already occupied, not surprisingly, all by women mostly middle-aged and older. I recognized some of the seniors from last night's debacle in the Emerald Lounge, but Mama and Lenore were no-shows. Not surprising. For my mother, crafting a scented hot pad couldn't compete with the allure of striking it rich at Bingo or in the casino.

The only man in the bar was the bartender, busy filling orders for coffee, tea, and the occasional Bloody Mary, mimosa, or cocktail of the day. I hoped my crafters stayed sober enough that they didn't accidentally cut themselves with the fabric shears or stab themselves with the embroidery needles they'd need to complete the hot pad.

Lily beamed as she glanced around the bar. "Nice turnout."

I exhaled a huge sigh of relief. Even though I'd received plenty of positive comments yesterday while making the sample crafts, part of me had still feared no one would show up and Lily would decide to cancel the remainder of the classes.

While I organized the supplies in piles along the length of the bar, Lily draped the tables with the plastic tablecloths. When she finished, she said, "I'm leaving the luggage cart in the corner. If I can nab a free crewmember at eleven o'clock, I'll send him to help you return everything to the stockroom. Otherwise, I'll be back to help you."

"Much appreciated."

"Oh, and one other thing..." She stepped around the bar and returned with a portable mic which she handed me. "You'll need this."

"Glad you thought of it." She helped me clip the device to my shirt and waistband. Between my chattering crafters and the background noise of hundreds of other passengers walking through the Atrium, the volume booster would prevent me from ending the hour with strained vocal cords.

Before leaving, Lily offered me a thumbs up, then waved to the seated women and called out, "Have fun, ladies!"

I waved goodbye to Lily, then took up a position where everyone in the bar could see me. "Good morning, ladies. Is everyone ready to have some crafting fun?"

The room filled with cheers and applause. When the voices quieted, I introduced myself and the project for the day. "I chose this scented hot pad as a way for you to dip a toe into the crafting waters without feeling the least bit intimidated. As you can see, my sample features a minimum amount of stitching. However, for those of you who shudder at the thought of having to sew on a loose shirt button, I'll be offering a no-sew option."

This produced another round of applause peppered with a few cheers. I clapped my own hands together. "Okay, then. Let's get crafting."

The women chatted, both with me and each other, as they worked on their projects. Not surprisingly, Victor Hogan was again the main topic of conversation this morning. And once again, not in a positive way.

I decided to wade into the conversation. "Victor Hogan is set to present a talk about his books this afternoon. Given his behavior of last night, do any of you plan to attend?"

"Definitely," said one woman. When I looked surprised, she added, "To give him a piece of my mind."

Around the room a chorus of voices rose in agreement.

"You all plan to show up to confront him?"

"Absolutely," said another woman. "I had no idea what a

horrible man he is. Not until I saw it with my own eyes last night."

"I don't know what he said or did to his date to set her off," said a third woman, "but he could have killed that poor woman who got in his way afterwards. She should file assault charges."

Nodding heads and a buzz of agreement followed her suggestion.

"That woman is my mother," I said.

Another chorus of voices filled the room, this time with words of sympathy and concern for Mama.

I assured them she hadn't sustained any injuries from her encounter with Victor Hogan. "She won't be purchasing any more of his books, though."

"Neither will I," said another woman. "As a matter of fact, I have his latest book with me. I thought about tossing it overboard, but I don't want some innocent dolphin choking on it."

This produced a wave of laughter.

After hearing from these women, even if Shane could produce a literal pack of wild horses on the ship, they wouldn't stand in the way of me attending Victor Hogan's talk this afternoon. It was promising to be the best entertainment on the ship.

When Lily returned an hour later, she found sixty satisfied crafters, finished projects in hand, beginning to spill out into the Atrium. "Well, ladies?" she asked a few who still lingered in the bar, "What did you think? Will you be returning for Anastasia's next class?"

They responded enthusiastically.

"Absolutely!"

"Great class!"

"Loved it!"

"Can't wait for the next one!"

"My sister is going to hate that she missed this one," said one woman. "She arrived too late to get a seat."

"Several of the women at breakfast this morning had planned to attend but also got here too late," said another woman.

Lily turned to me. "Would you mind repeating this class tomorrow for those who didn't get a seat today?"

An extra class meant an extra hundred dollars shaved from what I owed various creditors. With any luck, I might be debt-free by the time I became eligible for AARP membership. "I'd be happy to."

A few of the women clapped in appreciation.

"Tell your friends we'll repeat this class tomorrow," said Lily, "as well as have a second class with a new craft for all of you."

"Just as easy?" asked one woman.

I raised my hand and pinched my thumb and forefinger together. "Well, maybe just a wee bit more advanced. After all, with what you've achieved over the last hour, you've proven you're now accomplished crafters."

~*~

Lily folded tablecloths while I returned the unused supplies to the plastic tubs and bins. Then we both began piling everything onto the luggage cart. "I take it no one has found the missing passenger?"

"As far as I know, all available crew are still in search of Waldo."

"Waldo?"

"As in *Where's Waldo?*"

"You weren't given the passenger's name?"

"Of course, name and passport photo. But many on staff are referring to him as Waldo."

"Why?"

She shrugged. "Macabre ship humor."

"I'll say."

"Hey, you can't blame them. Most of these kids are only in their early twenties."

I stifled a chuckle over Lily's description of coworkers only a few years younger than herself. "And immature?"

She shrugged. "They signed on to work in areas like hospitality, sales, entertainment, spa services. It's not like corpse retrieval is listed as a line item under job description in our contracts."

"I guess that explains the three staff members I overheard planning Victor Hogan's murder."

EIGHTEEN

"Are you serious?" Lily dropped the bin of pinking shears she'd lifted off the bar. It toppled over a bar stool as it crashed to the floor. The lid popped open, spilling the contents around our feet. She stared wide-eyed and mouth agape.

We both dropped to our knees and began scooping up the pinking shears and depositing them back in the plastic bin. "I am, but I'm assuming they weren't."

Under her breath she mumbled, "I hope you're right."

Did she actually believe some of the crew would take matters into their own hands when it came to Victor Hogan?

I stood and placed the bin of pinking shears on the luggage cart. "I also had an interesting conversation with one of the cocktail waitresses yesterday."

Her expression grew wary. "About?"

"Also Victor Hogan."

Lily's mouth formed a tight frown. Without mentioning Bianca by name, I recounted what she'd told me.

She sighed. "Victor Hogan is the bane of our existence."

"So, it's true that the cruise line gives him license to sleaze?"

She chuckled, but the sound was hollow, and her expression showed no amusement. "You could say that. He's not unique, though. There are other Super Gems like him. They either drop thousands each voyage on booze, gambling in the casino, or both. They think that gives them the right to treat the female staff as only being onboard for their pleasure."

"Does their behavior ever go beyond inappropriate remarks and touching?"

"I've heard rumors, nothing more. Someone will leave suddenly, and no one knows why. I'm guessing payoffs and non-disclosure agreements are involved, but I have no proof."

Lily had confirmed everything Bianca had told me and then some. "Besides," she continued, "Victor is no different from the guys in corporate with their frat boy mentalities. Boys will be boys. Wink, wink." She illustrated her words with a double wink of one eye. "That goes for all the cruise lines, by the way, not just Gemstones of the Seven Seas. It's one of the deep, dark secrets of the cruise industry."

"Victor Hogan is hardly a boy. And no doubt, neither are any of the corporate honchos."

"True, but it's all about making money for the shareholders. We can be replaced a heck of a lot easier than a Super Gem. If they have to pay out a few thousand dollars to keep someone quiet?" She shrugged. "They consider it the price of doing business."

"Why work on a cruise ship, then?"

"Some of these kids can't afford not to. They make good money. It's an opportunity they wouldn't find anywhere else in the countries they come from. Many are supporting families back home. Others are saving for school. For some of us, it's a steppingstone toward an ultimate career goal."

I studied her for a long moment. "You're one of Hogan's victims, aren't you?"

She locked eyes with me. "There isn't a female crewmember under forty on this ship who isn't."

~*~

After returning the supplies to the storeroom, Lily locked the door and handed me the key. "I probably shouldn't do this, but the captain is running me ragged. This way you can gather the supplies for each class and return the bins afterwards, even if I'm in a meeting or something."

I pocketed the key and headed to the Crown Jewels Theater to catch Zack's eleven-thirty slide show presentation on Madagascar. I'd already viewed the photos from his two previous trips and heard all about lemurs and pochards, as well as other fauna and flora native to the immense tropical island, but I'd never had the pleasure of watching him give a talk to an audience.

Lily had scheduled a half-hour break between presentations and workshops to allow passengers time to move from one venue to the next, grab a cup of coffee, or answer the inevitable calls of nature. This enabled me to arrive with minutes to spare before the start of Zack's talk. I entered the theater to find a nearly packed house with only the occasional empty seat.

I walked down the middle aisle toward the front of the theater, scanning the sea of faces in each row on either side of me, hoping to find Shane or Mama, along with an empty seat for me. I finally found them in the front row along with Alex, Nick, and Sophie. There was an empty seat between Shane and Mama. "Is this reserved for Lenore?" I asked, hoping Mama hadn't invited Basil

213

to join her.

She patted the cushion. "For you, dear. We were hoping you'd make it in time. Lenore had other plans for this morning."

She didn't mention Basil, and I decided not to ask. I settled into the seat as the house lights dimmed.

Shane leaned over and whispered, "How did your workshop go?"

"Quite well. Lily asked me to add another class for the passengers we weren't able to accommodate."

He gave me a thumbs up as the cruise director stepped into the spotlighted circle on the stage. Once the audience quieted, Lily introduced Zack. "Our speaker this morning has traveled the four corners of the globe, documenting everything from the indigenous tribes of the Amazon to polar bears in the Arctic. You've probably seen his work in *National Geographic* as well as publications produced by the World Wildlife Federation and the Smithsonian. Today he's presenting a slide show on the natural wonders found in another part of the world, one most likely unfamiliar to many of you—Madagascar. Please join me in welcoming photojournalist Zachary Barnes."

The audience applause was accompanied by hoots, whistles, and foot stomping from the three teens in the front row. Zack pointed to them and said, "Ringers and yes, I paid them."

That solicited a burst of laughter from the audience. He spread his arms wide to indicate the laughing crowd. "I paid them, as well."

Who knew I was marrying a comedian? Too bad he didn't have Ralph perched on his shoulder. They could take their act on the road—as long as they didn't include a gig in Madagascar.

When the audience quieted, Zack launched into a brief

introduction of the island's unique ecosystem and began his slide show, peppering each slide with interesting facts and anecdotes about his experiences in Madagascar. An hour later he finished to a standing ovation.

"I had no idea Zack was such a fabulous speaker," said Shane, shouting above the din of rousing applause.

Neither had I.

Once Zack had removed his mic and handed it to one of Lily's assistants, he joined us. "Well?"

I rolled my eyes. "Tell me you're not fishing for compliments after that audience response."

He grinned. "Of course, I am."

"In that case, you were magnificent."

"Madagascar looks so cool," said Sophie. She turned to her father. "We should take a trip there sometime."

Zack's talk had not touched on the inherent dangers of traveling to Madagascar. My previous knowledge of the island had been limited to the animated movies. However, I'd done some research after Zack left on his first trip. As a result, I spent many a sleepless night until his return. Then he took a second trip to the island, which produced additional sleepless nights for me.

Zack's photography assignments always seemed to take him to places rife with social unrest, military coups, or drug cartels. Was it any wonder I believed his photojournalism was a cover for a completely different occupation? I caught his eye and silently conveyed my concern.

He got the message. "The government is discouraging tourism to Madagascar right now, Sophie."

"Why?"

"It's not the safest place to travel."

Her eyes grew wide. "But you went there twice. Why travel to dangerous places when there are plenty of safe places to take photographs?"

"Because he was on a mission," said Nick. "Zack's a spy."

"Nick!" I speared him with a Mom Look.

Sophie's jaw dropped as she stared in wide-eyed awe at Zack. "You are?"

Zack lasered his version of one of my Mom Looks at Nick.

Shane stepped over to his daughter and draped an arm around her. "Nick's teasing you, Soph."

Sophie studied Zack, then Nick. She glanced over at me before narrowing her gaze on Alex. "Is Zack really a spy?"

Alex shrugged. "He says only in Mom's imagination."

"Do you believe him?"

Zack laughed.

Sophie's head whipped around. "What's so funny?"

Zack spoke directly to me. "See what you've started?" Then he turned to Sophie. "I am not a spy, Sophie. I'm a photojournalist. Like any journalist, there are times I have assignments in places most tourists would find uncomfortable or unsafe."

"But you're safe when you go to these places, right?"

"I am."

Nick started to open his mouth, but I stopped him with one of the sternest Mom Looks I'd ever leveled at my son. Sophie had been through enough lately. If he dared tell her about the time Zack found himself staring down the business end of an Uzi in Guatemala, I'd ground him until he turned thirty.

Nick took the hint. He dropped the subject, segueing into a common refrain for all fifteen-year-old boys. "I'm hungry. Let's get some lunch."

Crisis averted. For now. Although I couldn't help but note that Alex had punted rather than directly answering Sophie's question.

~*~

The teens once again opted to do lunch on their own rather than hang out with us adults. I didn't blame them. When I was their age, I felt the same way. Now, though, I'd give anything to have had more time with my father. I never expected to lose him so early. Had he lived, he and Mama would be celebrating their fiftieth wedding anniversary in a few years. Instead, for most of my adult life I'd had a series of temporary stepfathers.

I wanted to catch Zack and Shane up on what I'd learned this morning, but I thought it best to do so without Mama. I had promised Lily I wouldn't say anything, but I made an executive decision that her request didn't extend to Zack. I knew neither he nor Shane would say anything. However, I couldn't be so sure about Mama, especially after she downed a few frozen umbrella drinks in the company of her new friends.

She had turned her focus to the various stragglers still making their way out of the theater. I placed my hand on her forearm to get her attention. "Do you have any plans for this afternoon, Mama?"

"I told Lenore I'd meet up with her for a seniors lunch event poolside—Trivia, Tacos, and Tequila."

My mother never ceases to amaze. "You plan to do tequila shots?"

She waved away my concern with an air swipe of her hand. "Don't be silly, dear. I take my tequila in margaritas." She glanced at her watch. "I'd better run. I don't want to be late."

Zack, Shane, and I watched as Mama sashayed up the theater

aisle toward the exit. "At least she's having fun in the midst of murder," I said, then added, "I think we should wait to tell her about the connection between Lawrence and Colton Brown."

"She doesn't know?" asked Shane.

"No, we didn't tell her last night. When we arrived back at the suite, we found her extremely upset over the video."

"Does your mother know uploading the video was your idea?"

I frowned as I shook my head. "I'll tell her eventually. For now, I'm opting for one crisis at a time when it comes to Mama. She's putting on a brave face right now, but I suspected she's still upset, not only with the video, but the events in the Emerald Lounge that led up to it."

"I agree," said Zack. "On both counts. I don't see what purpose it would serve to tell her about our involvement in the video or Lawrence's connection to Emerson."

Shane ran a hand through his hair. "You're sure that's a good idea? After all, there's still a killer on the ship."

"Mama isn't his target. Right now, she doesn't need the added guilt of learning her incarcerated ex is behind the release of Zack's father."

"Not to mention two, if not three, murders," added Zack. "She'll learn soon enough."

Shane nodded. "I suppose that makes sense."

"Good." Zack clapped his hands together. "Now that we've settled that, what about lunch?"

"Not the dining room," I said. "Someplace quiet and private. We need to talk."

Shane had pulled out his phone and was tapping away at the screen. "Let's head up to Deck Fifteen and check out the Amethyst Lounge. It's out of the way, and they offer a lunch menu."

Out of the way was an understatement. Even with the aid of the app's locator, we walked past the lounge twice before we found it nestled mid-ship between port and starboard, set off from any other area where passengers gathered.

We stepped from the outdoor walking track that circled the ship into the dimly lit lounge. Coming from the bright outdoors with its cloudless sky and the sun shimmering off the ocean, I needed a moment for my pupils to adjust.

The décor, with its dark polished wood wainscoting and floors, reminded me of an old English manor house. Framed botanicals lined the deep violet painted walls. Wooden tables and matching chairs, their seats upholstered in shades of purple and cream plaid, filled the center of the room. An amethyst geode lamp glowed from the middle of each table. Groupings of overstuffed loveseats, chairs, and coffee tables were strategically placed around the perimeter of the room.

Half a dozen people sat at the bar. Only a few of the tables were occupied. The bartender waved to us as he ran a rag over an unoccupied area of the bar. "Welcome. Sit anywhere, folks."

I suggested a table in the far corner of the room away from any of the other diners and led the way. The bartender, a guy who looked like he spent more money on tattoos than I made in a year, arrived a few seconds later with glasses of water and menus. His name tag identified him as Stefan from Canada. Once he placed the glasses of water on the table and handed us menus, he took our drink orders. I chuckled as he left.

"What's so funny?" asked Zack.

"Bar humor."

"I'll bite," said Shane, "but I've already heard the one about the rabbi, the priest, and the minister."

Zack slapped his back and laughed. "Only one?"

"There are more?"

"Thousands, my friend. Enough to fill entire books."

"Now I know what we should get Shane for next Christmas," I said.

"Okay," said Zack. "The floor is yours. Let's hear your bar joke."

I took a deep breath. "A gazillionaire, a spy, and a crafts editor walk into a bar..."

"I'm not a gazillionaire," said Shane.

"And I'm not a spy," said Zack.

I rolled my eyes. "Did I say you were? Chill, guys. It's a joke."

"So, what's the punchline?" asked Shane.

I shrugged. "Beats me. I haven't gotten that far. You have to admit, though, it's a great setup."

Zack fought to keep from smiling, but his eyes twinkled. "Don't quit your day job." Then he added, "Speaking of which, how'd your workshop go?"

"Packed house. Lily was thrilled with the turnout and asked me to repeat the class tomorrow for those passengers who came too late to get a seat."

Stefan returned with our drinks and took our orders, a cobb salad for me and burgers for Zack and Shane. Once he was out of earshot, I filled Zack and Shane in on what I had learned from Lily about the body that washed up on Fowler Island and how the captain had all available crewmembers searching every nook and cranny of the ship in search of Colton Brown, AKA "Donny the Duck" Rizzo.

"Lily suggested it's more likely the body is that of some guy who boozed it up too much on one of the fishing excursions and fell overboard."

"Not uncommon for charters like that," said Zack.

Was I the only person on the planet who had never heard of private resorts like Fowler Island that catered exclusively to men? Several times a year Dead Louse of a Spouse had attended vendor-sponsored sales conferences where wives were not invited. Had one of them taken place on Fowler Island? If so, that secret died with him.

"I'll bet most of those guys are too macho to wear life vests," said Shane.

"That wouldn't surprise me." I told them about Lily hearing Victor Hogan brag about his trip. "Anyway, Lily said the captain is really freaking out that the dead guy could be our missing passenger."

"I should think so," said Shane. "The way bodies are piling up around here, the Gemstone Empress is turning into a death ship. The captain's reputation is at stake."

"Or his job." I took a sip of water. "I suppose a ship's captain can only cover up so many suspicious deaths before eyebrows are raised at corporate headquarters."

Zack whipped out his phone. "If the body is Rizzo's, the authorities may already have made an ID."

"So quickly?" I asked.

"As a former prisoner, his fingerprints and DNA are on file in the FBI database. Did Lily say when the body was discovered?"

"No, I got the impression she didn't have any details. Or if she did, she wasn't saying."

"Isn't it possible that the body's been floating around for a week or more?" asked Shane.

"And may have come from anywhere?" I added. "Another

ship? A nearby island?"

"All possibilities," said Zack.

I took a sip of my water. "Sounds to me like the captain is grasping at straws."

"I found something." Zack read from his phone. "According to the *Post and Courier*, which is the local Charleston, South Carolina newspaper, a body was discovered on the eastern shore of Fowler Island two days ago."

"Does that mean it could be Brown, I mean Rizzo?" asked Shane. "All these fake names. I need cue cards."

I was beginning to feel the same way.

Zack shook his head. "The article states that the body was severely decomposed. We first set sail two days ago. It's winter. Bodies don't decompose that quickly in icy ocean water."

"Were we even that far south two days ago for the body to be Rizzo's?" asked Shane. "The current runs north. If the body was dumped overboard before we reached South Carolina, it wouldn't have drifted southward."

"We'd have to get hold of a navigation map," said Zack. "However, there's another consideration that makes it highly improbable that the body is Rizzo's."

"What's that?" I asked.

"Emerson is many things, but he's not stupid. If he killed Rizzo and dumped him overboard, he would know to weigh down the body to keep it from drifting to shore."

"Case closed, then," I said. "All indications point to the body being someone other than our phony Colton Brown."

"You know Colton Brown?" asked Stefan, coming up behind us with our lunch order. He placed the dishes in front of us. "Did someone find him? Alive I hope?"

"We haven't heard," said Zack. "What can you tell us?"

The bartender shook his head. "Not much. I was on one of the search teams this morning before my shift began. You friends of his?"

"We had a mutual acquaintance," said Zack.

Stefan furrowed his brow. "The dead guy?"

NINETEEN

I stared flap-jawed at the bartender, but Zack remained as cool as James Bond would under similar circumstances. Playing dumb, he asked, "Someone died on the ship?"

"Uh, yeah. Guess you hadn't heard, huh?"

Zack quirked an eyebrow. "Guess not. When was this?"

"Yesterday." Stefan twisted the bar apron tucked into his waistband. "Maybe I shouldn't have said anything."

I drizzled a small amount of vinaigrette onto my salad and stepped into the role of associate spy. "Given the number of elderly passengers on these cruises, I'm sure you must have passengers passing away all the time."

Stefan nodded a bit too vigorously. "Yeah, that's right. An older guy passed away in his bed."

Zack ratcheted up his questioning. "Why would you think he was the mutual acquaintance I spoke of?"

"Uhm, you said 'had', not 'have'? I took that to mean the guy is no longer alive."

"He's not," said Zack. "Does it matter?"

Stefan stared at a spot on the wall over our heads. He appeared to be debating with himself. Finally, he answered, "Mr. Brown was here having a beer shortly before we set sail. We got to talking because he was the only guy in the Amethyst at the time. We're so out of the way that most passengers don't find their way here until they've been on the ship for several days. Anyway, an older guy came in all angry like and demanded Mr. Brown leave with him."

"I see." Zack pulled up Emerson's passport photo and showed it to Stefan. "Was this the older man?"

The bartender scratched the back of his neck as he squinted at the image on Zack's screen, then raised his head to answer Zack. "I can't say for sure. Might've been. He was only in here for maybe a minute at the most."

"Look again," said Zack. "It's important."

Stefan looked down at the photo of Emerson once more and scowled. "Maybe."

"But you're not sure?"

He shrugged. "Hey man, you have any idea how many old guys are on this ship? They kind of blend into the woodwork, know what I mean? I only remember him because he was the only other person besides Mr. Brown in the lounge at the time, and he sort of made a scene."

"Did he threaten Mr. Brown?" asked Zack.

"No, nothing like that. He was just very demanding. Like Mr. Brown worked for him and wasn't supposed to be sitting having a beer. I stepped away from the bar when they started talking. I didn't want to look like I was listening in." He waved an arm to encompass the lounge. "Besides, look around. It's not like we've got great lighting in here."

"I understand," said Zack. "Did you see Mr. Brown or the older man after that?"

Stefan shook his head again. "Only that one time."

Another group wandered into the lounge. Relief washed over Stefan as he acknowledged them. "I'll be right with you, folks. Take any table." He turned back to us. "Look, I'd like to help you, but that's all I know."

Not quite. It was obvious Stefan knew Emerson hadn't simply *passed away* in his bed last night but had been murdered in Colton Brown's cabin. I smiled up at him. "Thank you, Stefan. You've been very helpful."

"Do you think he knows more than he's saying?" asked Shane as the bartender spun around and rushed off.

"Aside from what we already know?" asked Zack. "I don't think so."

Puzzlement settled over Shane's face. "Then why was he acting so nervous?"

I speared a forkful of lettuce and hardboiled egg, pausing before I slipped the fork into my mouth. "Considering what Zack discovered on the Internet about cruise lines covering up suspicious onboard deaths, I suspect crewmembers have been threatened with dismissal if they discuss such things with passengers."

~*~

Stefan kept his distance from our table for the next half hour until he returned to present our check. "This one's on me," said Shane. He handed over his cruise card.

Zack placed a twenty on the table. "I've got the tip."

Stefan's eyes grew wide as he stared down at the table. He quickly scooped up the overly generous tip, as if he feared Zack had grabbed the wrong bill from his wallet and would notice his error should the twenty linger for another moment. But Zack simply nodded.

We stepped out of the Amethyst Lounge, and I squinted as my pupils contracted from the sudden onslaught of bright sunlight. As we walked toward the entrance that would take us to the bank of elevators, I shaded my eyes with one hand while my other hand remained clasped in Zack's.

Once in front of the elevators, Shane pressed the Down button, and we waited until an elevator arrived. "I'm heading to the Diamond Lounge to take in the upcoming Victor Hogan drama. Anyone want to join me?"

"I'll pass," said Shane. "I don't want you guys starting to think of me as a third wheel."

"Never," I assured him. However, I did wish he'd widen his circle of friends beyond Zack and me. I realized he'd only moved from out west a little more than six months ago, but we appeared to be his only friends. If nothing else, the guy needed to find himself a girlfriend. I was seriously tempted to play Yente the Matchmaker and find the perfect woman for him.

"Thanks for that," he said, "but I thought I'd check out the singles mixer that starts in half an hour."

Aha! Perhaps some cosmic genie had read my mind. "Have fun!"

I turned to Zack. "What about you?"

"Looks like you're stuck with me."

I cocked my head and looked up at him. "You promise not to kill Victor Hogan?"

He winked. "As long as he keeps his hands off my woman. Otherwise all bets are off."

When the elevator came to a stop and the doors swooshed open, our ears were assaulted by the reverberating sounds of anger and chaos. As we made our way toward the Diamond Lounge, the noise increased to an uproar.

Zack and I stopped at the upper entrance to the lounge, taking in the sight of hundreds of women and some men, all shouting. Some waved their fists in the air. Others held makeshift signs that made it clear this was no Victor Hogan lovefest. The man was about to step out to confront an extremely hostile audience.

Or was he?

The massive lounge encompassed the entire bow of the ship. Stadium seating that included low cocktail tables surrounded by plush armchairs wrapped around three sides. All were occupied. Below, Lily stood in front of a wall of tinted windows that allowed for an impressive view of the water while blocking out the sun's glare. She looked close to tears as she tried to quiet the enraged passengers directing their anger toward her.

I stepped over to a group of women seated in front of us. "Do you know what's going on?"

"According to the cruise director," said one of the women, "Hogan has been taken ill." She illustrated her last two words with air quotes.

"Ill with Coward's Flu," said one of her companions. "He's probably cowering under his bed with a bottle of Scotch."

"I'll bet she warned him," said a third woman, jutting her chin in Lily's direction.

"I doubt that," I said. When all three contorted their faces into masks of skepticism, I added, "Lily is no fan of Victor Hogan."

"If that's the case," said the first woman, "why did she schedule him to speak?"

I waved an arm to encompass the crowd. "Perhaps she was hoping to embarrass him with a turnout like this."

The three women grew thoughtful. One picked up her Bloody Mary and nibbled on the stalk of celery. Another sipped from a champagne glass. The third stood. "If so, it didn't work since he's a no-show." She addressed her friends. "I see no point in staying here."

The other two women agreed, stood, and marched out of the lounge behind their friend. Others began following them. Not wanting to be caught in a mass exodus, Zack and I ducked out as quickly as possible.

Since we had spent all morning indoors, Zack and I decided to find a quiet spot in a shaded area of the deck to enjoy some fresh air and the gentle warm breeze drifting over the ship as it sailed slowly from nowhere to nowhere. After strolling halfway around the ship, we found two unoccupied deck chairs under an overhang near an outdoor bar and claimed them.

The moment we made ourselves comfortable, a crewmember in a starched white uniform with a nametag identifying him as Mario from Italy appeared. He held a tray of frothy cocktails layered in alternating pastel shades of yellow, pink, orange, and turquoise. A plastic skewer of mango, pineapple, and strawberry perched atop each glass. "Would madam or the gentleman care for a Coconut Rainbow Delight?"

Madam eyed the glass of pleasure, easily five-hundred calories. *Dare I?* I gazed longingly at the confection before I came to my sense. "I'll pass, thank you, but I'll take an iced cappuccino if the bar has a coffee service."

"No problem, madam. I'll have someone bring you that." He turned his head slightly toward Zack. "And for you, sir?"

"Same."

After the waiter walked off, Zack said, "You really wanted that Coconut Rainbow Delight, didn't you?"

"Was it that obvious?"

"Only to me and Mario. Why didn't you take one?"

"Because I need to make sure my pants still zip at the end of the cruise."

Not wanting to talk about my weight, I changed the subject. "I really feel sorry for Lily. It's bad enough she has to put up with Hogan's harassment, but from what I could make out from all the shouting, it sounded like many of the passengers in the Diamond Lounge blamed her for his actions."

Zack's lips tightened into a thin line, the corners of his mouth dipped downward, and he shook his head. "I know, but mob mentality is often illogical. It only takes one overly loud person to spout an accusation, whether true or not, before others immediately latch onto it. Next thing you know, a conspiracy theory is born."

"After we have our coffee, I'm going to head over to her office to see if she's okay."

"Want me to tag along?"

"Thanks, but I think the situation calls for a girls-only bonding session."

~*~

Twenty minutes later Zack and I parted with me off to Lily's office and Zack opting for a workout in the gym. I arrived to find no one manning the Guest Services desk. A sign on the counter read *Be Back Shortly*. Previously, I'd had to present my cruise card and state the name of the person I'd come to see. Then I'd have to wait while the crewmember on duty called Lily and got the okay to allow me entry into an area of the ship normally off-limits to passengers.

Perhaps nature had called, and the crewmember on duty had quickly rushed off to the little girls' or little boys' room. With no one to stop me and ask questions, I slipped behind the counter and through the doorway that opened into the corridor of offices. Unlike my earlier forays into the inner sanctum, the hallway was completely empty, although far from quiet. An angry male baritone with a slight Scandinavian accent boomed from the direction of Lily's office.

I rushed down the hall, and around the corner, stopping a few feet from the office door, and plastered myself against the wall. Lily's door was slightly ajar. I hadn't intended to spy, but I didn't think making my presence known was the best idea at the moment. I held my breath and listened.

"I don't care how you do it, but you'd better contain this mess."

"Me? How exactly do you expect me to do that?"

"Figure something out."

"You can't be serious. I wasn't the only crewmember who entered his room. For all I know one of the other two has already said something. You know how word travels around here."

"Make sure they keep their mouths shut. I don't want any passengers finding out about this."

"Isn't that *your* job, sir? Covering up murder is above my pay grade."

TWENTY

"We've already had two murders and a disappearance on this ship. If word gets out of another murder, you won't have a pay grade, Miss Moreau. None of us will."

Interesting. Even though Captain Halvorson had claimed Orson Gilbert's death was a suicide, he obviously believed otherwise. And now, there was another murder?

"I told the passengers in the Diamond Lounge he'd taken ill."

Someone killed Victor Hogan?

"We need something more permanent." The room went silent for a moment before the captain began to speak again. "We can announce he had a heart attack and didn't survive. Given his weight and drinking problem, no one will question that."

"How will the doctor explain the steak knife sticking out of his heart?"

"Leave that to the doctor and me. You worry about those two other crewmembers who saw the body."

"Yes, sir."

It sounded like Captain Halvorson was about to leave Lily's office. The last thing I wanted was for him to see me lurking in the corridor. Hoping neither of them saw me, I quickly scurried past the office and down the hall to the storeroom. After unlocking the door, I ducked inside and secured the latch behind me.

After waiting five minutes—my fingers crossed, hoping no one had a dire need for pompoms or macramé cord—I unlocked the door, opening it a crack to check the corridor. Hearing no voices, I inched the door open a little wider and stuck my head out. The hallway was empty. I stepped out of the storeroom, locked the door, and returned to Lily's office.

When I rapped on her closed door, I first heard her blow her nose. Then, in a shaky voice, she said, "Come in."

Lily looked shocked to see me. "Guest Services didn't call to tell me you were here."

"There was no one manning the desk."

The corners of her mouth turned down. "Odd."

I held my hands out at either side of my body, palms up. "Hey, when you gotta go, you gotta go, right?"

"I suppose." She composed her face into a smile that didn't extend to her red-rimmed eyes and motioned to the plastic molded chair across from her desk. "What can I do for you, Anastasia?"

I waited until I'd settled into the seat to respond. "I saw what happened in the Diamond Lounge. I was worried about you. Are you okay?"

She shuddered a sigh. "At least they were only carrying signs, not pitchforks and torches."

"Or tar and feathers."

She snorted. "Not that any passengers would have gotten past security with those, and they'd be hard-pressed to find such items on the ship." She paused for a moment. "Although, I suppose we do have tar stored somewhere below deck."

"I won't tell. At least none of them lobbed tomatoes at you. Those are much easier to come by on the ship."

Lily shuddered. "I hadn't thought of that." She glanced down at the crisp white shirt of her uniform. "Think of the cleaning bill!"

I nudged the conversation away from her and toward Hogan. "I suppose it's a good thing Victor Hogan took ill. Those passengers were out for bear."

She lowered her eyes and mumbled to a stack of papers on her desk. "Yes, good thing."

"Except he's not ill, is he, Lily?"

Her head shot up. She hesitated for a beat, as if trying to puzzle out the hidden meaning behind my words. Or whether I knew what really happened to Victor Hogan. Finally, she said, "I don't know what you mean."

"Yes, you do. We both know Victor Hogan is dead."

Lily gasped. "How on earth do you know that?"

When I told her what I'd overheard, her entire body deflated, and her eyes welled with fresh tears. "I can't be part of a coverup like this, but if I don't comply with the captain's orders, I'll lose my job. And if I do comply—"

"You'll be breaking the law and could wind up in prison."

She rested her elbows on her desk and lowered her head into her hands, her palms pressing against her eyelids. "What am I going to do?"

Lily cried silent tears. I reached for the tissue box and slid it toward her. She lifted her head, pulled a tissue from the box, and sopped up the tears streaking down her face. "I have no control over the other two crewmembers. If I tell them not to breathe a word of Victor's murder to anyone, what makes the captain think they'll comply?"

"Even if they agree not to say anything, you have no guarantee they'll keep their word."

"Exactly! All it takes is one beer too many. Besides, telling them not to say anything makes it sound like I'm somehow involved in the murder." She twisted the tissue into a ball and dropped it into the wastebasket next to her desk before reaching for another tissue and blowing her nose again. "Those crewmembers didn't take an oath to obey me. I'm not a naval officer."

"No, you're the designated sacrificial lamb in a worst-case scenario."

Lily's eyes widened, and a fresh batch of tears, spilled over her lids and onto her cheeks. "I'm not taking a bullet for the captain. It's not like he's ever had my back when it came to Victor Hogan. Besides, for all I know, word has already leaked out."

"That's good," I said.

She stared at me through her tears. "How?"

"If passengers and other crewmembers know that Hogan was murdered, you're only covering up a crime if you obey the captain. You don't want one of the other crewmembers ratting you out to the authorities."

"I'll still lose my job if word gets back to the captain that I disobeyed his order."

"Isn't that better than going to prison for obstruction of justice?"

"When you put it that way..."

"Lily, from what I've seen, you're extremely competent and

knowledgeable. You'll have no trouble getting another job. And a better one at that." I glanced around at her crammed, cubbyhole of an office. "What is it about working on a cruise ship that doesn't suck?"

She stared out her small porthole window in search of an answer before finally saying, "Truthfully? Not much."

"See?"

She grabbed another tissue and patted her eyes. "What do I do about Victor's murder, though?"

"We figure out who killed him. If he's locked in the brig, that's one less killer roaming the ship."

"*We?*"

"Would I be here if I didn't want to help?"

Lily leaned back in her chair and knit her brows together, her fingers twisting the tissue as she studied me. "I don't understand why you'd want to get involved. What's in it for you?"

"The safety of my loved ones." I told her about my connection to one of the other murder victims. "Four murders have occurred on this ship in the course of three days."

"Four?" Lily shook her head. "No, three."

"Four. I believe my fiancé's father killed the man you know as Colton Brown."

"Why?"

I explained my theory. "Some of these murders are connected. Maybe they all are." I had no idea how Hogan's murder might connect to the others, but the odds of two or more killers on one week-long cruise seemed too much of a coincidence to me. "There's at least one killer still loose on this ship, perhaps more, and we don't know if the killing spree is over."

Lily leaned forward, resting her forearms on her desk and

clasping her hands together. "But what can we do? It's not like you and I have any experience solving murders."

I smiled at her. "That's where you're wrong."

As I gave her a brief history of my life the past year, she eyed me with growing awe. "The problem is there are nearly fifty-five hundred passengers and crewmembers on this ship. Any one of them could be one of our killers. Even when we eliminate children and teens, passengers too feeble to commit these crimes, and those in wheelchairs, a staggering number of suspects still remain. We need to find some way to narrow the pool."

Lily picked up a pen from her desk and nervously drummed it against the desktop as she bit down on her lip and looked anywhere but at me. She might as well have a neon arrow flashing GUILTY pointing at her. "What aren't you telling me, Lily?"

She finally looked directly at me. "Can I trust you?"

I took a page from every cop show I'd ever watched and nodded. I'd decide later if I'd keep my word.

She heaved a huge sigh as she grabbed the cell phone sitting next to her coffee cup. "There's something you should see."

After tapping on the screen several times, she handed me the phone. "Watch this."

I pressed the Play icon and stared at the screen as a woman dressed incongruously in a silky flowing robe, stiletto heels, and a wide-brimmed hat with a veil walk up to a cabin door and knocked. In the crook of her arm she carried an ice bucket with what appeared to be a bottle of champagne and two flutes. A moment later, the door opened and after a brief exchange, she stepped inside. The video didn't capture the person on the other side of the door.

"That's Victor Hogan's suite," said Lily after I passed the

phone back to her. "She's the only person who entered Victor's suite last night."

"How did you get this?"

"From a crewmember who works on the bridge. She's one of Hogan's victims."

"Ensign McGuire?"

Lily's hands began to twitch. She clasped them together and lowered them onto her lap out of my sight. "How do you know that?"

I explained how the captain had assigned the ensign to help Zack view surveillance tapes after Orson Gilbert's murder.

Lily's face grew puzzled. "Was there a connection between the two men?"

"We think Emerson mistook Gilbert for a member of our party."

"Why?"

"We shared a dinner table with him and his family."

She nodded.

"Has the captain seen this video?"

"No!"

"Why not?" When she hesitated, growing even more nervous, I asked, "What more aren't you telling me, Lily?"

She bit her lower lip again. "Promise you won't tell?"

Once again, I mentally crossed my fingers and toes. "Of course."

"The tape no longer exists."

"What happened to it?"

She shrugged. "I guess it somehow got accidentally erased?"

Accidentally? I raised an eyebrow. "By the killer? Or someone protecting her?"

Lily shrugged. "I really can't say."

Can't say? Meaning she knows but refuses to tell me? "Do you think one of the female crewmembers assaulted by Hogan took the law into her own hands?"

She reluctantly nodded. "It seems likely, doesn't it?"

"What seems likely to me is the person who *accidentally* erased the tape believes so and destroyed evidence to protect the killer." Unless Ensign McGuire killed Hogan and erased the tape to protect herself. But if so, why would she send Lily a copy of the tape before destroying it?

"I suppose."

And I supposed Lily knew far more than she was letting on, but I decided not to press the issue. "There's a second possibility, the killer is the woman from the altercation in the Emerald Lounge last night."

Vigilante justice, either way. It now appeared highly unlikely that one person was responsible for all the murders on the ship. "How many people have seen the tape?"

"Besides Ensign McGuire and me? Just you."

I huffed out a sigh of frustration. "What guarantee do you have that Ensign McGuire won't share the video with someone else?"

"She won't."

Talk about naïve! "But she might. She's already shared it with you. How do you know she hasn't shared it with others? Someone else could leak it."

"She hasn't, and she won't."

I changed course. "What about your fear that the two crewmembers who also saw Hogan's body will spread news of his murder?"

"You've already convinced me I'm better off not saying

anything to them. If they talk, they talk. I'm not complicit in a coverup. Besides, no one will suspect the killer is a woman."

"You're still complicit in a coverup, Lily. You're protecting the killer. What happens when we dock back at the cruise terminal and you're questioned by the authorities?"

"Me? Why would the authorities question me?"

"You found the body!"

She shook her head vigorously. "The captain said he and the doctor would take care of things."

I rolled my eyes. "How? The moment the police view the body, they're going to know Victor Hogan was stabbed. I wouldn't be surprised if none of us is allowed off the ship until everyone is questioned. So, unless the captain and doctor plan to dispose of the body—"

Lily covered her mouth with her hands. "I didn't realize that's what he meant."

"How else will they cover up a stab wound to the heart? He plans to toss the body overboard."

"But how will he explain the body is missing if he plans to announce Victor had a heart attack?"

I ran this around in my head for a minute until I landed on the obvious scenario. The captain would announce that Victor Hogan suffered a mild heart attack this afternoon. Tomorrow he'd announce that Hogan had suffered a second, more serious attack while resting on his balcony this evening, causing him to lose his balance and fall overboard. I presented my theory to Lily.

She looked horrified by the idea. "I hope you're wrong."

"But he is planning to cover up the murder in some way. I fail to see how he can do that when the body is the evidence that indicates Victor Hogan did not die of natural causes."

Lily had no answer for that.

"There's something else you need to think about, Lily."

"As if all of this wasn't bad enough?"

"The captain is probably worrying that you or one of the other two crewmembers might try to blackmail him after he announces Victor's heart attack."

"Why would we do that?"

"Maybe you wouldn't, but he can't take that chance. A man who covers up murders might not have any qualms about committing some to protect himself."

I didn't think it possible that Lily's eyes could grow as wide as they did at that moment. "You can't mean—"

"Lily, your life is in danger."

TWENTY-ONE

"No." Lily shook her head emphatically. "The captain is a lot of things, and he irritates the heck out many of us. He's an old-school European chauvinist who really doesn't like women on his bridge, much less in any position of authority on his ship. But he's no killer. You're letting your imagination run wild, Anastasia."

Was I? I'd experienced the worst of humanity throughout the last year. Had I finally crossed the line into thinking all human beings were corrupt, ruthless, and evil until proven otherwise? Was this yet more fallout from learning of my husband's deceitful, secret life?

"Maybe you're right, Lily." For the life of me, though, I couldn't figure out how the captain would explain away a knife to the heart as anything other than a murder.

I stood and walked to the door. Before leaving I turned and said, "Do me a favor, though?"

"What's that?"

"Please be careful."

As I exited her office, I realized I was faced with an ethical dilemma. I had promised Lily I wouldn't say anything about Hogan's murder or the video. However, now that I knew about both, no way could I keep quiet. I had to tell Zack what I'd learned.

I pulled out my phone and shot him a text: *Where are you?*

He replied immediately: *Gym.*

I typed back: *We need to talk. Meet me back at the suite ASAP.*

He responded with a thumbs-up emoji and a happy face blowing a kiss.

Even though Karl had plunged me one step removed from living out of a cardboard box on a street corner, I'd won the lottery the day Zachary Barnes entered my life. I texted a kissy-face back to him.

~*~

I returned to an empty suite. The boys had texted earlier that they and Sophie had gone to the pool for a teen water volleyball marathon. Mama was off doing whatever, hopefully with Lenore and not Basil. With any luck, Zack and I would have the suite to ourselves long enough to hammer out what we should do.

Less than five minutes after I arrived, Zack rushed into the suite, stopping in his tracks as he dripped sweat, when he found me sitting on the sectional. "Are you all right? What's going on?"

I wrinkled my nose and pointed toward the bedroom. "It will wait. Go shower."

He cocked his head. "I take it that means I don't get a hug?"

I held up my hand to ward him off. "Don't you dare! I can smell you from all the way over here."

He laughed as he stripped off his T-shirt. "Want to join me?"

"Although I admire the view, I'll take a rain check."

He paused from stepping out of his gym shorts, his face

growing somber. "It's that serious?"

"Worse."

"I'll be back in five minutes."

He made it in four, still slightly damp but now clean. He dropped down beside me on the sectional and kissed me. "Better?"

I inhaled a combination of sandalwood and lemon. "Much."

He stood and performed a security sweep to confirm no one had bugged us since he'd last checked. Then he rejoined me on the sofa. "What's going on?"

I told him about the conversation I'd overheard between Lily and the captain, my subsequent conversation with Lily, and the video of the mystery woman entering Victor Hogan's suite last night. "Obviously, the captain and doctor have to be stopped from disposing of Hogan's body."

"Assuming they haven't already done so."

"I suspect the body is in the morgue. It makes sense that they'd wait until the dead of night—"

Zack raised an eyebrow.

"—no pun intended—to dump him overboard."

"Makes sense."

"If either you or I confront him, he's going to know Lily squealed. And we can't let on about the video—"

"Because that leads back to Ensign McGuire."

"Exactly. I can think of only one solution."

Zack offered a knowing nod. "Tino?"

"Tino. We need him to alert the cruise line, the authorities, and the media about the three murders and Colton Brown's disappearance. He should use that name since no one is supposed to know Brown is really Rizzo."

"Not good enough." Zack pulled out his phone and texted as

he continued to speak. "By the time someone acts, it may be too late. We also need him to send an anonymous text to the captain and doctor, warning them the authorities have been notified. That way they won't be able to dump Hogan's body overboard to cover up his murder."

He glanced up at me mid-text. "You realize, we're going to owe Tino big time."

"My guilt regarding Tino never seems to stop growing." Because of past history, I knew Tino Martinelli would do anything for me, even when the request meant skirting the law. He believed sometimes doing the right thing meant turning a blind eye to legalities. Even though he always claimed he'd never get caught, I still worried each time I asked him to put his amazing computer skills to work.

Within minutes of sending the text, Zack received a reply. He showed me the screen. It read: *Anything for Mrs. P. Keep her safe.*

As I blinked back the tears welling up behind my eyeballs, Zack pulled me close and planted a kiss on my temple. "Don't worry. We'll get through this."

"We still have two killers on the ship, and one of them could be after you. Or us."

"We'll figure it out. I promise."

~*~

Zack and I were cuddled together on the sectional, enjoying a glass of wine, when Mama arrived back at the suite. "Don't you two look comfy!"

"Would you like a glass of wine, Flora?"

She shook her head. "I have to get ready. Lenore and I are going to the Belle of the Ball Senior Soiree this evening. She's meeting me here. I just hope that horrible Victor Hogan doesn't show up and spoil the evening for everyone."

"I doubt you'll have to worry about that, Mama." I didn't dare tell her Victor Hogan wouldn't be showing up anywhere ever again. If I did, within five minutes, the entire ship would learn of his untimely death.

She paused at the entrance to her bedroom. "True, he probably wouldn't dare show his face after the way he behaved last night. He even bailed on his talk this afternoon. I suspect he took one look at the angry audience and fled. People had even made signs. Can you imagine!"

"I don't have to. We were there."

"Really? I didn't see you."

"We stood in the back. The place was jam-packed when we arrived."

"Well, I wish I'd thought to make a sign. Or asked you to make one for me. Anyway, no one believes for a minute that he suddenly became ill, no matter what that cruise director said."

"We got that impression," said Zack.

Mama opened her bedroom door and offered us a royal wave. "I'm off to make myself beautiful."

Zack and I were polishing off the last of the pinot grigio he'd opened for us when we heard a knock at the door. He got up and crossed the room to answer the door, giving Lenore an appraising nod of approval as he ushered her inside.

Lenore wore a black sleeveless silk sheath that hugged her body, black sheer stockings, and a pair of black silk stilettos with rhinestone bow clips. She'd worn her hair down, her chestnut waves cascading over her shoulders. A black silk fascinator adorned with several feathers and a short see-thru veil of decorative netting was perched slightly askew on her head.

Seeing the veil caused a prickle to creep up the back of my neck, but I shook it away. Nothing about Lenore's fascinator had any resemblance to the hat worn by Hogan's killer, other than they both contained veils. The killer's black chiffon veil had completely hidden her face. Lenore's veil was more a peek-a-boo fashion statement that accentuated her high cheekbones, aquiline nose, and cupid's bow lips.

Besides, Lenore had no reason to murder Victor Hogan. His killer had to be one of the crewmembers he'd victimized or his date from last night. Nothing else made any sense.

Zack offered Lenore a drink while she waited for Mama. She opted for a club soda with a wedge of lime, winking at me before taking a sip. I smiled back, acknowledging her pledge to stay sober around the ship's large contingent of single gentlemen of a certain age.

Mama had just stepped out of her bedroom when the ship's P.A. system sounded a series of bells. A moment later the captain came on to address the ship.

"Good evening, ladies and gentlemen. I'm sorry to inform you that due to unforeseen circumstances, we've been ordered to return to port in Bayonne, New Jersey immediately. The Gemstones of the Seven Seas Cruise Line regrets this unexpected and abrupt end to your vacation. Prior to disembarking, you will each receive a voucher toward a future cruise."

"Do you think there's something wrong with the ship?" asked Mama.

"If there were, I'd think we'd dock at the nearest port for repairs," said Lenore.

"Except the nearest ports are all in the Bahamas," I said, "and they won't let us dock due to that crewmember with measles."

"Even in an emergency?" asked Mama. "Surely, they wouldn't risk the ship losing power and drifting at sea."

"It's going to take us nearly two full days at top speed to get back to New Jersey," said Zack. "Whatever the reason, I doubt it has anything to do with the seaworthiness of the ship."

"I certainly hope you're right. This cruise has been one disaster after another." She graced Lenore with a beaming smile. "Aside from making a new friend, I'll be happy to see it end."

Lenore tipped her head in agreement. "We should consider a different cruise line for our next trip, Flora."

"You two are planning another cruise?" I asked.

"Absolutely," said Mama. "We've decided to keep our friendship alive with a yearly joint vacation."

With Ira footing all of Mama's living expenses, she could certainly afford to splurge on yearly cruises. I smiled at both of them. "That sounds lovely."

After Mama and Lenore headed off to their Senior Soiree, I turned to Zack. "You think that announcement has to do with the murders?"

"Don't you? Even though cruise lines routinely cover up suspicious deaths that occur onboard, I doubt any have ever had to deal with so many murders on one cruise."

"I feel like we're living through an Agatha Christie murder mystery. Have you happened to notice Hercule Poirot nosing around the ship?"

Zack chuckled. "We could certainly use his help. We've still got to get through the next two days without another murder."

~*~

That night I woke to what first sounded like a huge storm buffeting the ship. I rose and stepped to the sliding glass doors that opened onto the balcony and saw no signs of rain. A moment later Zack came up behind me. As he drew me into his chest, I said, "That's some racket. Maybe there is something seriously wrong with the ship."

He reached around me and opened the slider. The noise grew to a roar. We both stepped onto the balcony in time to see a helicopter flying low over our heads and making its way out to sea.

TWENTY-TWO

The dining room the next morning was abuzz with speculation. Apparently, the helicopter had awakened half the ship last night. The other half, including Mama and Lenore, hadn't turned in at that point and were still partying at the Senior Soiree. "At first we thought it would crash into us, the way those bright lights headed straight toward the ship," said Mama. "I was terrified."

"We all ran screaming from the lounge," added Lenore. "When we didn't hear a crash after a few minutes but continued hearing the whipping noise of the rotors, we walked out onto the promenade. The chopper had landed on the uppermost deck."

"Could you make out what was going on?" asked Zack.

She shook her head. "Not really. The lights blinded us. After a few minutes it took off."

"Ensign McGuire probably knows," I whispered to Zack.

"Maybe not, unless she was on duty at the time. I can reach out to her and ask."

"I'll see if Lily knows anything."

"What are you two whispering about?" asked Mama. "Do you know something you're not telling us?"

"No, Mama. We're as much in the dark as you are."

She eyed me in that way she does when she's trying to discern if I'm lying to her. In this case, I wasn't, and she finally gave up. Shaking her head, she lowered her eyes to study the breakfast menu.

According to the daily *GemEvents*, Lily had scheduled a repeat of my first class for ten o'clock and my second class for three-thirty. After breakfast I went directly to her office for the additional patterns and instruction sheets she had promised to run off for me.

"Everything okay today?" I asked after she ushered me into her office.

She offered me a huge smile. "A thousand percent better."

"Does your brightened mood have anything to do with the helicopter that landed on the ship last night?"

She waved her hand toward the chair in front of her desk. "Have a seat, and I'll tell you all about it."

Once I settled into the chair, she eyed me suspiciously for a moment. "You really have no idea?"

"None."

"Hmm...I thought perhaps you had something to do with this. If not, I don't know how the authorities found out, and maybe I don't want to know, but the captain is gone."

"Gone?"

"The doctor, too. They were escorted off the ship and onto the helicopter late last night."

"Are they under arrest?"

"At least according to the ship's rumor mill, but that may or may not be true. I wasn't there, and I haven't spoken with anyone who can give me a firsthand account. All I know for sure is that they were both relieved of duty. The cruise line flew in a replacement captain to take over for the remainder of the voyage. He's scheduled a staff meeting for later this morning. Maybe I'll find out more at that point. We also have a new doctor."

"What about the three bodies in the morgue?"

"From what I understand, they were loaded onto the helicopter."

"This is good news, Lily. You can't be implicated in a coverup."

"That's what the agent said. I feel like a two-ton weight has been lifted off me."

"Wait. What agent?"

"Along with the new captain and doctor, the helicopter brought a team of FBI agents. I've already been questioned. I'm sure they're going to want to talk to you and your fiancé, as well, given his father was one of the murder victims."

Tino had come through in spades. "No doubt. Did you tell the agent about the surveillance video?"

Shock spread over her face. "No, of course not."

"Why on earth not, Lily?"

"You know why not."

"Do you realize you're withholding material evidence in a murder investigation?"

"No, I'm not. I deleted the video."

"You've destroyed evidence."

"No, the person who erased the video destroyed the evidence. I simply deleted a text message on my phone."

A text message that contained critical information the authorities would want to see. I gave up trying to make Lily understand the severity of the crime she'd committed. If the Feds decided to charge her, she'd have to hope she could afford a crackerjack defense attorney because she was certainly going to need one.

All I could do at this point was hope Ensign McGuire had kept a copy of the video and turned it over to the authorities. However, since the ensign was either Hogan's killer or covering for the killer, I wasn't optimistic.

I stood. "Thanks for the heads-up about the FBI agent. I'd better start gathering the supplies for my ten o'clock class."

Lily bit down on her lower lip. Worry settled over her face as she absentmindedly fidgeted with a pen on her desk. "You're not going to rat on me, are you?"

"I'm not going to lie to the FBI, Lily, not for you or anyone. That's a crime. I'll answer all their questions truthfully."

She bobbed her head up and down, the worry draining from her eyes. "Okay, that's good. They won't ask about the video because they don't know it exists."

I wasn't about to tell her that the agents would quickly determine someone had deleted part of the surveillance recordings.

~*~

When I arrived back at the suite after my class, I found Zack speaking with a stranger. The two men cut off their conversation and stood when I entered the room. From his closely cropped military style haircut, dark suit, white shirt, and conservative tie, I immediately pegged the stranger as one of the FBI agents. He stood out on a cruise ship like a pallbearer in a mosh pit.

Zack made the introductions. "Sweetheart, this is Agent Aloysius Ledbetter. He's with the FBI. Agent Ledbetter, my fiancée Anastasia Pollack."

Agent Ledbetter tipped his head toward me as he whipped out his identification. "Mrs. Pollack."

I nodded back. "Agent. I heard the FBI landed last night. I take it you're here about the murders?"

"I am. Would you mind if I asked you a few questions?"

"Not at all." I motioned toward the chair he'd occupied when I entered the suite. "Please, take a seat."

As I settled onto the sectional, Zack said, "I'll leave you two alone."

"I'd rather you stayed."

Zack glanced over at Ledbetter. "Okay with you?"

Agent Ledbetter pulled out a notebook and pen. "Not a problem."

I studied both men, wondering if this was interagency courtesy, but I bit down firmly on my tongue. *Neither the time nor the place, Anastasia.*

"Before you ask me your questions, Agent Ledbetter, would you mind answering a few of mine?"

"If I can."

"Do you know who paid off members of the parole board to get Emerson Dawes released from prison?"

"I do. We've been investigating the circumstances around his release since it happened."

"Lawrence Tuttnauer?"

"Yes, I understand you suspected Tuttnauer from the beginning."

"I did. What I want to know now is what are you doing about him?"

"He's being transferred to another prison."

"Supermax?"

"No, but one nearly as restrictive."

I slammed my fists on the cushions on either side of my body. "Not good enough!" I felt the tears threatening behind my eyes. "Lawrence was already in maximum security. It didn't stop him from trying to orchestrate my fiancé's murder, did it?"

Zack reached over and captured my hands in both of his. I knew the gesture was meant to calm me, but it had the opposite effect. Anger consumed me. I turned to face him. "The only reason you're alive is because someone got to Emerson before he got to you."

"Lawrence won't have that opportunity again," said Zack.

"How do you know that? Whoever killed Emerson probably did so because he wanted to collect the full bounty on your head, not share it with Emerson and..."

I caught myself before blurting out the wrong name. I wasn't supposed to know Brown's true identity. "...and Colton Brown. Someone killed Orson Gilbert, I suspect because he thought he was a member of our family. Emerson's dead. Colton Brown is missing and most likely dead. Three murders, three suspects, and one unknown killer still somewhere on this ship."

Agent Ledbetter cleared his throat. "Which is why my colleagues and I are here, Mrs. Pollack."

I eyed him skeptically. "Do you have any leads?"

"I'm not at liberty to say."

I threw my arms up in the air. "Of course not." I failed miserably in keeping the sarcasm from my voice, but I really hated that standard law enforcement phrase. Realizing any further questioning on my part would be futile, I gave up and forced out a huge sigh. "What was it you wanted to ask me, Agent?"

"I understand you've seen a surveillance video of the possible suspect in Victor Hogan's murder."

I wasn't surprised Zack had already mentioned the video to Agent Ledbetter. I would have been surprised if he hadn't. "Are you juggling multiple cases, Agent, or do you believe there's a connection between Hogan's murder and the others?"

"We're exploring all possible leads."

"I don't see how there could be a connection. Hogan's killer is a woman, most likely one of the crew he sexually harassed or assaulted."

"Did someone confess to you, Mrs. Pollack?"

I shook my head. "That would be too easy, wouldn't it? I take it Zack has already informed you I was told the surveillance footage was erased?" When Ledbetter nodded, I continued. "I'm afraid the video I saw also no longer exists."

His eyebrows shot up to his receding hairline. "How do you know that?"

"The person who showed it to me yesterday told me earlier this morning that she deleted it from her phone."

"And that person would be?"

"Lily Moreau, the cruise director. She mentioned she'd been questioned this morning. When I asked her if she'd informed the agent of the video and turned it over, she said she hadn't because she'd deleted it."

Ledbetter scratched out some notes in his notebook, then raised his head and asked, "Why do you think she did that?"

I glanced over at Zack before I answered. "I think you already know why, don't you Agent Ledbetter?"

"Humor me, if you would, Mrs. Pollack."

"From what I've heard, most of the female crewmembers were

victimized by Victor Hogan. Lily and the person who erased the tape and sent her a copy both believe Hogan was killed by one of the crew. They're protecting their own because their complaints about Hogan were repeatedly ignored, both by the captain and the cruise line executives. So, unless the person who erased the tape kept a copy, it's gone."

"Do you know who erased the surveillance tape, Mrs. Pollack?"

"No, I was never told."

"But you have your suspicions?"

"I would think the person monitoring the surveillance cameras at the time would be a logical candidate."

Agent Ledbetter closed his notebook and rose. He reached into his pocket, removed a business card, and handed it to me. "Thank you for your time, Mrs. Pollack. If you think of anything else that might help in the investigation, you can reach me on my cell." He turned to Zack. "I'll keep you informed."

Zack receives an *I'll keep you informed*, but I get the standard *I'm not at liberty to say*? I studied both men as Zack stood and began to walk the agent to the door. Looks like I could add another checkmark in the Zack is a Spy column.

"There is one more thing," I said.

Agent Ledbetter turned around. "Yes?"

"If the killer didn't target Orson Gilbert because he thought Gilbert was a member of our party, there's another possibility."

Ledbetter strode back across the room and resumed his seat. Withdrawing his notepad and pen, he flipped to a blank page, ready to take notes. "Go ahead, Mrs. Pollack."

As the agent scribbled furiously, I told him of the conversation I'd overheard between Birdy and Bunny. "Maybe I'm reading too much into it, but it appeared Bunny knew more than she was letting on about Orson's death, and she and her husband did make up that story about Orson suffering from dementia."

He finished writing and closed his notebook. "Thank you, Mrs. Pollack. This could be pertinent information." He then rose to leave.

As soon the door closed behind Agent Ledbetter, I asked Zack, "Anything you want to tell me?"

"A full two-hours was erased from the tape. It's possible the woman you saw enter Hogan's room didn't kill him. Someone else may have entered after she left."

"Ledbetter told this to you but not me?"

Zack offered me a wink and a grin. "Male bonding?"

"Really? You're going with instantaneous bromance, expecting me to believe an FBI agent you've never met suddenly decides to divulge information about his investigation?"

Zack sighed. "Actually, Ledbetter and I have known each other for years."

Years? I crossed my arms over my chest and regarded him skeptically. "You do realize this doesn't look good for all those denials concerning working for an alphabet agency?"

"He's Patricia's cousin."

"You're ex-wife? That's some coincidence."

He held his arms out, palms up and raised his shoulders. "It happens."

I suppose I had no choice but to believe him. "He thinks the unknown third party killed Hogan?"

"It's one theory."

"But why would Emerson's killer murder Hogan? And why would he kill Hogan in a way that made it look like a woman had killed him?"

"You mean stabbing him in the heart?"

"Isn't that more indicative of a passion or revenge killing? Either by one of his victims or a woman scorned? It's also much messier." I scrunched up my face. "All that blood. Why not garrote him the way he killed Emerson?"

"Perhaps to toss a monkey wrench in the investigation. Our unknown killer may have paid the woman to bring the champagne to Hogan, then swooped in as she left."

"If that's the case, why would Ensign McGuire erase the surveillance tape?"

"She didn't."

"What? How do you know that?"

"Ensign McGuire wasn't on duty last night."

"Then who sent Lily the video?"

"Only Lily can answer that. However, the killer may have the computer skills to make it look like the video came from Ensign McGuire."

A person could get whiplash from all the theories being bandied back and forth. "The plot thickens."

TWENTY-THREE

"I'd like to catch Shane up on events," said Zack. "How about if the three of us head back to the Amethyst Lounge for lunch? Hopefully, it's as empty and quiet as yesterday."

"What about Mama, Lenore, and the kids? What should we tell them?"

Zack ran a hand through his hair, frowning as he furrowed his brow. "I'm still not sure we should say anything to your mother about Lawrence yet. Let's wait until we're back home."

"Not a bad idea." Mama harbored enough guilt when it came to her ex-husband. Knowing Lawrence had orchestrated Emerson's release wouldn't change our current situation.

"As for Hogan's death," continued Zack, "chances are word has leaked out by now, and your mother already knows."

"What about the boys and Sophie?" I still worried none of us was safe as long as an unknown accomplice still roamed the ship.

"They know to stick together and alert us of anything suspicious. Let's talk to Shane first and tackle everyone else after your class this afternoon."

I was torn about waiting a few hours, but I also wanted to discuss the situation with Shane before I said anything to Alex and Nick. Shane and I needed to be on the same page regarding how much we told the teens. I certainly don't remember Dr. Spock covering conversations about murder in any chapter of his child rearing books.

Zack was about to text Shane when his phone dinged an incoming message. "Seems word has already spread. Shane overheard two crewmembers discussing Hogan's murder." His thumbs tapped out a reply. "I told him to meet us at the lounge."

We arrived at the Amethyst Lounge a few minutes later. Stefan, the tattooed bartender from Canada, was once again on duty in the sparsely populated lounge. He waved a greeting, then pointed to where Shane already waited for us at the table we'd shared yesterday.

Shane grimaced as we joined him. "My daughter is already a basket case, and that was before this new murder. I'm not thrilled about having to tell her the latest news."

"Zack suggested we wait until after my class this afternoon to sit down with the kids."

Shane shook his head. "I asked them to join us for lunch. I don't want to risk Sophie hearing about Hogan's murder from some stranger." He raised his arm and waved. "Here they are now."

I turned to see Alex, Nick, and Sophie standing in the entrance. Alex pointed to where we sat, and they headed toward us.

I wished we had had some time without the kids to formulate exactly what we'd say to them, but we no longer had that luxury. As they approached, I said, "Why don't you take the lead on this,

Shane. We have some additional news we'll fill you in on once the kids leave."

After Stefan took our orders, Shane framed Hogan's murder around the events that had taken place in the Emerald Lounge two nights ago. "The dead guy was killed by his dinner date?" asked Sophie.

"It appears so," said Shane.

"Hmm, if Ralph were here, he'd squawk that hell hath no fury like a woman scorned."

Sophie took the news of Hogan's murder far better than Shane had feared. I didn't have the heart to tell her the quote didn't come from Shakespeare.

"I'm not so sure she was scorned," said Alex. "More like disgusted by whatever he said or did to her."

"Sounds like the guy had it coming," said Nick.

That produced a Mom Look from me. "No one deserves to be murdered, Nick."

"And no one has the right to take the law into his or her own hands," added Zack.

Nick mumbled an apology, and the conversation soon moved on to the teens' plans for the afternoon. Their matter-of-fact acceptance of Hogan's murder shocked me.

Had they become so inured to all the murders that had occurred around them this past year that they'd finally walled off their emotions? Or, as Nick so aptly put it, did Alex and Sophie also believed Hogan had it coming? Neither explanation sat well with me.

Once the kids had scarfed down their burgers and fries, they took off for a concert of current rock and pop music by some of the ship's musicians. After Stefan cleared our dishes and brought us coffee, Zack and I caught Shane up on what we knew to be the facts at this point. Half an hour later, I left the two men to prepare for my class.

~*~

With the ship heading back to port sooner than expected, my afternoon craft class would be the last I'd teach. Although disappointing, an extra three hundred dollars in my pocket was still a windfall I hadn't expected at the start of the cruise. Every little bit of extra income helped whittle down the financial quagmire I'd inherited from Karl's affair with Lady Luck.

The crewmember working the Guest Services desk remembered me from the morning and waved me toward the restricted door without calling ahead to Lily. As I approached Lily's office, I heard a conversation from within and paused to listen through the closed door.

"What video?" Asked Lily. "I don't know what you're talking about."

"Ms. Moreau," said a male voice, "we know you had a copy of the ship's surveillance tape from outside Victor Hogan's cabin."

"No, I don't."

"We can secure a warrant to seize your phone," said a female voice.

"You won't find anything on my phone. Here. Take a look for yourself."

"Because you deleted the file?" asked the male voice.

"I didn't say that."

"Are you aware," asked the female voice, "that we have the technology to access deleted phone files?"

I had no idea if this was true or not, but I knew law enforcement often lied to garner information from suspects and persons of interest. Lily was digging herself deeper and deeper in trouble. I wish she'd listened to me. If she continued on her present course, she'd find herself charged with interfering in a criminal investigation.

I'd heard enough. I could no longer help her, and I didn't want to get caught snooping. I continued on to the storeroom and gathered up the supplies I needed.

As I rolled the loaded luggage cart down the corridor a few minutes later, Lily's office door opened. A man and a woman, both dressed in conservative black suits, escorted Lily into the hallway.

Lily took one look at me and yelled, "This is all your fault. I never should have trusted you."

I stared at her face, red with rage and bloated from crying. "I'm sorry, Lily. I told you I wouldn't lie to the FBI. I pleaded with you to turn the video over."

"Victor Hogan deserved to die!"

I wanted to warn her not to say anything further until she had a lawyer, but I had a feeling it was already too late. As I watched the two agents urge her along the corridor in front of me, I noticed Lily was handcuffed behind her back.

Had Lily Moreau killed Victor Hogan?

~*~

I forced myself into a cheerful attitude for my afternoon class, although I felt anything but cheerful. The hour seemed to drag on forever. Even my crafters were distracted. They worked half-heartedly on their projects, preferring to spend most of the hour speculating on the identity of Victor Hogan's killer.

No one lingered at the end of the hour. I packed up the plastic bins of supplies and returned them to the storeroom. After I locked the storeroom, I handed the key to the crewmember working the Guest Services desk. "I'm not sure who to give this to."

"I can take it." After I turned over the key, she handed me an envelope. "This is for you."

"Thank you." Given Lily's untimely forced departure, I had wondered how I'd receive payment for the three classes. Luckily, she'd made arrangements ahead of time.

When I returned to the suite, I found Zack tapping away on his laptop while sitting on the balcony. Two glasses and a bottle of wine sat on the small table between the two lounge chairs in anticipation of my return.

He set his laptop aside, and while he opened and poured the wine, I told him about Lily's arrest. "Now I'm wondering if she killed Hogan. Although, from what I remember of the video, the woman appeared much taller. And if Lily did kill Hogan, why show me the video?"

"She also wouldn't have had access to the bridge to erase the tape."

"Which means if she killed Hogan, she had an accomplice. But why erase two full hours?"

"Hard to say." Zack took a sip of his wine while he thought for a moment. "You've spent time with her. Do you believe she's capable of murder?"

"Not unless her life were in danger, same as anyone. But she's so tiny. I don't see her overpowering Hogan, no matter how drunk he might have been. He was stabbed in the heart, not in the back. He would have seen her coming at him with the knife and easily stopped her."

"Unless he was drugged first."

I hadn't thought of that. "I guess the FBI agents will search

Lily's cabin for any substances that could have incapacitated him."

"Along with any other evidence tying her to the murder. There's another possibility, though."

"What's that?"

"Whoever sent Lily the video did so to set her up."

I sipped at my wine. "It seems all we have are three dead men, one missing man, a myriad of questions, and not a single answer."

"Are you telling me Nancy Drew is stumped?"

"Completely stymied. It's a good thing the FBI is on the case, given this puzzle has way too many missing pieces."

~*~

A gala dinner, followed by an evening of dancing, was planned for our last night on the ship. Passengers were requested to attend in formal or semi-formal attire. As inducement, the menu included fillet mignon and whole lobsters, with the ship's musicians performing live throughout both sittings. Anyone preferring more laidback clothing had their choice of the Pearl of the Sea Buffet or one of the other casual restaurants.

We opted for the dining room. For a lobster dinner, even Alex and Nick had no problem wearing the khaki dress slacks and navy blazers I'd insisted they pack.

I wore a boatneck black cocktail dress with chiffon overlay and lace cap sleeves, a purchase from back in the days before I discovered my life teetered atop a flimsy house of cards.

Mama had gone all out in a full-length iridescent jade satin gown with a flowing skirt, black ruched sash, and crystal bead-encrusted bodice. "New gown?" I asked when she exited her bedroom.

She twirled on her heels, the skirt billowing around her. "Isn't it to die for?"

Odd choice of words, given the number of deaths so far on this cruise. I turned to Zack and muttered, "I certainly hope not."

We arrived in the dining room to find Shane, Sophie, and Lenore already at the table. Birdie and the Marwoods showed up a short time later. Dennis wore an ill-fitting tux, Bunny was dressed in a loud floral print silk caftan, and Birdie had chosen a two-piece black crepe suit, easily three sizes too big for her emaciated frame. As usual, they did little more than offer slight nods when we greeted them.

I was startled by Birdie's physical deterioration since I'd last seen her. In my non-medical opinion, I doubted she had much time left. When the waiter brought the first course, she stared down at her plate, pushing the salad around without taking a single bite, no matter how much her sister urged her to eat.

Dennis, sitting on the opposite side of Birdie, paid no attention to his wife and sister-in-law, instead concentrating his full attention on his lobster, which he attacked with gusto. When the waiter had offered to remove the meat from the shell for him, he refused, stating, "Real men don't need help." He then proceeded to spray the table with lobster juice and bits of shell, and with each mouthful, he dribbled huge quantities of drawn butter down his chin. So much for an elegant evening repast!

We were on our dessert course of Cherries Jubilee when I noticed Agent Ledbetter and the female agent who had arrested Lily stride across the room toward our table. They stopped behind Bunny's chair. Agent Ledbetter caught my eye and offered me a nearly undiscernible nod before saying, "Mrs. Marwood, I need you to come with us, please."

Bunny at first ignored him. Dennis cast a quick glance toward the agents before continuing to shovel Cherries Jubilee into his mouth. If he knew why they were here, he didn't appear to care.

Ledbetter flashed his badge, his tone growing more threatening, but Bunny refused to budge. "I've done nothing wrong. I'm not going with you."

The female agent placed her hand on Bunny's arm. "I'm afraid you have no choice, ma'am. Now, please stand. You don't want to make a scene, do you?"

I glanced around the room and realized that ship had already sailed. Every passenger from the tables surrounding us had stopped eating, their attention glued to our table.

Birdie struggled to address Agent Ledbetter. In a very weak voice, not much louder than a whisper, she asked, "What's this all about?"

Ledbetter addressed Bunny. "Would you like to tell your sister, or should I, Mrs. Marwood?"

Bunny reached out and cradled her sister's hand in both of hers. Her eyes filled with tears, but her voice was firm and strong. "I did it for you, Birdie."

With fear filling her sunken eyes, Birdie said, "What have you done?"

Ledbetter and the other agent each grasped one of Bunny's upper arms and forcefully raised her from her chair. As the other agent cuffed her, Ledbetter said, "Bernadette Marwood, you're under arrest for the murder of Orson Gilbert."

Birdie let loose a banshee cry and passed out, collapsing against Dennis.

~*~

Hours later, after Zack and I had returned to the suite, someone knocked at the door. Expecting Shane, Zack swung open the door to find Agent Ledbetter standing in the corridor. "May I come in?"

Zack ushered him inside and pointed to the bar. "You off-duty?"

"Yes, and I'd love a double of whatever you've got. It's been one helluva day." He dropped onto one of the chairs in the seating area across from where I sat curled up on the sectional, having changed out of my cocktail dress and heels.

After Zack handed him a tumbler and took a seat next to me, the agent downed half the glass before speaking. Finally, he looked at me and said, "I came to thank you, Mrs. Pollack. That conversation you overhead proved pivotal in helping us with at least one of the murders that took place on this ship."

"Did Bunny push Orson over the railing?" I tried to imagine a scenario where Bunny would have the strength to overpower her brother-in-law, given Orson's height and weight. Only if he were drunk enough, I decided.

"No, she hired someone to kill him."

Zack and I exchanged a quick look. In unison we asked Ledbetter, "Emerson?"

"Possibly. Or his killer." He drained the remainder of the amber liquor from his glass and raised it toward Zack. "Mind if I have another?"

While Zack refilled his glass, Ledbetter continued, "We haven't connected all the dots yet. What we do know is that Mrs. Marwood engaged the services of a hit man."

"How?" I asked.

"On the Dark Web."

So much for stereotypes. Bunny Marwood struck me as a woman who wouldn't know how to turn on a computer, let alone own one. *Yet she knew how to access the Dark Web?* I didn't even know how to access the Dark Web."

"How did you discover that?" asked Zack.

Ledbetter waved an arm in my direction. "Thanks to your fiancée, we were able to obtain a warrant. Several of our agents spent a few hours this afternoon combing through the Marwood home in West Windsor. They found a treasure trove of evidence."

"I'm confused," I said. "I thought the whole point of the Dark Web was that it's nearly impossible to track online activity."

"Normally," said Ledbetter, "although the system does have some weaknesses. However, in this case we didn't need any forensic expertise."

"Why not?" asked Zack.

Ledbetter grinned. "Mrs. Marwood printed out all her research and correspondence. All the agents had to do was open a file cabinet and voila!"

"What about Dennis?" I asked.

"Totally oblivious to what his wife was up to. Both the evidence uncovered and our subsequent questioning of him late this afternoon, leads us to conclude Mrs. Marwood acted alone."

That explained Dennis's callous lack of concern over his wife's arrest. I hugged a throw pillow to my chest. "And Birdie?" Birdie hadn't simply fainted from the shock of learning her sister had a hand in Orson's death. After medical personnel arrived, they performed CPR before removing her on a stretcher.

Ledbetter shook his head. "She didn't make it."

From what I had overheard, Birdie had not lived a happy life even before she'd taken ill. Her sister had chosen an extreme way to show her love, but I understood her motive in orchestrating Orson's death. "I'm assuming the person Bunny hired didn't use his real name in their correspondence."

"Highly improbable," said Ledbetter.

"So, how do you find him, not to mention the other killers on the ship, before everyone disembarks tomorrow?"

Ledbetter frowned into his glass. "We're doing our best. Unfortunately, none of the crime scenes were secured as they should have been. The captain ran an extremely lax ship when it came to crimes committed on his watch."

"From what I've read online, that's pretty much SOP for assaults, murders, and disappearances on cruise ships," said Zack.

"Unfortunately, that's true," said Ledbetter. "The industry is more interested in covering up crimes than reporting them. It really hampers our ability to catch the perpetrators."

I didn't like the sound of that. "Are you suggesting you may never figure out who killed Emerson Dawes and Victor Hogan?"

"Afraid so. We'll do our best, but the odds are stacked against us."

I twisted my engagement ring. "Which means a killer will still be hunting Zack."

TWENTY-FOUR

Sleep refused to come that night. I couldn't wait to get off this death ship and return home, but I knew my worries wouldn't end once we'd returned to Westfield. The man with the price on his head seemed to have no such problem. When I slipped out of bed at two in the morning, Zack continued to sleep like a baby with a full belly and a dry diaper.

I was nuking a mug of milk when Mama finally returned to the suite. Her face had a flushed rosy glow to it. I hoped from gyrating on the dance floor and not on Basil's mattress. She took one look at me as I removed the steaming mug from the microwave and frowned. "You're up late, dear."

"So are you."

She waved her hand as if to dismiss my comment as unimportant. "I was having too much fun. I'm going to sleep in tomorrow morning. Lenore and I plan to meet for brunch at ten." As Mama headed for her bedroom, she waved once more. "Sleep tight."

I took a sip of milk. With any luck, it would provide me with a few hours of blissful oblivion.

~*~

Whether the warm milk worked its magic, or I finally fell asleep from utter exhaustion, I managed to get nearly five hours of z's before the sounds of ship activity woke me shortly before eight o'clock. After showering and dressing, I joined Zack and the boys in the living room.

They each greeted me with morning kisses, the boys quickly pecking a cheek, Zack lingering on my lips. "We're meeting Shane and Sophie for breakfast in about ten minutes," he said after ending the romantic moment. He glanced in the direction of Mama's room. "It doesn't appear Flora will be ready in time."

"She's sleeping in this morning."

"Let's go, then," said Nick. "I'm starving."

I laughed. "What else is new?"

Because the ship would dock in a few hours, the Pearl of the Sea Buffet was the only option for meals on this last day, although the bars and lounges were still open for beverages and light snacks. We arrived to find the buffet jam-packed. Luckily, Shane had managed to secure a table for all of us, but the cavernous room was too noisy for conversation. Alex, Nick, and Sophie scarfed down their breakfasts and headed off for a last few hours at the Teen Scene.

With the ship now sailing through winter seas, a stroll around the deck held little appeal, but with few other options this morning, Zack, Shane, and I decided to bundle up and brave the elements. When frostbite threated my fingers and toes, we ducked into the Amethyst Lounge to thaw. Around steaming cups of coffee, Zack and I caught Shane up on what we had learned about

Bunny's arrest.

We arrived back at the suite as Mama was leaving to meet Lenore for brunch. "Are you packed, Mama?"

"Yes, dear."

"Make sure you're back by two. That's when the ship is due to dock. We'll be able to leave shortly after that." She acknowledged me with a nautical salute as she exited the suite.

One of the perks of staying in such a luxurious suite was that, unlike most of the other passengers, we hadn't had to pack our suitcases and leave them in the corridor for collection prior to midnight last night. Our cabin steward would arrive with a luggage cart and escort us from the ship when it came time to disembark. Thus, we avoided having to hunt for our suitcases inside the terminal.

Rather than brave the hordes of people at the buffet for lunch, we decided to clean out the remainder of the finger foods left in the refrigerator. I texted the kids of our plans. When Alex replied that the ship had provided hamburgers and hot dogs at the Teen Scene, I reminded him to return to the suite no later than two o'clock.

We were polishing off the last of the crudités when my phone pinged an incoming text from Tino: *CALL ASAP.*

I quickly complied, hoping Ira hadn't taken a turn for the worse.

"Ira's fine," said Tino anticipating my question before I even asked. "So are the mini tyrants."

"What's going on?"

"Is Zack there?"

"And Shane."

"Put me on speaker."

As soon as I hit the speaker button, Tino continued. "I was digging around, trying to find someone on the ship with a sketchy background who might be your killer. None of the male passengers looked promising. A few had past misdemeanors, but nothing that raised my suspicions. So, I turned to the crew."

"And?" asked Zack.

"Struck out there, too. The only people left were the women on the ship, but I figured, you never know, right? Lo and behold, I hit pay dirt. Turns out there's a woman passenger who isn't who she says she is."

"What do you mean?" I asked.

"Like Emerson, she's traveling under an assumed name. Her real name is Greta Oberholtzmann. She's former Stasi."

"Stasi?" I tried to place the name.

"East German secret police," said Zack.

"Not only that," said Tino. "She's a trained assassin."

"Could she have set up shop on the Dark Web?" asked Zack.

"Could and did."

"What name is she using on the ship?" I asked.

"Lenore Rosedale."

I gasped, my hands flying to my mouth. "Mama!"

"I doubt she's in any danger," said Zack. "Lenore is genuinely fond of Flora."

"You know her?" asked Tino.

I forced words past my constricting throat. "She and my mother have been inseparable throughout the cruise."

Suddenly, all the puzzle pieces began to fall into place. "When I asked Lenore if she was a therapist, she said she prefers to think of herself as a people problem solver."

"Yeah," said Tino. "For a massive fee she'll eliminate any

people you have a problem with."

"She must be the killer Bunny hired," said Shane.

"Looks that way," said Tino.

"There's only one killer," I said.

Zack and Shane stared at me, questioningly.

"There is no unknown accomplice hiding on the ship," I explained. "Lenore killed Emerson and Hogan."

"Why?" asked Shane. "It seems too coincidental that she had three contracts on one cruise."

"She only had the one contract," I said. "She killed the others out of friendship for Mama."

"I don't follow," said Shane.

"I do," said Zack. "And it makes perfect sense."

"Absolutely," I said. "Mama told Lenore all about herself and her family—Karl, me, Lucille, Lawrence, Ira and his kids—she knew our entire history, especially everything we've gone through the last year. She also told Lenore about Zack and Emerson, how Emerson killed Zack's mother, his suspicious release, and showing up on the ship."

"Emerson was killed shortly after I texted Lenore his photo," said Zack.

"And she killed Hogan because he shoved Flora in the Emerald Lounge?" asked Shane.

"It makes perfect sense," I said. "Emerson killed 'Donny the Duck' and dumped him overboard, but Lenore was responsible for the three other murders."

Zack pulled out his phone and began texting. "I need to let Ledbetter know before she slips off the ship."

I placed my hand on his arm to stop him. "You can't tell him we know who she really is."

"Don't worry. Tino's secret is safe. Ledbetter will figure out Lenore's real identity on his own soon enough."

Mama walked in a few minutes later. Not knowing how she'd respond to what we had just learned, we had agreed to keep Lenore's true identity from her until after we arrived home. "Did you enjoy your brunch?"

She offered me a confused expression. "It was the strangest thing. Lenore never showed up. I thought maybe I misunderstood where she'd said to meet, so I texted her. She didn't respond. Not when I called, either."

"Did you go to her cabin?"

"I don't know where her cabin is located. We always met up somewhere, or she came here. I asked Guest Services for the number, but the woman on duty said she couldn't give out that information. She called for me, but no one answered. I was so worried that she finally contacted the cabin steward to check on her. He called back a few minutes later to say the cabin was empty."

"Perhaps she hooked up with someone last night," said Shane.

"Hmph," said Mama. "You're probably right, but she should have called or texted me to cancel our brunch plans. I feel like a jilted lover."

"I'm sure it just slipped her mind, Mama." Or Agent Ledbetter had figured things out before Tino's call and had already arrested her.

"Maybe so. She did seem quite enamored with someone she met last night." Mama shrugged. "I suppose I can't blame her. The poor dear really needs to find herself a man. She's been mooning over her dead husband far too long."

If she even had a dead husband. Along with her training as an assassin, Lenore had certainly perfected her acting chops. I wondered if the Dark Web gave out Oscars.

Lenore never responded to Mama's text and voicemail before it was time for us to disembark. Likewise, Zack hadn't heard back from Agent Ledbetter. We could only hope it was because he and his team had taken Lenore into custody.

Those hopes were dashed, however, as we walked off the ship and noticed two of the FBI agents closely scanning each disembarking passenger.

~*~

A week later I was back at work when I received a call from the receptionist. "Anastasia, a messenger just dropped off an envelope for you."

I received a constant stream of packages at work. Manufacturers were always hoping I'd feature their new products in a future issue of *American Woman*. Everyone clamored for free publicity, even in the pages of a third-rate women's magazine sold at supermarket checkout counters. Unfortunately, few of them ever shelled out to purchase advertising space. "I'll be right down."

A few minutes later I stared in puzzlement at the envelope, not a large padded envelope filled with fabric, paints, or glitter. I held in my hand a greeting card-sized cream-colored envelope of quality stationery. In perfect penmanship on the front of the envelope was my name. Nothing more. "How was this delivered?" I asked.

"By special messenger."

"Man or woman?"

"Man. Why?"

"Never mind." I thanked her and returned to my office.

I've often received invitations to receptions and other events sponsored by the crafts industry, but those invitations always came through the mail. I sat staring at the envelope for several minutes when Cloris McWerther, food editor and my best friend, popped across the hall with a bakery box. She flipped open the lid to display a dozen macarons. "Help yourself before I eat them all."

Cloris could eat all twelve macarons and not gain an ounce. I'd gain a pound simply by looking at them. However, because resistance is futile, I grabbed a raspberry and a lemon, my two favorite macaron flavors, and bit into the raspberry one. "Hmm, new bakery?"

"New online business. They want a plug in the magazine."

"Of course, they do."

"What's that?" She pointed to the unopened envelope.

I popped the remainder of the macaron into my mouth. "Not sure. Either an invitation or anthrax."

"I love your gallows humor—not. Why would someone send you an envelope of anthrax?"

I raised an eyebrow. "Really?"

"Yeah, scratch that. Ever since Karl died you've turned into a regular crime magnet." She helped herself to another macaron. "So, what are you planning to do?"

"A little investigating." I pulled a portable lightbox from the shelf above my filing cabinet, set it on my worktable, and plugged it in. I placed the envelope on the lightbox and switched on the light.

Cloris and I leaned over the envelope and searched for any signs of powder or other substances. "I don't see anything suspicious," she said.

I didn't either. After switching off the lightbox, I opened the envelope and removed a folded sheet of matching stationery.

Unfolding it revealed the same perfect script that graced the front of the envelope. It read:

You're welcome.
"Lenore"

TWENTY-FIVE

Cloris stared wide-eyed at the note. "That's the woman from the ship, isn't it?"

Other than Cloris, I hadn't mentioned the murders on the cruise to anyone at the magazine. I considered everyone else at work an acquaintance, but Cloris was the closest thing I had to a sister. She'd even saved my life once. "Yes."

"What do you think it means?"

"I don't know." Was Lenore, AKA Greta, saying she'd killed Emerson and Hogan for *me*? That sent shivers down my spine, causing the sheet of paper I held to ripple like a leaf in the wind. "I need to call the FBI agent."

My call went directly to Agent Ledbetter's voicemail. I left a message, informing him I'd received a note from Lenore and what it said. Then I called Zack. That call also went to voicemail.

The third call I placed was to Mama. "Have you heard from Lenore?"

"Thankfully, no." Having only months ago discovered her now

ex-husband was a mob kingpin, Mama had gone nearly ballistic when we'd told her what we'd discovered about her cruising buddy. "What is it about me that attracts murderers?" she had asked.

"Maybe it's genetic."

I had been joking, but she took me seriously. She offered up a huge sigh. "You could be right, dear. You've certainly stumbled across more dead bodies lately than most homicide detectives." She tilted her head thoughtfully. "I think I'm going to order one of those ancestry testing kits. Who knows? Maybe we're related to Wyatt Earp or Elliot Ness. That would certainly explain a lot."

Not really, but if that's how Mama wanted to spend her time and Ira's money, who was I to put the brakes on her fun? "You'll let me know if Lenore calls or writes you?"

"Really, Anastasia, I've already promised both you and that FBI agent, haven't I?"

"Just making sure, Mama. She's still out there somewhere." I decided not to tell her about the note I'd received.

Ten minutes later Mama called me back. She could barely speak, sputtering as she tried to get the words out. "Slow down, Mama. Breathe."

I heard her inhale sharply, then forcefully exhale. She repeated this several times with each breath growing progressively calmer until she was finally able to speak. "The warden at the prison where Lawrence was transferred just called me."

"Why?"

"Lawrence listed me as next of kin. He's dead. Murdered."

I gasped. That explained the note. Lenore had arranged for a guard or another inmate to eliminate Lawrence. Part of me wanted to break out in a happy dance. I'd no longer have to look over my shoulder, constantly worrying for my life and the lives of my loved ones. But another part of me was horrified at the thought that someone had solved my "people problem" by murder.

"Do you think Lenore is responsible?" asked Mama.

"Don't you?"

"I don't want to."

"I know." I hadn't wanted to, either.

At least now that Lenore had taken it upon herself to solve all of our "people problems," she'd be out of our lives, moving on to her next job.

Or maybe not.

What if Lenore had also decided to eliminate the huge communist thorn in Mama's side? Lenore knew all about the animosity between my mother and my mother-in-law. Was Lucille her next victim?

After hanging up from Mama, I placed another call to Agent Ledbetter and left a second message.

~*~

"I don't know why Agent Ledbetter isn't returning my calls," I told Zack as we prepared dinner that night. "As much as I wish I weren't saddled with Lucille, I don't want any harm coming to her out of Lenore's misguided sense of friendship and justice."

The commie in question wasn't home. Because she never bothered to leave a note, I had no idea if she was off galivanting with the other Daughters of the October Revolution or floating in the marshes of the Meadowlands, the favored dumping ground of New Jersey contract killers.

Zack ladled the stew he'd prepared in the slow cooker that morning into a serving bowl. "If Ledbetter's on a stakeout or in the middle of some other sensitive operation, he can't call.

Chances are, he's listened to your messages and will get in touch as soon as he's able."

From atop his perch on the refrigerator, Ralph squawked. "*He hath not fail'd to pester us with message. Hamlet*, Scene One, Act Two."

I pulled a fresh loaf of sourdough bread from the oven and began slicing it. Zack snatched the heel from the cutting board and offered it to Ralph. The parrot eyed Zack suspiciously before snatching the morsel from his fingers. Zack eyed him back and sighed. "I'm afraid he still hasn't forgiven me for leaving him."

I laughed at the drama playing out between man and bird. "He'll get over it."

Zack, the boys, and I had just gathered around the dining room table when we heard a screeching of tires, followed by a loud metallic crash. The four of us jumped up from the dining room table and ran to the living room window. Harriet Kleinhample's VW minibus had T-boned a car parked in front of a house two doors down and across the street from us.

Zack swung open the front door. He was about to step outside to check on Lucille and Harriet when two unmarked cars with flashing lights pulled up alongside the two vehicles. The occupants jumped out and with guns drawn, surrounded the wreckage. The driver's side door of a car parked next door to us opened. Agent Ledbetter stepped out, also with gun drawn, and yelled, "Stay in the house."

Zack immediately slammed the door shut. "Keep away from the windows," he said.

"Go into the den," I told the boys. "I want you as far away from flying bullets as possible."

"What about you and Zack?" asked Alex.

"We're right behind you."

The minutes ticked by as we hunkered down in the den. Instead of gunfire, we heard more sirens. Zack ventured into the living room, returning a minute later. "Two ambulances, an emergency fire vehicle, and a fire truck. They're removing Lucille and Harriet from the VW."

"Are they alive?"

"Hard to tell but given the EMT activity, I'd say yes."

"Was Lenore in the other car?"

"Lenore or someone working for her from the response we witnessed. Why else would the FBI be here?"

After another ten minutes, Zack received a text from Ledbetter: *You can come out now.*

I told the boys to stay in the house. Zack and I grabbed our coats and stepped out into the chaos.

Lucille and Harriet were strapped to gurneys and being loaded into one of the ambulances. Both were conscious and haranguing the medical personnel. "Will they be all right?" I asked one of the EMTs standing nearby.

"They're badly bruised and both appear to have whiplash," she said, "but no apparent broken bones. They should be fine." She tilted her head toward what was left of the parked car. "Can't say the same for the third victim, though."

I glanced at the other vehicle. Harriet had plowed directly into the front driver's side of a dark Buick. I can only assume she'd skidded on a patch of ice and lost control. The victim never stood a chance.

Zack was nearby speaking with Ledbetter. The firemen continued to work the Jaws of Life to extricate the body from the Buick. I thanked the EMT and joined them. "Is it Lenore?"

Ledbetter nodded. "Her assassin days are over. You can sleep easy tonight, Mrs. Pollack. And thank you."

"For what?"

"For solving the murders. How did you figure out they were all connected?"

I certainly couldn't tell the FBI that I never would have connected the dots if not for Tino's hacking skills. I wasn't even supposed to know Lenore's true identity.

Zack saved the day. He hugged me to his side and said, "I'm marrying a modern-day Nancy Drew."

Ledbetter reached out and offered me his hand. "If you ever want to change careers, Mrs. Pollack, get in touch with me. I could use someone like you on my team."

I accepted his hand. "Thanks for the offer, Agent Ledbetter, but I've had my fill of dead bodies."

And cruises.

ANASTASIA'S SIMPLE SEWING CRAFTS

Waste not, want not. That's what my great-aunt Penelope Periwinkle used to say, and now that I'm counting every penny, I realize how right she was. But even before pauperdom walloped me upside the head, I always saved all the scraps from my sewing projects. You never know when you'll need a 2" x 3" piece of felt or a 5" length of grosgrain ribbon for a project.

Here are directions for the two projects I taught on the cruise.

Tip 1: Cookie cutters make great patterns when you need simple shapes.

Tip 2: The heat from a hot dish will release the scent from the essential oils when the dish is placed on the finished hot pad. If you prefer to make an unscented hot pad, omit the oil.

Scented Felt Hot Pad

Materials: two 9" x 9" squares of felt; two 8-3/4" x 8-3/4" pieces of quilt batting; large heart-shaped cookie cutter; decorative fabric slightly larger than cookie cutter; embroidery floss in a contrasting color; essential oil (your choice of scent), straight pins; scissors; pinking shears (optional); embroidery needle; water-soluble or disappearing fabric marker; fabric glue.

Trace cookie cutter onto wrong side of decorative fabric. Cut out shape with either scissors or pinking shears.

Using fabric glue, glue shape centered over one piece of felt. Allow to dry.

Glue a layer of quilt batting centered on remaining felt square. Add a few drops of essential oil to the batting. When glue is dry, glue second layer of batting over first layer and add a few more drops of essential oil. Allow glue to dry.

Pin felt squares, wrong sides together, matching outer edges.

Using all six strands of embroidery floss, stitch around perimeter of squares in blanket stitch. Using three strands embroidery floss, quilt 1/8" from edge around heart.

Note: For no-sew version of hot pad, glue squares together along outer edges. Use a permanent fabric marker to draw quilting stitches on heart.

Felt Heart Pocket

Materials: small, medium, and large heart-shaped cookie cutters; two 9" x 12" sheets of felt in one color and one in a second color (or scraps left over from other projects); embroidery floss in a contrasting color; 12" of 1/4" wide ribbon or decorative braid; embroidery needle; assorted metallic decorative buttons or charms; needle-nose pliers; jewelry glue; straight pins; scissors; water-soluble or disappearing fabric marker.

Using the fabric marker, trace two large hearts and one small heart from the larger piece of felt and one medium heart from the smaller piece. Cut out hearts.

Pin medium heart centered over one large heart. Pin small heart centered over medium heart. Using four strands of embroidery floss and a running stitch, stitch around small and medium hearts close to cut edges.

Pin stitched heart over remaining large heart. Stitch together with four strands embroidery floss and running stitch along sides, starting and stopping even with top of medium heart on both sides to form opening for pocket.

Stitch braid or ribbon to inside of pocket on both sides for hanging loop.

If buttons have shanks, use needle-nose pliers to cut them from buttons. Glue buttons randomly to hearts, centering one on small heart.

ABOUT THE AUTHOR

USA Today bestselling and award-winning author Lois Winston writes mystery, romance, romantic suspense, chick lit, women's fiction, children's chapter books, and nonfiction under her own name and her Emma Carlyle pen name. *Kirkus Reviews* dubbed her critically acclaimed Anastasia Pollack Crafting Mystery series, "North Jersey's more mature answer to Stephanie Plum." In addition, Lois is an award-winning craft and needlework designer who often draws much of her source material for both her characters and plots from her experiences in the crafts industry.

Connect with Lois at the following sites:
Email: lois@loiswinston.com
Website: http://www.loiswinston.com
Killer Crafts & Crafty Killers Blog:
http://www.anastasiapollack.blogspot.com
Pinterest: http://www.pinterest.com/anasleuth
Twitter: https://twitter.com/Anasleuth
Bookbub: https://www.bookbub.com/authors/lois-winston

Sign up for Lois's newsletter at:
https://app.mailerlite.com/webforms/landing/z1z1u5

Made in the USA
Middletown, DE
23 October 2021

50865844R00184